DEBATABLE LANDS

edited by
John Murray

an anthology
of modern
world writing

PANURGE PUBLISHING
Brampton, Cumbria
1994

DEBATABLE LANDS

first published 1994 by
Panurge Publishing
Crooked Holme Farm Cottage
Brampton, Cumbria CA8 2AT

EDITOR John Murray
PRODUCTION EDITOR Henry Swan
COVER DESIGN Andy Williams
EDITORIAL ASSISTANT Janet Bancroft
Typeset at Union Lane Telecentre, Brampton, Cumbria CA8 1BX
Tel. 06977 - 41014
Printed by Peterson Printers, 12 Laygate, South Shields, Tyne and Wear NE33 5RP
Tel. 091-456-3493

ISBN 1 898984 05 0

All fiction submissions must be accompanied by
SAE or IRCs. Work is considered all the year
round, and talented new writers are
especially encouraged to submit.

British Library Cataloguing in Publication Data.
A catalogue record for this book is available from
the British Library.

PANURGE PUBLISHING
Crooked Holme Farm Cottage,
Brampton,
Cumbria CA8 2AT
Tel. 06977-41087

P A N U R g E

Anthology Number 21

CONTRIBUTORS

FIRST PUBLISHED STORY

Margaret Dunglinson won 2nd prize at Bridport 1991 with her Panurge story. She lives in Aspatria, Cumbria, and has had poems in *Stand* and *Iron*. She has won numerous prizes for her poetry. **Adèle Geras** was born in 1944 in Jerusalem and has published many children's books. She has been an actress and singer. **Barry Hunter** is 38 and will be starting a screenwriting course at the National Film School soon. **Tim Love** was born in 1957 and works in Cambridge as a programmer. His poems have been in *Stand* etc. **Derek Neale** teaches Creative Writing in Norwich where he also did the famous M.A. He was born in 1957. **Tom Saunders** was first encouraged to write at Kingston Poly when doing a mature degree there. He also did the Norwich M.A. Aged 47 he lives in Oxfordshire. **E.H. Solomon** is 78 and lives in Saxilby, Lincs. He is a great admirer of Lorca and does much Spanish translation. **Terry Tinthoff** born 1955 is an American living in London. She has just finished her first novel.

OTHERS

Ivy Bannister is an American living in Stillorgan, Eire. She has won the Hennessy Award and also the Mobil Ireland Playwrighting Award 1993. **Cecil Bonstein** has had work in *Critical Quarterly, Panurge, Sunk Island Review* and *Best Short Stories 1990* (Heinemann). He lives in Wimbledon. **James Brockway** born 1917 has had numerous translations of Dutch poems and stories published in British magazines. He also appeared in Panurges 2 and 5. He lives in The Hague. **John Cunningham** published *Leeds to Christmas* with Polygon in 1990 and has had stories in previous Panurges. **Julia Darling** was a founder-member of Poetry Virgins, Newcastle. She has won awards for both her plays and stories, plus a Tyrone Guthrie Award in 1994. **Geoffrey Heptonstall** lives in Cambridge and writes for the *Contemporary Review* and *London Magazine*. **Rhys H.Hughes** is a Cardiff writer born 1966 and also an electronic engineer. His work has been in *Sugar Sleep* and elsewhere. **Philip Sidney Jennings** lives in London and was born in 1946. He teaches Creative Writing and did a Writing M.A. in New York. His stories have been in *Panurge, Sunk Island Review, Encounter* and *Punch*. He published a teenage novel in 1992 entitled *Dome*. **Dick McBride** is an American living in Worcestershire. Formerly with City Lights Publishing, San Francisco, he has been in the booktrade and also been a one-man distributor in the U.K. He was born in 1928. His stories have been in many magazines. **William Palmer** is 49 and a Birmingham writer whose novels *The Good Republic* and *Leporello* both came out with Secker and Minerva. **Anna McGrail** has had stories in *Iron* and *Connecticut Quarterly* and lives in Hove. **Honor Patching** is from Fife. Her work has been in *London Magazine* and *New Writing Scotland*. She was born in 1948. **Frans Pointl** was shortlisted for the premier Dutch literary prize with his story collection *The Chicken That Flew Over The Soup* (1991). **Philip Wolmuth** has most recently been working in Cyprus as a photographer. **Howard Wright** lives in Portadown where he was born in 1959. His stories have appeared in *New Welsh Review* and elsewhere. He teaches at the New University of Ulster.

Cecil Bonstein

A Dybbuk Or Not A Dybbuk

In Jewish folklore the Dybbuk is a pest; a catastrophe; a poisonous, disembodied, evil spirit. Because of sins previously committed it has to prowl forever, wherever Jews are to be found, hunting for a suitable host. When, after possibly years of desperate searching, such a host is found, the dybbuk takes parasitic refuge there and forces its unfortunate victim to become irrational, vicious, bellicose and sullen.

*

Six months had passed since I had been demobbed from the RAF. The time was round about February or March 1947. Three married couples, friends of the family, had arrived almost simultaneously. They filled the narrow passage of the small East End house with the mayhem of their voices. Once the first pent-up flow had been released and they had calmed down, the routine required that the men should play cards while their wives enjoyed three hours or so of unbridled conversation. Led by my mother, the women entered the kitchen and closed the door. We could hear the mumbling warmth of their voices livened by periodic bursts of laughter or argument. There was an occasional clatter as my mother shovelled coal on the fire.

The pack of cards lay on the circular, highly polished table. The gas fire hissed and overheated the small room. The three men, their jackets draped over the chair backs, sat looking at my father; waiting for him to start shuffling the cards. I sat outside the circle.

But there was a complication. My father had a cold. He seemed to be indifferent to the rest of us. He appeared to be meditating; concentrating on all the unpleasant symptoms torturing his body. He kept sniffing, clearing his throat, coughing, sighing, blowing wetly into his handkerchief. My mother had generously layered him with Vick. It steamed off his chest. The small room concentrated the smell of the vapourising ointment and trapped us in his illness.

They asked when he was going to start the game.

"Do you expect me to play with such a cold?"

"What has playing cards got to do with a cold? Have you lost your hands, God forbid?"

"You should never have such a cold."

Leo said: "Last year I had a cold. It was so bad I nearly got pneumonia."

"So what stopped you? And if it was such a bad cold did you

Theresa Gaffey's Wedding, Dundalk, Eire 1991

Philip Wolmuth

play cards?"

"Play cards! I went to work."

My mother came in just then. "Excuse me everyone. Benny, darling, shall I make you another lemon tea?"

"Maybe it will help," my father said in a weak voice, "and perhaps a teaspoon of honey."

My mother hurried off promising to return with the drink plus a scarf to help him sweat a bit more. The voices in the kitchen softened. I had the impression that, briefly, serious colds had become the main topic of conversation. After all, breadwinners had to be nurtured and worried over. On the other hand, more realistic than we appreciated, they may well have been repressing their laughter; joking in whispers about my father's tragic behaviour.

*

They did not play cards. They sat looking at each other. My father wearing a heavy grey cardigan and a long red scarf, sitting near the gas fire oozing sweat and nasal discharges, was the centre of attention. He suddenly decided that this was a special occasion. That he needed the only cure worth having. He asked me to apportion good measures of whisky.

Gradually, as they loosened up, the four men began to confide in each other and to divulge their main concerns. Concerns about their children - I was my father's main problem - their boring jobs and their wives.

Of course, their wives looked after them. They had their faults. Could you expect a wife not to have a few faults? But they looked after them - apart from one. They cooked good traditional dinners - one did not. They were patient and self-sacrificing like all good Jewish wives and mothers - apart from one. The odd one out, surprisingly, was Sadie, Leo's wife. We were intrigued. Sadie, the youngest of the four women was, without doubt, the most attractive. She had a style of dressing which, though modest, gently asserted the agreeableness of her plumpish figure. She knew how to use musky perfume economically, yet in sufficient measure to entice men's noses toward her. When she listened, wide-eyed and with the gentlest of intermittent wiggles, and occasional leg crossings, to the important words leaving the lips of roused men, she was irresistible.

Yet here was Leo telling us that women change. When they were being courted they were marvellous. You only had to touch an elbow. An elbow? Not even an elbow, and they would look at you as if you were Rudolph Valentino. But now ... What? After fifteen years of marriage ... Fifteen years! Sadie shouted at him, disagreed with him ... And her cooking! She didn't cook what he liked any more, only what she liked. "Look at the way Benny's Ruth looks after his cold. If I get a cold what happens? I can't even stay in the same room. She's afraid she'll get a red nose. A red nose! Is Benny's wife afraid of a red nose?"

We were intrigued. My father said, glancing quickly at me. "But when you go to bed ...?"

Leo ignored the question. "It's like she's got a dybbuk inside her ..."

My father looking wise and thoughtful said, "Ah, a dybbuk. I could tell you about a Polish dybbuk. But whoever heard of a dybbuk here, in England? In Whitechapel?"

"It's all right for you to make jokes. You're not living with Sadie. I tell you she's a changed woman."

The conversation continued about Sadie and women generally until I decided that I would show them how clever I was. "Of course," I said, "Freud would have found your Sadie an interesting case."

"Freud; who is this Freud?"

"He's a psychiatrist. You know, a doctor for people with mental problems."

"You think my Sadie is mad?"

"Of course not."

"So why should she see this Freud?"

"Freud's dead."

"So you want Sadie to see a dead doctor for mad people. All right, now I understand."

"Leo, I'm sorry. Let me try to explain."

"Am I stopping you? My Sadie is mad and she's got to see a dead doctor for mad people. What is there to explain?"

I had got myself in a mess. "Leo, please listen. Freud discovered that the only thing wrong with a lot of his neurotic women patients was ... sexual frustration."

My father mischievously perked up. I had given him too much whisky. "You mean Leo's got a toiter schmekel (a dead penis)."

Leo was furious. The others laughed. "So now we must take advice about married life from a writer who no-one wants to read and hasn't even got a girl friend and a dead doctor. This is what the modern world has come to."

My father excitedly intervened. "You're right Leo. I apologise for my son. He's got a wrong answer for everything. He can't help himself. Best thing is to ignore him like I do." My father, by annoying me, gradually placated Leo.

Eventually, glancing quickly at me as though he wondered whether I ought to hear what he had to say, my father told us the following story. He may well have made it up. He had a peculiar sense of humour.

"Listen Leo, you mentioned your Sadie and a dybbuk, let me tell you a true story about a dybbuk. One day, in our small town in Poland, my father - your grandfather," he said looking accusingly at me, "was playing cards. I was reading a school book. All of a sudden one of the players, Schloima, began to cry. Such crying, so many tears ... I hope you never hear such crying."

"What's the matter Schloima?" they all asked. After much encouragement and the dropping of many tears, Schloima gave them the skeleton of his troubles. I pretended that I was studying my school book. Sighing and wiping his eyes every few seconds, he told them that his wife, Pasel, was making his life unbearable. She had a dybbuk inside her. He was sure she had a dybbuk. Even Rabbi Kolchinsky thought so. Hadn't he arranged a special exorcism ceremony? But despite the united prayers of ten men, the reading of the ninety first psalm and a loud command by the rabbi for the dybbuk to release her; what had happened? Nothing. Absolutely nothing. To tell the truth things had got worse. Maybe they had annoyed the dybbuk?

In the weeks that followed the prayers, Pasel went on screaming at poor Schloima for the slightest reason - or for no reason at all. If he got a hole in a sock, she screamed. If a little soup dropped out of his lips - can a man drink soup without opening his lips? - and touched the tablecloth or his trousers, she screamed. If the oil lamp smoked, she screamed. Sometimes in bed when, exhausted after a hard day's work, he was trying to go to sleep, she would kick him. What had he ever done to deserve to be kicked in bed? Or she would push herself so close to him that he had no room in the bed. She would lie so close that he had to hold the side to stop himself falling out.

Once, on a hot night, she was lying next to him without shame, nearly naked, restless and sweating - can you imagine? - she had suddenly completely lost her temper and bundled him out of the bed.

While he lay on the floor with a nearly broken arm - he showed everyone the small bruise - she had shouted such terrible words about his failings as a man and a husband that he thought she had gone mad.

Poor Schloima, working from early morning until late at night - just like you Leo - repairing shoes. He needed his sleep. He couldn't afford to have his nights broken like this. "Life, of course, is hard," Schloima said. "When do people get what they deserve? With their last breath they might just have time to whisper, 'God what for?' Still, a man who works hard should have some nachas. Some joy." Everyone agreed and tried to give him advice but he just shook his head and told them they did not understand.

In the end, Schloima, a deeply religious man, went to see a tzaddik. Now, as you know, calling a man a tzaddik - a holy man of such great goodness he can even make deals with the supernatural - doesn't guarantee he is one. Why? Because if he is a tzaddik he would not be able to say he is without losing his special powers. For the tzaddik to say he isn't a tzaddik would also be impossible because then he would be telling a lie. So, as you know, we have to guess that a man is a tzaddik. We have to go by his reputation and his holy way of life.

A few days later the tzaddik, Finkel Fagel, came to our house. He was a tall thin man. His face was a wide brown beard and two watery brown eyes. He wore a black hat and a long black cotton coat. Under his arm he carried an old, decomposing prayer book. My father stayed in the room to support the very nervous Schloima. I was told to leave, but I watched through the keyhole of the closed door. My mother had gone on a talking visit to a neighbour.

Finkel Fagel, sitting with his right hand on the book and the left one over his heart, asked questions about Pasel's age, which was thirty-three, and her eating habits and sleeping habits and the kind of things she did which made Schloima so unhappy. He asked for her most recent photograph and stared at it for many minutes. Eventually, stroking his beard and gazing sadly at Schloima, he sighed and agreed that Pasel's body had been penetrated by a dybbuk. A dybbuk of the worst kind and very difficult to deal with. After all, had not the noble Rabbi Kolchinsky tried and failed?

He said there was only one method which might work. He had learned about it during his lengthy and laborious studies in the great city of Warsaw. To help the poor woman he was prepared to try it even though it was not without some danger to himself. But who worries about personal danger? Does not a person have a duty to help others? He spoke the way you would expect a tzaddik to speak. He went on to describe the few simple things he would need to - with God's help - bring happiness back to the marriage. A good meal beforehand to give him strength. A dark room with a bed, a window which could be opened for just one inch and quickly closed again, and a table with a lighted candle. A large glass of vodka when he finished would help restore him but, of course, it was not essential.

For the ceremony it would be necessary for Pasel to lie on her back on the bed. She would have to wear a thin white cotton nightdress and nothing else. There must be no other garment, absolutely nothing that would stop the dybbuk from fleeing the orifices of her body.

Schloima, wearing his prayer shawl and head covering, would have to sit on a hard wooden chair outside the bedroom. To protect him from the dybbuk, should Finkel Fagel succeed in forcing it out, the door would have to be firmly closed. It would be useful if the legs of the chair on which he sat were cut to half their length. Then, while Schloima prayed, Finkel Fagel, also praying and trusting in the Almighty's protection, would force his body to lie upon Pasel's. Once his body had managed to settle he would slowly increase the pressure as best he could until he squeezed the dybbuk out - and hopefully, into poor Pasel's mouth. As soon as he thought it was there he would cover her mouth with his and suck out the dybbuk. He would then run to the window, blow through the one inch gap and quickly close it. The dybbuk would in this way be sent on a new search which would, with the gracious Almighty's loving assistance, go on forever. Success would show itself by a small crack in the window or a red spot which would appear on the inside of one of Pasel's thighs or on one of her big toes.

"Isn't it dangerous?" asked Schloima.

"It's dangerous but for me it's a mitzva. It's my good deed, please don't think about it. It's like I'm giving the Almighty an extra prayer."

"You learned all this in Warsaw?"

"Where else?" he said as, with an appreciative gulp, he drained the large glass of vodka my father had placed near his hand.

*

From what I overheard - the whole town was talking about Pasel's and Schloima's problem - this is what happened.

Schloima didn't agree that day. But then he had a terrible night - a night such as I hope none of us ever have - when a nearly mad Pasel woke him up, wrestled him out of the bed, punched and scratched him and even tried to bite him. After this Schloima ran to Finkel Fagel and begged him, for the sake of his marriage and his health, to rid his beautiful wife of the terrible dybbuk.

Finkel Fagel, good man that he was, agreed immediately. Once he started he became obsessed to cure Pasel. Everyone spoke about his dedication. That such a scholar from Warsaw should risk his body to help a simple man and his wife in a small town was remarkable. Could tzaddiks come any nobler than this?

Each time, before he started, Finkel Fagel ate a full dinner. His favourite was chicken soup with lockshen followed by chicken and roast potatoes and chrane. His favourite sweet was stewed fruit. After serving him with the dinner Pasel went to the bedroom and got herself ready for the exorcism. Of course, she did protest at first - wouldn't your wife protest - but she was won over by the charm and obvious goodness of the tzaddik and Schloima's tears.

Three nights a week he went to the house. While Schloima prayed - they said he was a wreck, poor man, what with his long hours of work and his praying and the smoke from the oil lamp and the cost of the dinners and the vodka, Finkel Fagel, also getting weaker - what can you expect? - as the days passed, went on ordering his bony, holy body to rest full length on Pasel's warm, soft, dybbuk-riddled one.

On each occasion, when he thought the critical moment had arrived, he would bravely put his lips over Pasel's lips and with both their mouths wide open he would try to suck out the dybbuk. Sometimes, some of the more superstitious villagers listening outside thought they heard tiny moans and screams. Rumours? Who knows?

As day followed day people began to notice that Pasel was getting better. Sometimes she stroked cats and if children's heads came near she patted them and complimented their mothers on what they had produced, and she wasn't so irritable. Some days she hardly noticed people. Although she was awake she looked as though she was breathing flowers. And although she still screamed now and then at poor Schloima it was more through habit than real hatred.

At the end of each session Finkel Fagel, very tired - he wasn't a strong man - would slowly lift his body off Pasel's and after a short rest and a few more prayers would call Schloima. Together the two men each holding a lighted candle and wearing their prayer-shawls and skull-caps would carefully examine the window for a crack, and all over Pasel's white thighs - when did these thighs ever see four searching eyes before? - and her toes for a blood spot. Now and again, when he felt desperate, Finkel Fagel would get an orthodox friend to sit with Schloima outside the bedroom, and while Schloima prayed the friend would blow as hard as he could into a ram's horn. To those who heard it, it sounded as though the noise was coming from a furious dybbuk. But as we all know, from when the shofah is blown on Yom Kippur, this is the most powerful way of getting God's attention. After each examination the exhausted Finkel would restore his strength with a good measure of vodka. I don't think he could have got home without it.

Twice Finkel Fagel thought the dybbuk was in his mouth. As his puffed out cheeks, like a hairy coconut with candle glowing eyes, floated in front of the window, the pious villagers whispering outside, screamed and ran away. They screamed so loud you would have thought the cossacks were after them. On those two nights they say dogs howled in the dark alleys and cats spat and climbed to the tops of trees. But maybe he did not close the window fast enough because each time Finkel Fagel, sighing and praying, had to go back to the unfortunate Pasel. Sometimes he went into the bedroom with weights on his back in the hope that this would help to squeeze out the terrible spirit. To everyone's surprise, no matter what he did, Pasel never complained. They say the dinners she cooked for him were delicious.

Of course, we don't know what clothing Finkel Fagel took off before he forced his body to settle on Pasel's. Buttons and braces pressing on someone can be very uncomfortable, even painful, and Finkel Fagel couldn't bear to hurt anyone. But whatever he took off, as a religious man who was praying all through the ceremony, he would most certainly have had to wear his hat or his skull cap. For, as you know, prayers without a covering on the head is like taking an examination without an examiner They don't count."

Leo interrupted my father at this point. "You say this is a true story. So what about the schmekel? Can a man take his clothes off and lie on top of a beautiful woman with nearly nothing on and not have a schmekel like a broomstick?"

My father, looking thoughtful, said, "That's an intelligent question. To tell you the truth Leo, I don't know. Was I in the bedroom? For some men such a thing would be impossible, but for a tzaddik ... Who knows? We are talking about a man in a million. A million? Maybe a man in ten million."

"Could you do it?"

"Me! Even with my bad cold I couldn't do it."

"So what happened?"

"I don't know for sure. A few months later we left Poland. We came to England. For a few years there were letters but my father was not a good letter writer. He was a good talker but he wasn't a good letter writer. They said that Schloima stopped working overtime. He bought Pasel flowers every Friday. That even without a cracked window - only the tzaddik and Schloima know whether there's a spot on Pasel's thighs - the dybbuk went away. Pasel became like the woman of the early years of their marriage. Oh, and there was more good news. Just before Finkel Fagel went away she became pregnant. Hadn't she been trying for years? She cooked Schloima his favourite meals again and she went back to singing at parties and organising party games. Her voice, it could empty a room but she was good to look at so people ignored their ears. Schloima was so happy with Pasel that he hated leaving her to go to work. He even hired an assistant ... It was like he was in love for the first time.

The story goes that Finkel Fagel, when he saw how good his Warsaw Method was, travelled to all the ghettoes of Poland looking for women with dybbuks.

What more can I tell you? My father died. I married and had a son. Is he perfect? How many of our children are perfect? What happened? We all know what happened in Poland; in Europe. From there, for Jews, all the stories have got the same finish. We're the lucky ones. We came to a civilised country."

The others nodded sadly.

At this point the wives, anxious to return home, surged noisily into the room. My father, remembering his cold, coughed and touched his red nose with a handkerchief. Leo hurried to help Sadie with her coat but she missed the sleeve opening. "Look at him," she cried, "he can't even find my arm."

Leo apologised, but made matters worse by accidentally striking her breast with his elbow as she turned to see why her diving arm had met only air. Glowering, she wrenched the coat away. My mother said, "It was an accident Sadie. Let me help you." But my father, sweating, sniffing, reeking Vick, got there first and with the flourish of a matador held the coat before her. "Thank you," she said. "You know, Ruth, you've got a real treasure for a husband." My mother warily watched my father's hands as he draped the coat around her. Leo's devoted, spaniel face looked crestfallen.

*

I heard a rumour that Leo had gone to a rabbi to discuss his marital problems. There was even talk of a minion and prayers being said for the exorcism of the dybbuk. But I did not believe these tales. I could not imagine a minion of ten men being able to keep such a prayer meeting secret. We were virtually living in village communities of streets; of friends and neighbours and families. A few words secretly dropped into an eager ear would quickly have spread from community to community, bringing to life a twittering spring season of gossip and droll speculation. I, for example, was the butt of jokers throughout the district. The story was that I had tried to get Leo to see a mad dead doctor about his schmekel. It was the kind of racy Cockney humour that seemed to appeal to everyone.

A few weeks after Leo's disclosures about Sadie, I was approaching their small grey terrace house. It was early evening. Leo, as usual, would have been working late. As I drew near I saw my father step out of the house. He walked away quickly and furtively. I had the feeling that in a fleeting sideways glance he had glimpsed me.

I had been on my way to the Whitechapel library. I wanted to research bits of the war and of the Bengal famine of 1943 which I had witnessed from the comparative comfort of the RAF. Shocked at seeing my father, I sat in the reference library and did no research. I sat and speculated about integrity and selfishness and sex and, more relevantly, about my limited understanding of human nature.

*

The sequel to this story came some two months later. Another card game. The same players but now, from the kitchen we could hear more sounds of argument than of easily digestible conversation. Even my mother, normally a patient, gentle woman had recently become tense and subject to spasms of ill-temper. Only Sadie's voice sounded calm and conciliatory.

The pack of cards lay unopened on the table. The men, usually subdued, hearing the strident voices from the kitchen, were complaining desultorily about the way their wives had changed. Leo suddenly said, "Maybe they catched something. Who knows what happens to women sometimes. Sometimes they go a little bit mad." Leo spread his arms and shrugged. "Then all of a sudden, like my Sadie, they get better. A dybbuk or not a dybbuk. If they get better should we care? Do you know what I say? I say let's enjoy our wives, and when the madness gets into them ...? Wait. Be patient. Wait. Wait till the madness flies away. It's like an illness. Has Benny still got his cold? Does my poor back still hurt? You remember my bad back? People get better." He stared hard at my father and the other two, challenging them to disagree. A challenge they would normally have accepted with gusto. But they did not answer. They nodded their heads. They sighed, looked hangdog, and avoided his eyes.

I had known these men from childhood. I had assumed that what I saw and heard was all there was. I had ignored something fundamental. I had ignored the compelling, amoral power of the schmekel. Or should I say schmekels?

I realised I had a lot to learn. That was the day my attempt at a writing career ended. The next week I took a job as a clerk in the post office.

Pushover Quiz

Answers to Panurge 20 Quiz.
It was **Eça de Queiroz** who worked in Newcastle's Portuguese embassy and who wrote *The Sin of Father Amaro.*
The winner was **David Rose** of Middlesex who got a £20 Book Token.

Panurge 21 Quiz. Only one question. Which Frenchwoman in 1973 published a bestseller called 'Boy'? First correct answer wins £20 Book Token. Deadline 5.11.94. Answers to Pushover Quiz, Panurge, Crooked Holme Farm Cottage, Brampton, Cumbria CA8 2AT.

JOINT 2ND PRIZE

Bloodlines

Julia Darling

The letters are all blue and flimsy. Airmail is so unsatisfactory. Not like vellum. Sometimes I don't even open them when they arrive. I just put them straight into the carrier bag behind the stereo. The writing is always the same, and they inevitably begin with ... 'I hope you are well.'

Sometimes I am not well. Sometimes I have been dreaming about savage dogs, or pavements with cracks in them. There are days when I find this city quite alarming and can't bear to look at it. It's full of leaking arcades that have been dampened by foul outbursts of rain, and car parks that loom up when you least expect them, and shops with huge cavernous mouths that pull you in. On such days I generally stay in bed and try to write letters back to my father in Madrid.

He would like me to go and see him. But I am uncomfortable with my father. He is too big. He cuts the light out of rooms. I remember his loud voice making me jump when I was a baby, or I think I do. My mother won't speak of him at all since the divorce. She has married an interior decorator called Paul, and lives in Hertfordshire.

My father writes and tells me that he will pay the fare, with his golden card with the eagle flying across it, and that he has a spare room and a housekeeper.

The first time I read about the housekeeper I was on the train going home. I live at the end of the line, and every day I step neatly onto the buzzing yellow train that sweeps into the morose station where I live. Candycoats, Hawkersville, Mankerton, Subside Village, Overflank, Middleclaw, Wegsfield, Fallowsyard and then Barberstown, which is the centre, where I limp out, like a mole burrowing out into a builder's yard. After five minutes I am blasted with dust particles, and nearly flattened by women with large bags.

I started reading about the housekeeper as we drew into Subside. It was the first interesting thing my father had told me in five years of correspondence. He said, drily, that she was an excellent, if uneducated housekeeper, apart from during the full moon, when she changed dramatically and he had been forced to lock his drinks cabinet.

I laughed. It was the thought of my father; large, English and unshiftable, being prey to the unstable cycles of a Spanish country woman. I was sure she drank red wine.

I work for the Dock Refurbishment Council on a temporary contract. Coincidentally, I often call in sick, due to my own monthly cyclical problems. I heave and weep and generally swell.

At the moment we are building a great embossed tower in the middle of a mosaic-paved square. It will glitter in bright sunlight.

The aim is to attract foreign guests to this rather infertile city. I phone people up and describe the tower in great detail. I talk to strangers as if they are my oldest friends. We're launching the tower, like a space rocket, on the night of the Summer Solstice, and there will be a dazzling firework display with rockets and even a head of a Northern man drinking a pint of beer illuminated across the rotting harbour.

I am very attached to the tower. Sometimes I feel it belongs to me, in all its ridiculousness. I am familiar with every part of its making; its inner rubble, its window measurements, its oak interior, its hidden foundations, and even the number of tiny glass mirrors pressed into its Gaudiesque body.

It is the work of an architect from Brazil. I like to think of how much it has cost the government. I like to watch it growing from blue lines on paper into this solid edifice. It will always be there. Even when I am old.

Publicly, I am the woman in a small suit who rustles behind joking business men with a file full of coloured paper. Sometimes they turn to me and place their big palms across my back in a leaning, almost caring way. How I got into this kind of employment beats me; I was Head Girl at school, maybe that's the root of it.

I will also tell you that since those heady days at Walthamstow Girls Grammar, I have always been attracted to other girls. I'm a dyke, a lemon, a lesbo, a queer. Perhaps that's why I am uncomfortable with my father.

Like most people I know, my love life is a series of incomplete disasters. Unlike them, I do not have fantasies about the right person, and I have never advertised in the Guardian Lonely Hearts column, or contacted a dating agency. I prefer the condition of lovelessness, to be honest; I am at home with it.

When the letter came about the housekeeper I was single, but soon after that the wine bar opened on the river bank and I met Sandra Diaz.

I went to the wine bar after work in order to fortify myself for the long shuttle home. Da Vincis reminded me of my father, sat in his Spanish hat, waiting for his housekeeper to appear with an omelette, or a flagon of Sangria. It was a superficial connection ... strings of onions, and raffia-coated bottles. The pictures of bulls reminded me of my father though.

The Dock Refurbishment Council had invited artists from European countries to create public works to coincide with the launching of the great tower. Although I wasn't in charge of that particular set of files and complicated phone numbers, having no linguistic skill, and no knowledge of modern art, I did realise that the woman in reflective sunglasses was probably foreign, and probably artistic. She drank Newcastle Brown with interest, and kept looking at the ceiling. Also she smoked Parisiennes which stank of the French underground and foreign ashtrays.

I was mid-cycle, so my sense of smell was heightened. Then Gordon came in from Artworks, which was the department next to ours in a prefabricated hut, and said hallo to me and Sandra simultaneously, so I had to sit down and join in the fragmented conversation. I wasn't surprised when she said she came from Madrid; after all, one thing follows another, once you start thinking about omelettes, or babies, or dogs they seem to be everywhere. They even come out of the radio as you say them. That night it was *Learn Spanish* on Radio Four, and the day before I had been to Safeways and every tin I put in the trolley turned out to be of Spanish origin.

The minute I saw Sandra I knew she was loose. She was the kind of woman who just floats into situations acting alarmed, but in fact is entirely at ease with the oddest liaison. She had very short Spanish blonde hair and a defined forehead. Her English was polished and aesthetic. She made encrusted textiles, she said, and had work hanging in the Museum of Modern Art.

"So what," I thought. The stink of her Parisiennes was getting me down. I felt a sick note coming on. Gordon slavered all over her anyway. He talked about Art the way other people talk about meals; as if he consumed it daily.

In order to change the course of the conversation that was centering on an airtight fishtank, with sonic tapes booming overhead, I mentioned to Sandra that my father lived in Madrid and she looked at me as if I was accusing her of something.

"What does he do, this father of yours?" she said.

"He's a linguist, and who knows what they get up to?" I chirped.

Then, with a slight sense of disloyalty, I told her over the next half an hour, about the housekeeper and the fits she had during menstruation. Since the first letter my father had written again, describing a drinks party with colleagues from the Institute of Latin Studies.

Things had been quite unexceptional at first, with Rosa bringing trays of cocktails onto the balcony, demurely and subserviently. Then gradually, she had gone downhill, and started to stagger. Finally, like some Grace Pool lookalike she had fallen onto the floor clutching her matted head and moaning.

My father hadn't sacked her, although he said he had been stern, but 'the poor woman is in the throes of the moon, and seems to have no will of her own at certain times.'

I thought the story quite amusing, but Sandra whistled through her white teeth, and shook her head. Then she took off her sunglasses, exposing black diamond eyes. Sandra reached over the straw beermats and grasped my wrist.

"Country women are very suspicious."

I think she meant superstitious, but I was looking at her slim brown hands and feeling a bit shaky. Nothing had touched me apart from the palms of business men, for nearly three years. Her touch had a smell of some exotic Spanish brandy, or bay leaf, or eucalyptus.

Gordon coughed and left, though we hardly noticed him.

In the end we tottered back to the underground together, and slid down the escalator at Barberstown, singing the *Internationale.* By Middleclaw we were holding hands, and by the time we touched Hawkersville her tongue was behind my ear. Luckily she looked like a boy in her anonymous shades, or we might have regretted our actions at Candycoats, when a metro inspector had to shake us apart, like dogs, to tell us that the train terminated here.

The only other thing I remember about that night is that it was a crescent moon and for a while we lay in the back garden looking up at it surrounded by nettles, which miraculously didn't sting me.

The next day, while red wine still coursed through my throbbing veins, a letter arrived from my father, saying that Rosa was much improved and had just made an excellent paella, having apologised profusely for her behaviour.

The summer continued with raw passion and modern art intertwining like my and Sandra's legs as we rolled about, always with a bottle of some cheap wine half empty by the bed. I wonder now how I ever got to work at all, but somehow the beautiful phallic tower continued to be built, and the mosaic artists stuck their little golden bits all over it, and Sandra made her indecipherable artworks of strewn grass and mud, and I wrote to my father, and he wrote back.

I remember one day quite vividly.

Sandra and I took an unopened letter from my father down to the new business park, that reminded me of a neat shanty town, with its empty blocks of dusty offices, and half finished sculptures. The river was very oily and smelly, and I saw a rose floating down sadly amongst a mass of other debris. We sat on a deserted promenade and opened the letter.

I hope you are well. I have some excellent news. Perhaps I didn't explain to you that I have been ill with a virus for some weeks (he had, but my father always tells me everything several times). *Rosa has been looking after me. I don't know what I would have done without her. She is much better generally. Her appearance is quite lovely, and as far as I know, she no longer drinks, and her other problems are much abated.*

The rose was nearly out of sight by now, and Sandra didn't seem to be listening.

The upshot of all this is that I have proposed to her and we are to be married next month. I feel that we can be companions to one another in our old age. It will be a small wedding. Of course I would be delighted if you would like to come over, but I understand this may be difficult for you ...

From where we were sitting the mosaic tower glinted maliciously. I felt slightly disturbed by the news of my father's wedding. It suddenly occurred to me that since my passion had been roused my menstrual cycle had been considerably quietened. Then I thought about my father in bed with his dark, superstitious housekeeper and felt uncomfortable.

Sandra took the letter and deftly folded it into a small blue paper boat, and dropped it down into the water.

It sailed off.

"Good luck, daddy," she said morbidly, and I suddenly wanted to be alone, on my way home, on the shunting train. Going back to the end of the line.

As we walked back I was stung by several nettles that the corporation gardeners had left behind.

The next week it was the great launch, and everyone at work became quite frantic with bits of paper flying in all directions. There was a lot of arms on shoulders and heads on desks, and tears in the toilet. I had pre-menstrual tension and I avoided Sandra. She kept on phoning up with her insistent Spanish voice, which irritated me beyond belief. I wrote to my father, congratulating him on his engagement. I sent him a postcard of the tower ablaze with light.

When the day finally came I put on a maroon suit, and stuffed my shoulder bag with sanitary protection, as my lower abdomen was dark and heavy, like before a storm, and my breasts were like concrete balloons. I was just about to leave the house, when the phone rang. Of course it was Sandra, who I was beginning to wish I'd never met. I could smell her Parisiennes down the phone, and the stale pong of her clothes.

Sandra was wailing.

"Oh for God's sake!" I said curtly.

Then she stopped her wretched braying, and whispered nastily.

"I curse you then."

Actually, I heaved a sigh of relief when she said that. All I was thinking about was the colour of my shoes and if they really matched my maroon suit.

"Fair enough," I quipped, and put the phone down.

On the way to work I counted women who smiled. There were two. One was in her demented eighties, and other was a pre-pubescent schoolgirl who looked out of the train window grinning. All the others were miserable as Christmas.

As soon as I got to the quayside I knew something was wrong. I saw Gordon through his prefabricated window, pacing up and down with a mobile phone pinned to his ear. Then I saw the tower. It was splattered with red paint ... running into the gullies of its sparkling golden sides. There was a crowd of people gazing at it and shaking their heads. I looked across the square and could have sworn I saw Sandra, glowing ferociously in the shadows.

I started to run towards her; my stupid shoes twisting on the cobbles, but she was gone. There seemed to be paper blowing everywhere ... reports and clip files, and transparent paper holders, and memos. I was hot with rage. I felt as if I was foaming at the mouth ... trapped and blown and uncontrolled.

Then Gordon grabbed my arm. He looked oddly calm amongst the wreckage. I looked at him bluntly.

"There's a phone call for you," he stated. "International. Madrid."

I caught a sudden smell of tapas when he said that, and felt immediately nauseous.

Gordon had turned. I was supposed to follow him. I hobbled back to the office. All around me police and passers-by were muttering. It began to rain ... suddenly and intensely, and as I walked to the phone I saw that the water was washing away some of the paint, and red puddles were appearing on the ground.

"It's only acrylic," Gordon was saying, conversationally.

I picked up the receiver and spoke dumbly into it.

"Yes."

It was a thick, Spanish voice. A woman. She seemed to be crying, but it was hard to know the difference between the sound of the rain and her voice.

"Your father. He has a heart attack. He has passed on."

I suddenly thought that it was Sandra, playing some ghastly trick.

"Who is this?" I said angrily.

"Rosa." Then I realised how her voice slurred, and that she was drunk.

"What do you mean. Passed on?"

Then there was a loud noise. A clap of lightning or something, and I dropped the phone. I'm not quite sure what happened after that. I think I was sick.

I'm at home now. I'm lying in bed, and bleeding. None of the fireworks would light, so the day was a wash out, and there will be no tourists flooding to see the pinkish tower. My contract is ended.

Tomorrow I will fly to Madrid and sort out the funeral. I can't imagine my father in a coffin. He will never fit. I can't stop thinking of unspiritual things.

I am cursed. In Madrid a Spanish housekeeper called Rosa is waiting for me. I am pathetically afraid of her.

And I wish Sandra would come, and stroke my head and help me drink a bottle of red wine, but I am completely alone, here at the end of the line.

The last letter from my father was a boat, a blue boat, sailing off down a river, that will have disintegrated by now.

And there will be no more letters.

I lie here with the carrier-bag emptied over the mattress, under a sea of thin blue paper.

Success

William Palmer

'I was Max Bialystock. Five shows on Broadway. Two hundred dollar suits. Dinner at del Monico's. Look at me now - I'm wearing a *cardboard belt...*'

*

I quote from memory Zero Mostel's wonderful lament for lost success in Mel Brooks' film *The Producers.* The character he plays is tormented by the idea of success, endlessly in pursuit of it, and hatches a plan to seize his greatest success from a careful manipulation of failure. I wasn't actually wearing a cardboard belt when *Panurge's* invitation to write about Success dropped through the letter box. But with it came a letter from the bank manager regretting he could not increase my overdraft as I 'seem to have no fixed and reliable means of earning.' Perfectly true. Neither have actors, or producers of plays, or snooker players, or ballet dancers, or anyone else who takes life in his or her own hands or voice or body and tries to live on the one thing they can, or think they can, do best.

Success, say the politicians, is only failure deferred. Failure, say the writers and others, is only success withheld. I don't know what it is in strictly material terms. Those differ by expectation, after all. I read last year a pathetic piece by some 'writer' in the Guardian, telling how he had decided to give up writing because his chums in the City were all earning filing cabinets full of money and he judged himself incredibly ill-paid for his output - which seemed to consist of a handful of short stories. Come to *Panurge* - they will print your stories in good, sometimes wonderful company - and pay you virtually nothing for the privilege. Because that's what it is. Nobody asks a writer to write, an actor to act, or anybody to do anything at all. You can make as much or as little in a job or on the dole. Writing is a profession only in so far as so many people profess to be able to do it, and then get angry or confused or bitter because nobody will agree with them. The success is in the work - any other Success is usually, though not always, coincidental.

*

A case history. My own, because it is the only one I know intimately and every other one is different. There are no career paths to the top, middle or bottom. I began writing when a lot of people do, in adolescence, when poetry is partly a glandular response to sex and the suddenly burgeoning world around. I read hugely, omnivorously, devouringly. (This - the library, the bookshop - is the only university, the only workshop a writer can go to in order to learn his trade. A person who reads English at university hoping to become a writer is like a swallow reading ornithology in order to fly.) Poetry, as I say, came with all the other baggage of adolescence. At thirteen I wrote a 200-line blank verse poem in the style of Browning; it was, if I remember, the dim ruminations of an Arab shut outside a city's walls and dying of thirst. At fourteen I wrote incredibly complex metrical impersonations of Gerard Manley Hopkins and Dylan Thomas. At fifteen; tart, elliptical Audenesque ballads. At sixteen my first poem - about the death of Oscar Wilde, God bless us - was published in a little magazine. The editor called. Fame beckoned.

My next poem was published fifteen years later in 1976, and my first story a year later. I was incredibly backward in the way of all self-educated people. But I had travelled a good deal, still reading endlessly, and absorbing what I thought of as 'Life'. I won't go into the reasons for the long time lag - they are many, and both common and peculiar to myself. I still wrote poetry all those years, submitting occasionally to magazines poems which were returned with those depressing printed rejection slips, poems which were printed years later, some of them. I subscribed to magazines, especially to *Stand* which was a lonely Northern beacon in those days. But from 1976 on I published stories and poems in magazines with less and less resistance. I don't want it to seem that editors publish work because you have been published elsewhere. Editors sometimes have cliques and favourites, but they are usually the bad ones - there are editors who remain, against all odds, extraordinarily fair and open, despite writers' complaints. What happens I think is that your work does actually become better after you are published - it is very difficult to work without hope year after year. The prospect of publication is in itself an animating factor. Of course, the dangerous corollary to this is that you write to please an editor. That way lies a real and hideous success.

Back to the story.

All this time I'd earned a living from the array of jobs in offices, factories, hospitals etc., that you could readily obtain before the economic miracle of the Thatcher era. I continued to do these jobs while starting to publish in the little magazines. Another sort of success began to press on my heels. I was getting older and there was a pressure on anyone of any sort of intelligence to progress upwards, to show ambition, to make a career, in the places where I worked. I resisted by switching jobs, by journeying from one place to another, by simply lying low as long as I could. I began to feel like Melville's clerk, Bartleby, muttering - 'I would rather not' - when offered promotion or extra responsibility. I knew what I wanted to do - which was what I had always done, was increasingly *doing,* that was to write. By now I was married, with a young child, and the pressures began to build financially too. I was making little money from writing. I was unhappy, drinking too much, writing late into the night. A novel. Another. They were no good - mean, exhausted, derivative efforts. I had also, in 1981, got taken on by an agent - I'm going back a little now. This came about after sending some stories to Bill Buford at the newly restarted *Granta.* He was very kind - he liked them, but said they were not for him. He recommended that I get myself an agent. I said I didn't know any agents. He gave me the name of one, who I still have now. Like poor Peter Piper in Tom Sharpe's *The Great Pursuit* - the first quarter of which is required reading for anyone aspiring to be a literary agent, if not a writer - I bombarded my new accomplice with various versions of novels Mark I and Mark II. He couldn't, and I am profoundly grateful he could not, sell these. He did sell quite a few stories for me however. The third novel was a huge improvement, not being about me. But this was again too short and too indebted to other novels to succeed. By now it was 1987. Fortunately, I was sacked at the end of that year from my last employer - after a long and exhausting struggle for him to do so - so that I could pick up some redundancy money. My wife had gone back to work. In the glow of burning bridges - which are very warming for a time at least - and with no kind of financial future, I at last got down to writing.

As they say, the prospect of being hung in the morning concentrates the mind wonderfully. This is no joke - I do believe that unless your temperament drives you to do something to the exclusion of all else, to refuse to be distracted, you will not succeed in any way at that thing. It is no good waiting or moaning or explaining your silence - to yourself, or others. Particularly to others. So, where was

I? I had about 120 opening pages of promising but flabby and rambling material towards my novel, *The Good Republic.* Over a weekend I boiled that down to 30 pages and sent it off together with a detailed synopsis of the rest to my agent. Within a week he had an offer from Secker and Warburg. I am exaggerating a little, come to think about it. They did want to see more pages, but I had been thundering along and these quickly followed. The whole novel clung pretty closely to my original synopsis. This is not to demonstrate any idea of writing to fulfil the expectations of a publisher, or my own rigidity of thought. For me a novel, or story, or poem, has a structure that is 'given'. However dimly apprehended it exists as a house exists; it is architecturally whole and however you knock it about and light its rooms and place its occupants, it is palpably there in the mind; the work is in holding the structure steady, and in moving the occupants from the front door to the back, from entrance to exit. With this house still only half built, and half illuminated, I went down to meet my publisher.

I stood, flushed and important, in the Editorial Director's office at Secker and Warburg. I couldn't help wilting a little, looking at the names on the bookshelves around. He had gone out to get me a beaker of coffee from the machine - I'd expected a china tea set at least. I looked down at his table loaded with manuscripts and saw one with the title *The Van.* Fat chance, I thought smugly. What a bloody naff title. What sort of idiot sent *that* in with any serious hope of success?

I went back home to the Midlands and finished up the book. When the last draft was finished it was sold to Viking in the USA. I sat back and waited for publication, and the inevitable, unavoidable, ineluctable triumph. Did it come? Not exactly - not in those terms.

I went down on publication day, in June 1990. I lunched with my publisher, and was whisked away to Bush House to do an interview for BBC World Service. Disaster. It was my first interview - and the first for my interviewer. I *think* she had read the book. I was already highly nervous and so slightly belligerent. Her first question: 'Why did you write this book?' is one of the totally unanswerable questions, after 'Why the hell *did* you marry me then?' I sat numb-brained. I spluttered. I shouted nonsense. She asked me about the political background to my novel. I started to gabble ... It is all too painful to recall. Coming out, along the long dingy corridors, with the very nice young woman Seckers had provided as my minder, I said, 'If they can get anything out of that they're bloody geniuses,' and looked back to the see the producer right behind us, glaring at me with professional and personal hatred.

But the book was quite widely and mostly very well received. The variations in reception were the most interesting. One reviewer singled out my gift for characterisation. Another praised my sometime poetic prose. Another said the action was gripping. The reviewer in the TLS said I could not write action, or dialogue, or create character, which was pretty comprehensive. After a few weeks, and the last review, an awful silence descended.

How did it sell? More than I'd hoped - and not what I'd hoped. It was not a disaster. It sold out its first small hardback run. The paperback is still in print. It astonished me at first that anyone would buy a book for the price of a decent bottle of Scotch by someone they had never heard of - and then I felt aggrieved that more of them did not do so. Mercifully, you don't know for a long time - unless you have a best seller on your hands - how many copies a book has sold. Anyway, I was already busily into my next novel.

I wrote this throughout the back end of 1990, and all of 1991, delivering it in January 1992. In 1991 I had a good year. I was awarded an Arts Council Bursary, and received a larger advance for the second novel than for the first. I also caught chickenpox in France. This is not recommended for adult persons, being much more severe than the childhood version, and it is rather difficult to write while suffering from a raging fever and a body load of ghastly pustules. I think though that on balance it may have rather enhanced the descriptions of my hero dying of syphilis. At least it gave me some first hand experience. This second novel, *Leporello* came out in the autumn of 1992. By this time, the bookshops were ghost towns rapidly destocking on ghosts. The book had several excellent reviews, one or two polite ones, and some actively hostile. Again, the differences between reviews are most interesting to the writer of the book. It again sold out in its hardback run, and is doing quite a lot better in paperback than the first book.

Where does all this leave me now? In what way is it the success that *Panurge* asked me to write about? In the past fifteen years I have had a score of short stories, several dozen poems, and two novels published. I have a contract to produce another novel which should be out in 1994. Since 1988 I have made a living - with the endless and marvellous support of my wife, Gill - out of writing. I'm still living, though in debt for doing so, like everyone else. I've had some critical enthusiasm, and some antagonism. If you haven't heard of me, I hope you will. If you haven't bought my books, I hope you will rush out and buy one or other of them.

But success?

I began with a reference to film, and will finish with that. Film is the dominant art form of our century. In D.J. Taylor's recently published book on the English novel he laments that contemporary writers have not the same breadth of vision as the great novelists of the nineteenth century. True, but he is looking in the wrong place. Our equivalents to Dickens and Trollope are not novelists, but film directors such as Orson Welles and John Ford. And the tragedy of film for the individual creator is that it is a collaborative medium, and you can make a personal work usually only in the teeth of the greatest opposition from your collaborators. Orson Welles has been put forward as the film-maker who most approximated to a writer, in that he attempted, at great personal cost, to shape his films in the way a writer shapes his material. He is also held up as the supreme example of early success and hubris - and subsequent calamitous failure. As something of a tragic buffoon, reduced to advertising with his physical bulk and orotundity the virtues of cheap wine on television. The truth is that Welles remained for all of his life a great artist of a high and fine intelligence. He managed, in often appalling circumstances, to make five or six pictures of astonishing power and poetic beauty. If this is failure, what is success?

Welles is viewed as a failure because he attempted so much and fell sometimes short. But his ambition was a noble one - to create works which would illuminate, enrich, question - in the current sociological jargon, to 'empower' his audience. I have to go to a film-maker, and a dead one, for such an example, because I cannot think of a living English writer who would admit to such ambitions, let alone try to accomplish them.

Many younger writers go into television and film because they think it will give them a far wider audience than the seemingly ever dwindling world of readers. And to make money. But to succeed as a writer, pure and simple? In what way? Financially? You would do better plugging away at the eight draws on Littlewoods. Money flows in the direction of public demand - witness the same parade of names at the top of the bestsellers list each year. Such success is not easily imitable. It takes a great effort to write like Jeffrey Archer; not as great as, say, Joseph Conrad, but an effort nonetheless. The difference is in the man. Between a lump of coal and a diamond. But if such success is required it is probably better to try for that job in the city.

The Author is supposed to be dead. Well, not quite. Critical orthodoxies are comforts for fools. I do not believe that novels and stories and poems are only tricks and toys to wile away the time until the Millenium, when we can all get down to the really serious business of computer games and virtual reality sex. Writers, whatever their relative failure or success, should be on the side of the angels. What otherwise is the point of their endeavours? What else shall they do? Join the bloody enemy?

Tom Saunders

A King In His Crooked Castle

The Nostrum House was designed in the late 40's by an artist named Aroldo Maniscalconi, a Confrontationalist committed to challenging all modes of conventionality, his battle cry being: 'That which is New cannot be normal.' Observing, like dozens before him, that the straight line was both a tyranny and a contradiction of nature, he denied each room, each embryonic box, the safety of the horizontal and the perpendicular, causing the entire structure to sag and bag like some colossally ugly clay pot that had collapsed in on itself in the heat of the kiln. Resulting in a building that was, if some of the critics were to be believed, perfect in its imperfection, a triumph of the imaginative over the sensible, a Maniscalconi pure and difficult. A work of art that was mercifully unsullied by any utilitarian influence, with a kitchen in the attic and two toilets in the basement; bedrooms on the ground floor and bathrooms on the third. The only irony being that the best tradesmen had to be used to realize the artist's grand lack of design because the routinely incompetent could not be relied upon to yield up their worst work to order. Bricklayers whose walls habitually veered out of plumb were prone to produce the exact opposite when the plans required it of them. Carpenters and plumbers who had spent a lifetime not knowing what they were doing and where they should be doing it became very confused when confusion was the rule and were inclined to go badly wrong by going right.

It was a job that every one of them would remember for the rest of their lives. Walls and floors came together at deranged angles, no door or window was the same shape or size as its neighbour and, by the time the final bend was bent and the final joint was wiped, Maniscalconi's creation had more pipes running through it than the human body, a labyrinthinely-veined circulatory system of its very own. Water streamed in from the main and was sent on unimaginable journeys, gushing out of taps with spouts sculpted in the shape of slack penises and helter-skeltering round and round the intestinal convolutions of a plexus of ribbed and lobed radiators that panted and wheezed like clogged lungs first thing in the morning and last thing at night.

Peter Shanks-Damson commissioned the house. My research told me that fact. But when I asked permission to address him as Peter, he waved an index finger with a hooked grey nail and complained long-sufferingly: "Not Peter, P-ierre. It sounds like affectation but you must take into account that I'm one eighth Breton swineherd on my step-mother's side."

I met him initially when I was asked to write an article for an up-market style magazine with thick, glossy pages and even thicker and glossier pretensions, one of a stop-go series on architectural curiosities in and around the city. "Come in, lad," he said on the doorstep, "only too glad to give you the tour. Who did you say you were again? Of course, Smith, I'm sure I served with a chap called Smith in the Blues. Probably your dear old dad. I wouldn't mention it to him, though, he'll only deny it. For some reason they always do."

Later, I would find myself irresistibly drawn back to the place whenever I was in the area, making my excuses and asking that I be permitted just an hour or two more to wander its absurd corridors. Because it and its owner had rooted themselves in my mind, teasing my need to explain everything and everyone to some invisible third party, foiling all my attempts to understand them, like a madman's cryptic aside or a whodunnit with the final page torn out.

In my piece I wrote that he was a man who had been sporadically rich, a description he approved of so much he swiftly appropriated it as his own. Never being required to do a day's honest labour in his long life he got by on a relay race of allowances and bequests that came his way as, one after the other, his wealthier relations succumbed to everlasting peace. "My multitudinous uncles and aunts had nothing in common, other than a pathological fear of sex and a thoroughgoing hatred of the young," was how he explained his good fortune. "God bless them, they had no alternative but to leave all their loot to me because it was inconceivable that it should go to a stranger." Not that he managed to remain solvent for more than a year or two at a stretch. When he had funds he spent them with the abandon of a gluttonous sultan who is yearly granted his weight in gold and diamonds by a grateful populace. "I'm happy never to have known the value of hard-earned cash," he would say "I was bred to it. And where would the world be without fellows such as I? I'm a one man redistribution service."

Pierre was reclusive in that he preferred not to go out, but he appeared to like company well enough. I assume he was one of those happy band of egotists who, because they are wholly fascinating to themselves, see nothing unnatural in being asked to be on show. In all my many visits, I never for one second got the impression that my presence was unwelcome. Of course, the pause while the old chap found his way from whatever far corner of the house he happened to be in when the bell was rung put most callers off. It was a house of far corners, where everything you might want and everywhere you might want to go managed to be as far away from where you actually were as possible. I discovered this myself the first time I stayed the night. There was no point in hurrying. It was best just to set out hopefully and enjoy all the twists and turns and surprises and not be too disappointed if you ended up somewhere other than where you had planned. Flexibility of purpose was the first rule, as was the second, third and fourth.

Pierre and Maniscalconi never got on. The artist was famous for his temper tantrums and Pierre was famous for his placidity, which put them somewhat at odds, though only the former showed any signs of recognizing this fact. Regrettably, offensiveness, if it is to be enjoyable, demands that someone should be offended. By the time the building work was finished, Maniscalconi, warned by his doctor in regard to his rocketing blood pressure, felt he could no longer afford to risk another infuriating confrontation with his patron's affable smile and left forthwith, leaving instructions for his fee to be forwarded to him via the mail. When he received it, Pierre's assertion in the covering letter that he was a 'charming chap' all but did for the Italian. Certainly, this calumny, when circulated by his detractors, played no small part in the artist's subsequent decline from favour.

When Pierre opened the lopsided oak door to me that first day I was struck, as he brushed the grime and cobwebs from the scattered white strands of his hair and smiled at me with his long carthorse teeth, by how much he resembled Max Schreck in the film *Nosferatu.* A resemblance that was accentuated by the way he carried his hands high on his chest, the way his shoulders were humped and his spine was bent. He had shrunk, as he was heard to boast himself, 'into a frightener of old biddies and young snotnoses' over the years, the kink in his back largely due to the hammock made of parachute silk he always slept in. "Wouldn't, nay couldn't, sleep a wink anywhere else," was his explanation. "The touch and the smell of it reminds me of the wedding dress my wife wore when we were married in April '41. Lovely girl, very capable, sewed the frock herself, stayed up until three in the morning stitching. Used every scrap of material she could. Told her when it was finished that all that was missing was the ripcord and the red beret. Poor darling didn't have a clue what I was going on about. She was Austrian, you know, as are all the best sweet things. Refugee. Socialist parents, came over after the *Anschluss,* driven out by the bastard Schickelgruber. Blond hair coiled in plaits on top of her head like a Valkyrie, like ropes of the finest golden thread. Eyes so awfully blue you quickly forgot about her squint. Ran off an hour after the ceremony with a Polish Hurricane pilot with teeth like pearl buttons and cheekbones and a Morgan three-wheeler with a supercharger on the front. Friend of a friend, the perfumed sod. Something of a blow to one's self-esteem as you can doubtless imagine. Still think about her ... Rosa was her name ... almost every day. Haven't wholly ruled out the chances of a knock on the door and a tearful reconciliation. What a surprise it would give her to find her husband in such a striking setting. Can you believe she once wrote in a letter that she thought of me as philistine and boring?"

Which one of us suggested that I should catalogue the treasures Pierre had surrounded himself with other the years? Probably I did. But my curiosity fed his hunger for an audience. We dove-tailed in our concerns, you might say; we had a mutual gratification society all to ourselves.

All of the important pieces had been sold by then; the sketches by Matisse, the statuette by Giacometti. What remained, whether it was stacked against the decaying plaster of a forsaken room or in one of the tea chests still scattered everywhere, said not much at all about art and a lot about Pierre's uncertain taste. Of course, he had an excuse for each and every misbegotten item. Listening to him, I wondered at the innocence of his enthusiasm, an innocence I do not allow myself. (An ex-girlfriend of mine used to claim that I would not buy the things I truthfully liked because I knew that if I did people would know what to think of me.)

My own nights at the Nostrum House were spent in the same room; once I had successfully memorised the route it seemed foolhardy to confuse matters by changing the arrangement. Which is very British of me I know, but a bed you can be sure of finding is the only bed worth having in my book. Besides, I rather liked the room. I liked to think it suited me. Remote from the rest of the bedrooms on the improbably rambling ground floor it stands proud of the blind rear wall, a blunt brick pimple, either an afterthought or a beginning, flouting Newton, hanging in the air, the vertiginous prospect from its window an enticement to suicide or euphoria, maybe even both. Most satisfactory of all there is the seasick cant of its floor, a perilous gradient that obligingly tumbles your weary bones between the sheets at night and stops you - should you be stupid enough to need stopping - from shunning their cosiness in the morning, aware that any movement on your part will entail an uphill struggle. But for the nagging thought that Pierre might enter at any moment with a scalding hot cup of tea and lose his footing there is an even money chance I would be there still.

Maniscalconi and Pierre met in Paris after the war. The artist was designing scenery for a new production of Stravinsky's *Apollon Musagète* and sleeping with a mysterious woman who had slept with a man who had slept with one of the few women who had not slept with Picasso. At least, not up until then. Pierre 'simply loved' Paris, it was, he said, his favourite foreign city. "Couldn't live there, though. Couldn't live in anywhere so uncivilised they can't cook a proper roast lunch with thick brown gravy and a wedge of Yorkshire pudding. The French spend more time talking about food than they do eating it ... a bit like the Americans and sex."

The Nostrum House was launched, figuratively, with a new bottle of wine, the third bottle to be exact; ordered by Maniscalconi and drunk, largely, by Pierre. The two men had been introduced earlier in the evening by a gallery owner-cum-agent, acting, in the purest of ulterior motives, as a go-between. Pierre wanted a painting, at least he thought he did. Terminal illness - Aunt Bill, a rabid old fox-hunter and five-star misanthrope, had recently maimed her last insolent peasant - had brought a healthy flush to his bank account and the money very much needed spending. As he was in Paris and he could afford something a little grander than the usual postcard of a street scene by Utrillo, a painting for his rooms in the Albany seemed like a good start. A painting that rather disliked the idea of itself, something large and unattractive that people would find hard to ignore, that would sock them in the eye or make them laugh or make them feel ill. A Maniscalconi in other words.

In his ignorance, Pierre had expected the artist to be grateful to him for his patronage. Not one bit of it. "Where exactly would the picture hang?" Maniscalconi asked aggressively. "Would it have its own room?" And the inquisition did not end there. How was he to know that Pierre wouldn't surround the work with the worst kind of kitsch? What proof did he have that Pierre was not some vulgar speculator interested only in procuring a profit? Would he cherish the painting and make sure it was preserved for the good of future generations? Did he appreciate what he was asking? Was he without a heart? Wasn't he able to see that each completed canvas was like a fistful of flesh torn from the artist's guts, an essential part of his being, that to buy one of them was an act of trust?

Listening to this and helping himself from the virgin bottle of wine placed on the table by the waiter, Pierre had to concede that Maniscalconi had a point. When he proposed what appeared to him to be the answer, the artist, who was by then peering about him in an aggrieved fashion and addressing the entire restaurant, came close to choking. "A house?" he said. "You want me, a painter celebrated by the few critics of perception, to build a thing of bricks? For you? In England?" He leant forward, his eyes bulging in disbelief. "You expect me to make *art* in England?"

Pierre's voice appeared louder than it was in the pregnant hush of the room. "Do you know," he said, "I really rather think I do." After an audible intake of breath there was a small cheer from the other diners. People then began to rise from their tables, filling the aisle with bodies as they waited with beaming faces to shake hands with both artist and sponsor. Nodding like an automaton as they congratulated him, Maniscalconi was left looking stunned.

He took no part in the negotiations that followed, and once the price had been settled upon, he was shepherded in the direction of the door with a diplomatic show of force from the mysterious woman and the gallery owner. Turning his head from one to the other, his feet pedalling slowly in space as they lifted him, he protested in an operatic whisper: "Build *him* a house? Create something timeless and beautiful around *him*? Why, the man has the aesthetic allure of a dung beetle, a cockroach."

Although, on the night, Pierre was no less shocked by his offer than everybody else around the table, the more he thought about it the more it appealed to him. It would be the perfect answer to his problem. No longer would he be haunted by the vague suspicion that the life he had made for himself was a work of imitation, not only worthless but inauthentic. With the building of the house he would bring into being something potent and original that would, but for him, never have existed. He would be assured of his place in other people's heads forever. He would ring like the true coin.

More than this, the project transgressed against everything the Skanks-Damson's as a family had believed in or thought meaningful, everything that Pierre had ever had a desperate need to transgress against in fact. The very idea of Aunt Bill's dusty old cash being used to succour and encourage the avant-garde was delicious in the extreme. It was tantamount to drawing a big black moustache on the Mona Lisa, though to tell the truth Aunt Bill, in the considerable largeness of what she at least liked to think of as her life, had been no oil painting and a second moustache, whether big and black and waxed or curly and carroty red, would have been something of a redundancy on her already well-tufted upper lip.

The story of how the house came to be commissioned was one of Pierre's favourites and I heard it many times. He liked to tell me about himself while I was eating dinner. A scraggy-necked vulture in his fraying black suit and yellowed shirt front, he would perch on the edge of his chair, a glass and a bottle of Calvados on the table by his hand. As he spoke he watched the movement of my fork, pausing for me to respond only when my mouth was full of food and then smiling to himself when I spluttered and coughed.

In the manner of many of his contemporaries, Pierre was, in his own unassuming way, a drinker of professional competence. Somebody who had settled, in relation to his own image, for the profoundly pickled rather than the well-preserved. Somebody who smelt like an old brandy cask, his breath and sweat stale yet sweet. Instead of choosing to become drunk he chose not to be come sober, sipping at his drink, imbibing for sustenance rather than pleasure, rationing his intake like a traveller who knows that he has a limited supply of water and a very hot desert to cross.

Eating for him was a spectacle, a curiosity. He took no part in the cooking or serving of food. Hungry guests at the Nostrum House were expected to fend for themselves. The first time I was invited to stay for dinner I was advised to go to the kitchen and see what I could find. There I discovered several dozen frozen meals in the freezer compartment of a coffin-sized fridge, a stockpile that was never replenished, leaving me with less and less to choose from as my visits went on. How they had got there was an unsolved mystery, Pierre would never say. He always affected great surprise at what he saw when he hung his nose over my plate. "What exactly do they call that?" he would ask. "Really? From India. And you just pop it in the oven do you? How wonderful." Often he would get me to fetch the box so he could read the ingredients off of the back. His wolf grey eyes sucking up the names of every spice and flavour enhancer with the avidity of a scientist poring over new data.

As for himself, he adhered to what he called the Ben Gunn diet: pongy brown Stilton eaten with a slice of dry bread. The last time I spoke to him he was nibbling away in this fashion, crumbs on his lips and waistcoat. He looked frail, delicate, like he might break if you put your arm around him. It was late on a Sunday evening in April. When we got on to the subject of my departure the following morning, I tried to get him to fix a date for my next visit but he seemed uncharacteristically reluctant to give me an answer. "Went to spend a week with a friend, years ago now, haven't wanted to go anywhere much since," he said. "Couldn't get used to the house. It was all over the place. Kitchen downstairs. Bedrooms and bathrooms together. Most off-putting. Couldn't damn well find my way around. Wasn't what I was accustomed to, you see. I've grown accustomed to living here, just like I've grown accustomed to being who I am. It isn't about choices, choices are brutish. It's about becoming, you become what surrounds you." He brushed himself off with a flick of his thin, mottled hand, the bird bones beneath the skin protruding whitely. "I'm near to being used up, my dear old chap. I've got shoes older than Queen Liz, ties older than you."

It was a weird night, that night. I know I would say that now, but believe me it was. It was difficult to sleep after what Pierre had said. He had sounded and looked ill. He had left brandy in his glass. Needing light, I scaled the snowy incline of the undersheet and switched on the lamp. Rolling back and propping myself up in a nest of feather pillows, I could picture his bewildered expression as he swung open all the wrong doors in his friend's home, baffled by its conformity, the needle on his inner compass spinning wildly out of control. How frightened, how stripped of substance, he must have felt without the bizarre certainties of the Nostrum House to reassure him. And what is so very awful about that? Everyone needs somewhere of their own, somewhere that belongs utterly to them and no-one else.

No-one else? Well, not quite. Woken from a doze by the distant flushing of a toilet, I jerked my head around with a shiver when I suddenly became aware of the shadow of a spider as big as a beach crab in the corner of my eye. It was scuttling with hesitant steps across the slope of the ceiling. Horrified, I lay tense to my toes and watched as it felt its way slowly down the wall behind me and vanished behind the bedside cabinet. Knowing it was there, waiting to run over my face, kept me wide awake for hours; when the pipes gave up their groans with a sigh I could hear the papery patter of its eight long legs every time it moved in my direction.

The house was so silent in the morning, I sensed instantly what had happened. There was nothing morbid about this, nothing psychic or paranormal: when someone gets up and quits a room their absence is often felt as strongly as their presence. I knew as surely as I was alive that my host was not, the cold rooms and corridors spoke to me of that.

The hammock was swinging gently in the breeze that blew through the cracks in the crooked window frame. I had used the faint creak of the ropes suspending it as a homing signal. Pierre was lying on his back, his arms folded across his chest. He had a peaceful look on his face, but there was what I took to be the crusty residue of two large tears streaking his gaunt, grey-stubbled cheeks. He was all got up in a pair of purple silk pyjamas, his monogram, *P.S-D.*, embroidered in golden thread above the breast pocket; the front of the loose jacket had a ladder of frogged fastenings in the Chinese style. His few wisps of hair were held in place by a hairnet woven from criss-crossed pink filaments. Cradled in the bend of his left elbow was a mangy blue teddy bear with amber button eyes, its lips compressed in a hard, stitched line.

The great equine fangs that had once grinned at me from between Pierre's lips smiled at me still from a glass standing on the high table near the hammock. The yellowy liquid in which the teeth were steeped looked, at first, disturbingly like urine, but when I bent closer I could tell from the smell that it was brandy. Also on the table was a book in a ripped paper cover, a collection of poems by Henry Newbolt, dedicated to Thomas Hardy and published by Nelson, price 2/6d. Picking it up, I leafed through it until I came to the pages divided by Pierre's curling leather bookmark. The poem there was called The Old Superb:

The wind was rising easterly, the
morning sky was blue,
The Straits before us opened wide
and free;
We looked towards the Admiral,

where high Peter flew,
And all our hearts were dancing
like the sea.

There was no other furniture in the bedroom save for an upright parlour piano, a golden-veneered Broadwood with silver candlestick holders. Along the top, crammed together so that the obscured one another, were a dozen or more photographs, Pierre's face prominent in all of them. There was Pierre wearing a bowler hat and standing with Rene Magritte; Pierre sitting with raised glass at a table at the Cafe Flore with Jean Paul Sartre and Simone de Beauvoir; Pierre pretending to illustrate to a cooly unamused Miles Davis, his face hidden within an ectoplasmic cloud of cigarette smoke, the correct way to play the trumpet; Pierre as a baby, sans clothes and teeth; Pierre at school, his stance awkward and shy; Pierre at Cambridge, his stance slouching and bohemian, a meerschaum pipe in the corner of his smiling mouth; Pierre in his best dress uniform outside the church on his wedding day, his stance parade-ground smart.

The day of the funeral, the only other mourner for the majority of the service was the distant cousin Pierre had left the Nostrum House to. He arrived in a black suit and a check cloth cap, which he took off and tossed on to the passenger seat of his Range Rover before joining me at the door to the church.

We had advanced as far as the grave side, the vicar having just completed the 'Ashes to ashes, dust to dust', oration, when two fey looking individuals of uncertain age garbed in jester's motley and smelling of gin and rose water came sidling across the churchyard. "We got held up," said one. "Are we too late?" asked the other.

The distant cousin shrugged his shoulders as if to say, I don't think it matters all that much now, do you? and avoided making eye contact with them.

"Almost," I said.

"Would you like to say a few words?" enquired the vicar.

Both jesters shook their heads, the tiny bells on the points of their coxcombs jingling in tempo. "We came to dance," they said in unison. And dance they did, circling the grave with hops and skips and kicks, their arms and legs moving convulsively as if they were suffering from a severe nervous condition.

The show lasted for thirty seconds or so, by that time they had run out of breath. Wheezing horribly, they linked hands and took a deep bow, inclining first in the direction of the open grave, then towards us, their live audience, then backing away awkwardly along the path separating the plots. Before turning, they called: "We'll meet again,

P-ierre. Don't know where, don't know when." Lingering at the church gates they tugged at the crotches of their costumes, which, due to the exertions of their performance, were now hanging down below their knees.

"Thank you for coming," panted the distant cousin as we walked, trying to disguise our haste, towards our cars. His large red nose had an unhealthy blue cast to it. "I never had the pleasure of the old fella, myself."

"You missed something."

"One of a kind, eh?"

"One of a kind."

He stared at me piercingly, head tilted to one side. "I suppose you're a fan of this ..." he made a show of searching for the right word, "house, I've been lumbered with?"

I told him the truth, hoping Pierre would forgive me.

The cousin laughed. "Too bloody true. What a nightmare. Imagine locking yourself away in a place like that."

"I take it you won't be moving in then?"

He started as if I had stuck a pin in him. "Good Lord, no."

"Not really," I said, stifling a grin and agreeing solemnly with him, "your style."

He sighed. "Have to unload it as best I can."

As I commiserated we shook hands.

In my rear-view mirror, I watched the last hope of the Skanks-Damson's as he climbed into his car. Turning the ignition with one hand he leant over and picked up his cloth cap with the other and screwed it back on his head, lips puckered in a whistle, thoughts once again encased and earthbound.

Several weeks later, when the work on the headstone was finally completed, I supervised its installation as Pierre had asked me to do in his will. (A task I was more than happy to undertake: guilty of not always taking him seriously while he was alive, I felt duty bound to do the opposite now that he was not.) Tracking down a monumental mason who was sure enough of his own ability to take on the job was the chief difficulty. Nevertheless, in the end, Pierre was fittingly remembered according to his own strict instructions; the stone was manufactured to perfection and laid in place. It was made from pink Italian marble and carved in outline and relief to resemble the front elevation of the Nostrum House. The inscription read:

PIERRE SKANKS-DAMSON. 1918-1992.
PATRON OF THE ARTS.

Howard Wright

The Necrographer

[I]

Claire and myself were in bed watching *Top of the Pops* when they broke in, banking on the music to cover the racket. Three of them, three masked men, burst in, leapt on us both, slapped Claire about a bit, gagged her, then hit me, stuffed a gag into my mouth and tied my wrists and ankles. The more I resisted the more I was slapped and told to shut up.

I was dragged on to our landing by the quiet couple, leaving the talker with Claire. I struggled to stay but got a cosh on the ear for my trouble. My upside-down view made me dizzy, then nauseous, as if I'd just stepped off a roller-coaster. My stomach was forcing its way into my throat; the pain was like a spike in my temple.

My hands were tied to the banisters and both legs got sat on. The figure who had tied me stepped back suddenly, into the landing dark, as if hesitating, and the fella on my legs told him to do it. The procrastinator stretched his coat-lining taut so it wouldn't ride up when he withdrew his hand. I watched that gloved hand bring out a pistol and that's when I started screaming through the gag. I heard the words in my head. The legman shook me hard and told me to shut up; then he too watched the gunman.

From that first hesitation, it was somehow inevitable that this figure should stoop and touch my head with the barrel. I quietened down as I was supposed to. I was on a different planet. I cared only that that cold gleam should disappear. It moved on, to my throat, my ribs, halting above my right knee.

I couldn't conceive of the pain. It would arrive in any case so I closed my eyes and clicked my teeth over the cloth. The legman prevented me from swinging the offending limb out of range. I thought this would never happen in my own home - you know, the castle syndrome, but then, thank God, I'm not English. I remembered Claire. Both gloved hands snarled around the rubber handle; the scarecrow skull butted in, another hesitation and now we all shouted for the eejit to do it.

Claire was the only thing in my head. The sudden noise intensified the instant, and the music. He drilled a narrow hole through the carpet, underfelt and floorboards - crushing, splintering, burning, bloodying. Killing me. Others talk of feeling nothing - well, for some seconds, yes, then it falls like an avalanche on the whole body as if pumped with liquid pain.

And tears don't ease the pressure; I had to rip out the banisters or surrender. Then I could absorb no more. Sparkles fizzled on the ceiling. I arched my back until it came away. I heard more voices. My left side itched and I realised they had reached that side as well. More music seeped through. Their train had left me with two viscerous stumps. Everything tingled uncontrollably till I couldn't accept anymore. There was the taste of sick and the vision of tilting walls. And someone still singing ...

Is pain enough to kill someone? I've asked myself that many times in the interim and concluded, well, yes.

As you might say, I'm dead already.

Heaven is antiseptic and tiled white; a hospital outside the walls. They had the good sense not to put me on the second floor. The nurses were sympathetic agricultural girls who had seen it all, twice, and my anger and complaining was another part of a day's work, though they still listened and humoured me.

I had to understand I was nothing special, and only when I came to terms with that did things move more easily, even to the extent of getting to squeeze the tight muscles beneath their frilly sleeves. I was told if I was making beds, turning fifteen-stone men and wheeling wheelchairs, I, too, would have a physique like theirs.

Yes, they made me laugh, and I grew content because their industry at curing pain was very funny. Here I was - immobile, patella-less and all I could imagine were ways of inflicting agony. I thought about knees; I felt for the nurses' knees through their smokey 15-denier. Legs of smoke and bronze. It tickled them. Then they'd slap me if I went higher. I thought about Claire, her face and her legs, and about the spaces that had been my own knees; about the space in someone's head, their facts mixed up, and about that someone being Jimbo, and how much I hated him.

What had I done? Your guess is as good as mine. I'm no grass; I'm not disloyal. But as it was Jimbo gave the orders, made the security, started the businesses, ran the clubs, the machines and women. I had crossed him once and received a reprimand and a fine. *We have to pay for our sins one day, he said, and I'm not talking heaven.* Jimbo was a real philosopher and as such had no common sense. This knee-capping episode was a far more serious misunderstanding, speaking as one who felt the repercussions; so obviously I couldn't forgive. *He* would pay *me*. My certainty conjured up the energy to overcome my injuries and indulge in a gluttony of revenge.

This gave my physio cause to be pleased. She was a strong, capable woman in her thirties, with broad shoulders and spikes in her bleached hair. When she told me her name was Lesley I said it couldn't be anything else, causing her to smile apprehensively. I was a strange character then - Lesley blamed the shock. The fierce callisthenics brought me down to earth. She was gentle at first, then, after a couple of months, was throwing me around like a teddy bear, or stretching my limbs on a weight-frame or walking me, like an old man, between two mahogany beams. Revenge fed me.

However, all was forgiven when I took that first step, unaided across the gymnasium floor. I hugged Lesley, taking her perfume on my cheek, while the other patients cheered. A week later Claire was over with a hold-all and brought me, and my crutches, home. Naturally I had to give Lesley my word of honour that I would rest. But of course me and Claire got down to business at once. My brave wife had worked overtime to buy a gun.

[II]

This is where Neville enters the story. Bad Man Nev. He would do anything for money except lose it. I heard he had a hand and a leg in beating up his cousin for courting a girl of the other sort. It gained him respect and no harm at all. Not even a fine. Who was Jimbo to worry about stuff like that? Nev asked no questions, told the useful fibs and worked a brief sojourn with the 'right' people, namely Jimbo and his mob. That's where I knew him from.

I rang Nev's house as soon as Claire had sorted out money and I had arranged the equipment. He did not recognise my voice after all these years, but I convinced him with a few shared memories, and limped over the next evening, catching the bus part of the way, to talk turkey.

A pristine union jack flopped from a socket high on the front wall. This was odd as the month was March. His door was closed on a bolt and chain and the wooden panels sandwiched steel plates. I remembered him fat; now he was gangly, just as tall, though he looked at you with a less than confident sideways stare as if sussing out your next answer and it wasn't what he wanted to hear. When he answered, he blinked. Perhaps the divorce was to blame. His second wife - 'The little woman' - Adele, stayed in a back room.

The only time he left me was to collect two tea-mugs and have some words with her. Then I heard footsteps above my head.

Nev was a good listener, especially, like I said, when money was brought into the conversation. He enlisted immediately. I asked him to see about getting a gun. What size? Nine millimetre. Hundred and fifty now, hundred and fifty on delivery. I was to come back in a week and lay off the telephone. I didn't look him in the eyes once. When he expressed concern for my condition - meaning was I up to the job - I shrugged and stressed I couldn't possibly live with my wife or with myself if I didn't show Jimbo he had picked on the wrong guy for such patently flawed reasons. It seemed the right thing to convince him it was Jimbo. But feeling it best not to be too buddy-buddy, I refused his offer of a lift.

Back at the bus stop, as in the shops and bars, I was pressed forward ahead of others with a silent wave of the arm or head. These city people miss nothing and say nothing. They are affable to deflate any aggression but also, more importantly, to suss the person out. Me, I'm the legendary victim on their door-step - the example from the news bulletins. Or maybe they don't think of me at all. What's another cripple with the paraplegics and quadraplegics who even I stare at? Of course they suspect what has happened and I'm prepared to play for a bit of fun, and get my own back. Life's hard enough, I say. So I'm recovering from a Tyrolean skiing accident, or have recently had both cartilages out after years rowing for the university. Nobody really gives a damn, and well, I thought, if they believe all that guff they will believe anything - no harm to them.

No harm to them, I needed Jimbo's address.

We had little to go on. Lesser mortals called him James and he lived in North Belfast. We were only on first name terms. Any surnames given were by order false, usually of a colour - Brown, or Black or Scarlet; only leaders could give themselves the title White, and that's how we knew Jimbo. Nobody chose Green as far as I can remember. He was on the dole and separated from darling Phyllis, staying late most evenings at the 'headquarters' in Ballyhackamore, a squalid flea-pit of a venue, covered in illiterate emblems, where our merry band of outlaws drank ourselves paralytic under the iron tables while, in the cellar, homemade weapons and army surplus uniforms and equipment lay wrapped for the light of the 'Glorious Day'.

Nev had left before the move to Ballyhack so I gave him directions, telling him to follow Jimbo home and then come back and tell me.

Unfortunately, though it was good Nev was a stranger that far east, it also meant he was easily lost. I should have gone with him but it was my massage night with Lesley. I couldn't work out if Claire was more unhappy about Nev's failure or this weekly tumble with Miss Spike Top. I trusted Nev - no reason not to. It was a trust not misplaced - though he must have been like a fish out of water; either Jimbo clicked or as Nev confessed, he just lost the play on the one-way system - I didn't press the point. Damn it, though, another week was lost ... Next time out Nev would be my chauffeur.

I brought the goodies - flask, sandwiches, Mars Bars, rope, masks, gun, cricket bat. We used the secret compartment under the rear seat in case the Brits stopped us. Our observatory was up a side street at a dead-spot. Nev finished a sandwich while simultaneously looking through binoculars, when the last group came out, effing and blinding in the harsh light from the shaded bulb over the red, white and blue armour-plated door. Jimbo wore his perennial sunglasses.

Nev suggested an attack, which with hindsight might have saved us a load of trouble. However we would have been in the open and as I was still on a stick, my legs were not up to crossing the broken ground at any speed. Nev could quite easily have taken the three of them but I resisted the temptation - Jimbo was bound to go home some time.

According to Nev they went the same route as the previous night, the 'commanders' dropped off in stages. We knew he was heading north, so I restrained Nev. Then, with the last crony dispatched, Jimbo roared away. I allowed Nev free rein through Belfast, startling lechers in doorways, avoiding wine victims dancing at the leaning clock. I counted passing headlights and tried to read street names. God, I thought, some of these people wouldn't know the underside of the city unless it hit them on the head (or knee-caps).

Nev was doing well by this time. He wanted to know if we only wanted Jimbo's address; I said, barring accidents or a road-block, tonight's the night. I consulted my steel partner and he agreed. Nev was grinning like a frozen fish; I broke into a Mars Bar.

The dual carriageway between docks and factories swept under our wheels. Nev allowed another car to slip in between us and Jimbo. I massaged my knee from being cooped up for so long. The overhead lights flashed by in sudden moments of day and night and vehicles from the other direction thumped up and past, while I noticed Helen's Bay and Holywood, on the opposite low-lying shore, were swallowed by the black lough which allowed no reflections to splash up from its polythene surface. On this side, strung beads of municipal streetlighting tore lines across Cavehill's lower slopes, and the crest, Napoleon's Nose, was a black hump against the red sky of Glengormley and Mallusk.

At last Jimbo took off down a tributary to the Shore Road, veered through junctions and signals, and eventually, after another long stretch and the excitement of passing a night patrol, entered Rathcoole's concrete lava flow. Unknown territory to Nev and me. However it was well-lit and the canny folk had parked their vehicles under the lamp-posts. Softly, softly.

Jimbo slowed right down, took a left at a T-junction, gained the brow of an incline and stopped. We stayed back and sidled to a halt at a low cement wall. I opened the door and luxuriously clicked my etiolated joints. The urban escarpment shone like candles in a chapel making the sky a meaty pink, but punctured by faint stars; no clouds, no moon.

Nev put on his mask while I hunted for the other accoutrements. I checked my own mask and immediately it irritated my skin. Nev was out and at the corner, watching Jimbo lock up his car and sink the radio aerial into the chassis. He patted his pockets for the keys of the house. "Go!" I hissed, and Bad Man Nev flew across the front lawns, leaping small privet hedges and Castlewellan firs.

Jimbo was up the path. Fly, Fly, Nev ... Closer, closer. Don't turn, please God, don't turn. It must have taken seconds. But Jimbo turned and saw terror falling. He reached inside his coat and backed to the door. Ten yards, five yards. Too slow, son. Nev smashed into him, flung a hand over the mouth knocking off the glasses, threw the body to the path, stomach down, arm close to breaking. I recomposed myself, checked up and down - not a flutter. Maybe this was normality in Rathcoole. At least my dreams had come true.

Feeling serious again I limped on the cricket bat towards my feast, stooping once to retrieve the sunglasses, which weren't sunglasses but tinted spectacles. I steamed and polished them, and put them in my pocket. By now Nev had the poor sod tied and gagged. When I ambled up to them, the door was opened and our happy trio fell into the sepulchral hall.

[III]

I played safe and assumed someone would be upstairs. Jimbo shook his head. And right enough we heard nothing. Regardless, Nev set Jimbo in a big chair and went up to investigate. I plugged in the sidelight, and for a minute we were alone - mystery versus fear. Those weak eyes. A cuffuffle above our heads. Jimbo realised what had occurred and struggled so I had to hit him a hard slap on the mouth.

Things had gone quiet and Nev came down with a disjointed mannequin over his right shoulder. He held her chin up and I nodded approval, then he tied her to the banisters where he could keep an eye on her. She hung there like a symbol of something, feet off the ground, arms straight, her modesty vaguely covered by chiffon negligee.

We began.

I replaced Jimbo's glasses - seeing fear, after all, was half the battle. I took out the bat. It had Ian Botham's autograph on the willow. Jimbo was caught between this wood and Neville at the door. I called him names, and brandished the silly gun, forcing Jimbo to linger on the colour and sheen, but it was all show. He thought I was going to use it; so did I, in fact, until reality dawned. I had no silencer, but that was just an excuse - secretly I hadn't the nerve to experience the whole ordeal again. The money was peanuts though not entirely wasted. I always thought the bat had more threat in it, much more of what Jimbo himself would call 'the personal involvement'. Claire is better at these things than I am because she thinks ahead.

I pocketed the gun and tried to forget the money, and picking up the bat in both hands, began to call him an airhead, a soft man, a little big man. I talked too much. I forgot his men were the silent type. I ordered Neville to check the ropes and I went into my Capone act, tapping the meat of the bat in the palm, saying this was real justice not like the kind from his amateurs, scared of their own shadows.

The head was shaking almost continuously now. I gave a bow and tidy salute when it occurred to me that a soldier - for what else was I? - must have the timing of a good comedian. My face straightened, gave a hesitation - yes, his lads knew the power of timing - and by pure talent, in a lightning whiplash, brought the meaty club into his right knee-cap. A six! The pain was silent as I knew it would be; he rocked backwards, foaming around and through the gag. I felt the nerves go through the wood, the ligaments, the crumbling marrow. Nothing was left. Neville wobbled the seat back into place. Once more - this was justice, I said nobly, eyes for eyes and teeth for teeth. I was feeling great.

"A knee for a knee," proffered Neville ironically. We were both in our glory. You couldn't beat it with a big stick.

I pleaded with Jimbo to believe what I said about fair-play and decency and checking the facts before acting, and as I pleaded, I carried the club back and through to his left knee like an axe-man cleaving a trunk. Jimbo was well out of things this time; he passed out completely and my gloating was finished.

I pulled off the itchy hood and shouted at Neville for getting woollen ones. Adele had knitted them, he explained, and he didn't want to hurt her feelings by refusing them. I shrugged it off and unplugged the light and went to the door. Neville looked back almost with regret, saying it was nice while it lasted. I repeated the joke about beating it with a big stick. I had to drag him out when he stopped to inspect the woman on the banisters. Jimbo hadn't much taste in women but Neville wasn't fussed. I read later about the 'necrophilic urge'. A nice word, *necrophilic*, like *necrologist, necromancer, necrobiosis, necrolater* ... We stood in the street checking we had everything.

"What about him?" Neville asked. "He can still give his orders".

Jimbo wouldn't grass on us and anyway killing wasn't my intention, honest, but Bad Man was right this time. The consequences had seldom been clear beyond the satisfaction of revenge, but now Neville's head was on the block. Indeed it was a pity Neville was even there.

"You do it then," I said. "Use the cushion and leave the woman alone".

The cold ached in my dead knees as I crossed the pale, windless road. I became conscious that I was leaning on the bat. I came to my senses, and realised bad luck adds up until one decision is made and everything is all right again. That's why I was standing in the middle of Rathcoole on a clear night. Neville was still in there doing what he does best. I thought then the world would work out and that would be an end to it. Claire was fantastic. I opened the driver's door and placed the bat in the rear seat compartment, checked the gun again, and switched it to my right pocket.

Derek Neale

Land Of Their Fathers

To Begin ...

The town sits under grey granite scree: its roofs glimmer like the teeth of a saw, cutting deep into the outcrop of the mountain. The quarries lie dormant: no millstones grinding, no wailing sirens or belly blasts. Only a dirty green grass silently reclaiming the pits of dust and sweat ...

*

Before he reached school age his father sat with him at the bench nearly every day. They modelled little animals and people from spare lumps of muddy clay - lions, boys and goats, and a girl they named Rhiannon in honour of their new home. Like all the others she found a space in the kiln for the biscuit firing but went without colour or glaze. The joy lay in the mud, and in the wheel: spinning, splashing, bowls rising from nothing, strange shapes giddily pirouetting. The water, warm to young hands, chiselled the arthritic joints of his father, so even then it pained him to play with his son. Even then, in the slime of his daily work, his father's hands ached for the wheel to slow and for the water to stop running.

When she was a child, her dad read from his most precious book: of moonless night in a small town, starless and bible black. And he told her it was off to the south - this sloe-black, crow-black land - as if grey, the slate grey of their town, was a shade closer to heaven. He sang to her in his halting asthmatic rasp of princesses and princes, and of Y Ddraig Goch, the dragon on the mountain who guarded the valley. He told her of a time before the quarries, of the farm on the mountain, with his father, and his father before him. But when she asked why he kept the shotgun in the wardrobe, he gave no farmer's talk - of pests and crows and rabbits - but said it served to keep the Devil and his witches at bay.

*

The town sits under granite grey skies, waiting for more rain and the sanctuary of dark: coal black night to be lit inside by flickering TV screens, and lit outside by Stryd Fawr's orange streetlamp halo. Above the mountain, above the clouds, the banished moon rides the night alone ...

Gathering Moss ...

She stopped gathering moss from the mountain after the robbery. She was no gunman but she had fit the description, dressed as she was - 5'8", medium build, ruddy complexion, dark hair and moustache. The blue hat that Mam, *cariad* Mam, had knitted before her stroke hid the bulk of her hair. One of Dad's green army sweaters, hanging halfway down to the knee of her jeans, concealed the shape of her body. The police, with their prodding fingers and beady eyes, had touched on a raw nerve when they came across her, there on the mountain. So she forgot about their uniforms, forgot about the DHSS, the Fraud Squad. *Cariad* Mam was all she saw, even when the police realised their mistake and warned her about the gunman: *cariad* Mam lying there, all alone.

A man wielding a shotgun had robbed Jones the Post Office on the Saturday. She was glad. When she cashed her fortnightly cheque there - £99.03, including £40 mobility allowance for Mam - Jones always asked:

"Have you got your personal identification love, so's we can conform to the regulations?"

And sometimes, when she was going through the door, she heard him whisper to his wife:

"Only the bad berries get left on the tree to winter."

A real hero: he stopped the gunman making a clean get away by locking himself in his new Volvo, while his wife handed over the money, the gun at her head, the car keys in her apron. The gunman was seen heading on foot towards the mountain, while Jones cowered under his steering wheel, praying to the accelerator. A real hero: a bastard, like the rest of them.

The Jones's were one reason why she dressed as a man when she went on the mountain. They were all bastards - Jones the Post Office, Jones the butcher, Jones the chemist. They all looked - for breasts as she leaned to sign her cheque, up her skirt as she reached for tins of soup (in Kwik Save where the manager was a Jones), at the curve of her backside as she put the cornbeef in her basket. All bastards, wanting personal identification. It was safer by far, walking on the mountain as a man.

She lived with *cariad* Mam in a two-up-two-down on the edge of town, on a street where the quarry houses retreated from the mountain like defeated soldiers, their uniforms muddy grey, helmets bloody and wet. She had tried to stick up the peeling wallpaper, the fallen yellow and red roses, with sellotape. There were slates off the roof, soaking the walls, she knew, she had told Jones the bank, the agent for her landlord. But he had denied it, said it was condensation

Bridesmaid, Dundalk, Ireland.

Philip Wolmuth

- "You should open a few windows, love. Get a bit of fresh air in." A brown, leathery fungus prospered in the kitchen, on the sweating slate floor. She swept it into the backyard and shovelled it up on Saturdays. It didn't bother *cariad* Mam, smiling there under her crochet blanket, saying nothing but "thankyou" and "there's lovely", every day a smile. Nothing bothered *cariad* Mam. The black mould covering the bathroom walls had grown thick since Dad had died. He used to scrub it off, but what could she do - open a few windows? Let the dank, putrid smell out? Then the kids would shout in, like they shouted on Stryd Fawr: "Bandy Blodwen, busty Blodwen, don't point your third nipple at us Blodwen, lend us a balloon Blodwen, take us to the moon Blodwen."

She went up the mountain to the lake on Sunday mornings when the Jones's were sure to be in chapel. The disguise guarded against one of them playing truant, and against the Fraud Squad. She picked mosses from around the lake for Mr. Worthing, who owned a garden centre in Birmingham or Liverpool, she could never remember. He also owned the house next door but was only there on summer weekends. He told her - "Some people like to make their plots look like wild rockeries." Plots he called them. She knew nothing about that, but knew that he paid a good price for the mosses and heather - pocket money for the mattress, for Christmas, money for coal when the nights drew in, money for when Mam, *cariad* Mam, lying there ...

She had heard they were about - the DHSS, the Fraud Squad. If they caught her working, gathering moss, they would snap up her benefit, the furniture, everything, snap it up they would and where would she be then? Where would Mam be then? When she heard they were about she bought the black moustache from the junk shop on Stryd Fawr, just to make sure.

She walked from the road to the lake in half an hour, sometimes less. Beads of sweat dripped from the cauldron of her hat, smarting her eyes, making her scratch so that her forehead, her cheeks, her chin, all grew red and bothered. She went straight to work, gathering the moss from the boulders on the near shore first, placing the bright green sponges in the black bin bag and trying to keep out the sticky brown peat. When she had lined the bottom of the bag she would sit on one of the granite slabs, the remnants of a farm burnt out after the war and now smoked with sage green lichen. From where she sat she could see anyone coming before they saw her. The bowl of the cwm flattened out into a saucer at the lake. Purple heather spiked with saffron gorse, rampant ferns and reddening rowan berries, all fleshed the walls of the cwm like left-overs from an exotic feast. She just saw the horizon, the bent hawthorn where the path met the lip of the cwm. She would wait a few minutes, make sure, then hold her breath as she removed her sweater and her blouse, then her boots, her jeans, her socks and her vest. Last to go were the black moustache and the hat, always with one final glance to the horizon.

Stumbling in, the ice water clothed her, encouraged her to move, so her arms and legs became radials of a compelling force, pulling, pushing, tossing, gliding. She forgot about the children on Stryd Fawr shouting, calling - lanky, bandy, busty Blodwen. She forgot about the cry that died with her dad - get yourself a man, Princess, get yourself a good man. She swam through it, washing, erasing, as trickles of sensation returned to her spine, her thighs, down to her toes and out to her finger tips. She swam to the far shore of the lake where the lilac bell heather grew, sheltered by the tall cotton grass. When she rose out of the water she forgot about the horizon behind her. She looked up past the bilberries to the mountain's summit, feeling the water trickle down, looked up and beyond to what she thought was heaven. Y Ddraig Goch, the dragon, lived up there and he was the only one to see. He would keep the Jones's and their beady eyes at bay, of that she was sure. Then she brought the bell heather back to the near shore, plant by plant, swimming with them above her head.

The day after the robbery she was collecting moss from the lake. She rubbed herself dry with ferns and ran to get warm on the soft grass of the sheep tracks, avoiding the barbed heather and gorse. She had replaced only the hat and moustache when she heard it. She was fully dressed apart from her sweater by the time it landed, swirling the fragrant gorse around in a dry mechanical storm. When they reached her she was wearing the sweater and was about to dump the bag of mosses in the lake.

But the bag dropped to the ground as her hands rose automatically, pointing up to the queuing clouds.

Made of Clay ...

Kerry was three when the Hertz-Randles moved to the valley from London. They opened a pottery in the old quarry manager's house, welcomed by Jones the Post Office who, for their first three years, asked - “Are you enjoying your holiday?” - whenever they bought stamps from him. They enjoyed a meagre summer trade, serving the holiday makers with painted clay sheep and Japanese brush strokes on ‘Made in Wales’ mugs. Kerry’s slouch was born in the winter of his seventh year, when his father took to the pubs. Jones the Post Office saw it coming:

“With a name like Hertz-Randle what do you expect? There’s German blood there somewhere, mark my words.”

Kerry’s mother, as if in response, devoted herself wholeheartedly to the task of mothering her son:

“Have you got your sandwiches? Kerry Hertz-Randle, what are we going to do with you? Do you want an apple today? It’ll fill you up. Do the other children take apples? Never mind that, you have one.”

At first he tried to answer but time saw his posture change to that of a slinking cat: he slipped into the ease of “Yes Mam”, “No Mam” - until she grew so utterly tired of the valley that she asked - “Who is this MAM? Who is she, MAM?” When he mastered “Yes Mummy” without a stutter and when appropriate, “Yes Mother”, he knew she wouldn’t tire of those.

He was at Yscol yr Berwyn by then, marked apart by a secret in his bag and by his ‘Mummy’, who picked him up after school, so he never walked along Stryd Fawr with the others, never passed the fags around at number 37, the derelict house; knew nothing of it, or of the songs they sang when they saw Blodwen and followed her. Bandy Blodwen was a name scrawled on the blackboard, joined by a heart and arrow to another name - Jones, Parry, Owen, Jones - it could have been anyone. His mother dragged him home day after day, as if she were taking him back with her, to London. His father worked in the morning, stopping the wheel at twelve precisely, when the Owen Glendower opened its doors. Kerry had no need to answer him, there was nothing to answer. He heard them arguing late at night, his mother screaming - “Not only did you bring us to this cursed place, you can’t get us out - look at you!”

His father, slurred and feeble - “You wanted to come to Wales as well” - blasted by his mother screaming louder - “I wanted to live by the sea, not in this bloody grey hole.”

Kerry spent his lunchtimes in a corner of the playground, whispering to Rhiannon and picking at his mother’s sandwiches. Rhiannon was his daughter: 4" high with an apron and dress of uniform, almost flesh, brown - an unpainted clay doll, the only one he had kept. She lived for the most part in his school bag, propped up between his pencil case and exercise books. They had made a vow to protect each other, there in the corner of Yscol yr Berwyn playground. Long before he started running on the mountain, long before the Bangor game: they had scratched each other's arms. No blood, but Rhiannon was his sister.

Some taunted him - "Cracked pot", "teacher's pet", "piss pot" - but no one thumped him. The teachers steered clear of him, looked at his hunched shoulders and excused him from games without a note: a liability, having a lad like that on the rugby field, and in the changing room -

"Something wrong with your back, lad?"

"Sir."

He had learned quickly that 'sir' served as yes and no in the same breath; yes, I submit, no, I'm not listening.

His apparent privileges brought recriminations. Books were stolen, once his sandwiches, and regularly scrawled on his desk was the recommendation that he should 'Piss off back to Notre-Dame'. The day of the Bangor game someone got serious - planted a half-smoked Benson and Hedges in his desk and sent an anonymous note to Parry-Jones, the games teacher infamous for his abhorrence of nicotine.

"A private puffer are we?" - for once Parry-Jones was blind to Kerry's slouching shoulders.

"We'll see how well you can puff, lad - the 3rd team are playing Bangor this afternoon, and it just so happens they're a centre short. Don't think I've ever seen you run. I'll make sure you've got a kit."

Kerry had watched them play rugby from the sidelines, seen them coveting the ball like a golden egg, firing like green bullets from one end of the field to the other. He had seen the ones with headbands, the forwards, lumbering like overfed carthorses - groaning, moaning as they stirred the pitch into a stew of sweat and spit and mud.

The mixture of sweat and embrocation made the changing room smell like a stable. The carthorses greased their brows and ears with vaseline, splashed liniment on their legs, and he was told, "If you get the ball, get rid - straight away, there'll always be someone behind you, but always behind mind." Then one of the carthorses grabbed the waistband of his green shorts and poured liniment down into his pants, shouting - "That'll make you run, Potter." - as they all cheered. It soaked into his shorts and looked like he had wet himself: it began to burn, and he held his shorts and pants away. It was too late to change them now, so he ran out on to the pitch burning, carrying the smell of the stable with him.

The carthorses were high-spirited into the first scrum, as the rain swept down, and the fresh white lines sank into the morass. He hopped around his fire as the ball stuck to the feet and bodies of the carthorses: skulls grinding, collar bones flexing. It was getting hotter, seeping into cracks and crevices. Would it ever stop? "No, no!" he thought as he held his shorts open for the rain to fall in. "No, no!" as the ball bobbed from one green shirt to another, spiralling and twirling at the peak of its final arc. It came towards him, falling slowly as if it had lost its way. Letting go of his shorts, "No, no!" he thought: he held out his hands in front of him and closed his eyes. Only when he felt it finally clutched still against his stomach did he remember - "always behind". He opened his eyes, looked and hopped, saw nobody and ran.

There were shouts on either side of him; getting hotter, skin was peeling, "No!" he thought, "No!" Head down, faster, cooler, hugging tighter, head down, faster, cooler, soon be there. Oh, Rhiannon! Faster, tighter, hugging closer. He ran towards the posts chased by a posse of green and yellow shirts; please help, faster, cooler, please! He was beneath the posts when he heard one of the shouts - "POTTER, THE OTHER WAY YOU IDIOT - THE OTHER WAY!"

He turned in a large circle so the posse were stranded; head down, down blind, faster, cooler, his shoulders hunched naturally around the ball; head down, faster, faster, the carthorses left muttering amongst themselves; faster, faster, the yellow and green strung out the length of the pitch; faster, faster, no-one to stop him but how was he to know; head down, cooler, cooler, head down and it would go away; deaf to the cheers behind him, deaf to the carthorses shouting, "Go on, go on ... You show 'em". Oh, Rhiannon, please, head down, faster, cooler, faster, faster; deaf to Parry-Jones' final shout from the touchline - "WATCH OUT FOR THE POSTS, LAD - MIND THE BLOODY POSTS!"

Surrender ...

Helicopters had been drafted in to help with the search for the gunman. When they spotted the insect-like figure by the lake they were confident they had got their man. They aimed their guns with even more certainty when, through their binoculars, they saw his moustache. They fanned out in a wide arc from the helicopter's whirling blades, advancing from boulder to gorse bush, then back to boulder, calling through a megaphone -

"This is the police. You are surrounded. Put your hands in the air and remain still."

When they saw the hands pointing upwards they stopped their darting runs and took aim. All still. Until the crackling voice advanced, persisting with the chase -

"Don't move a muscle - it'll get you nowhere, there's nowhere to go."

The megaphone rose from behind a bush, like a strange beetle, and the others stood upright, revealing their faceless antennae, the beads of their guns all converging on the moustache.

They were about to handcuff her when one of them noticed the moustache was false. They started to prod. She grew stiff; she had heard about the police, about the DHSS, and about the Fraud Squad.

"GET OFF, YOU ... LET ME ALONE!" Take the moss, take the benefits, but leave me be. "GET OFF ... GET OFF!"

One of them mentioned a gun. She'd never taken it out of the wardrobe, not since Dad died. Did Mam tell them? How could she? Dad always kept it in the wardrobe, hurting nobody, keeping the Devil and his witches at bay. Mam knew nothing about it: Mam, *cariad* Mam, lying there, underneath her smile.

One of them let her hair out of the hat, as another discovered the bag was full of moss and heather.

"No loot here, lads."

"What do you want?" They knew, she could see they knew. She could see it - sitting in prison, the house empty, nobody to sweep the kitchen floor, nobody to keep it tidy, and *cariad* Mam in a home, nobody to make her tea, nobody to tuck her in. Nobody! She saw it all. But for *cariad* Mam she might have given in and told them, told them everything. As it was, she forgot about the Fraud Squad, forgot who she was talking to, and pushed their arms and guns away as they asked:

"Why're you dressed like a man, love?"

"Why're you dressed like a man?" she snarled back. They all laughed and stopped their prodding, but still she pushed them away, until they edged back into a cautious circle around her. They found nothing to charge her with, so they took her address and warned her,

"I should go straight home if I was you, love, the bloke we're looking for is dangerous."

She buried the moustache deep in her pocket. No Fraud Squad, the prodding had stopped, but still she waded into the lake and emptied the bag of mosses into the water. The bell heather floated for a while then followed the moss to the bottom. As the ripples closed, the wind from the helicopter settled and she heard a skylark, singing high above. She looked for the bird's perch in the clouds, wondering if it could fly higher than the grey; up above the dark cumulus ceiling, way up with Y Ddraig Goch. And as she scoured the sky, a stone fell in amongst the boulders and slabs of the old farm. She jerked around, clutching the empty bin bag to her chest. Another stone fell, louder this time, pounding through her whole body, confirming some terrible suggestion. She ran, her wet jeans sticking like a second skin to her thighs, her hair falling from the nest of her hat. At the lip of the cwm she looked back and thought she saw a shadow, a man running from boulder to boulder around the ruin. Her bin bag caught on the hawthorn as she ran: down, down to *cariad* Mam.

They never found the gunman. Jones the Post Office got a new security system installed and made arrangements to park his Volvo around the corner. She forgot about the Fraud Squad and about the mosses: Mam caught one of the flu bugs that was around, the sort that Jones the chemist was always talking about. On into the autumn she spluttered and coughed, until she stopped talking altogether - not even "thankyou", not even "there's lovely". *Cariad* Mam lying there silent: she started messing the bed so every morning brought a warm stench, steaming the windows and shutting out the world. But just before Christmas the junk shop on Stryd Fawr provided the ideal presents: a new hot water bottle for Mam and a pair of black framed sunglasses, just right for the mountain.

She didn't take a bin bag this time but found bits of her old one stuck on the hawthorn at the lip of the cwm, together with a few crimson berries withering like congealed drops of blood. The lake was frozen and a frosted green lichen covered the grass and moss where the snow hadn't dusted. She looked for tracks but even the sheep had retreated to lower ground. She crept up to the ruin and waited inside the broken walls, listening to the rise and fall of her own breathing until she heard the cry coming, bellowing around the lake, rising from her own mouth. The echo left a hollow in her stomach, a hole in the sky. And as her eyes searched up through the hole, her sunglasses fell to the ground -

"Y Ddraig Goch!" she cried, picking up the sunglasses: "Where were you, Y Ddraig Goch?" as she raced past the hawthorn and back down into the valley.

The kids on Stryd Fawr still shouted - "Bandy Blodwen, busty Blodwen, show us your tits Blodwen", and some, as word got around - "Take us to the moon Blodwen and your mossy bed". Jones the Post Office sometimes lamented after she had cashed her fortnightly cheque - "Some are born to be mothers and some are born to care for others." But only when his wife replied - "Yes, bach" - did it sound like a double-headed curse.

The Mountain's Scream...

Kerry went to the hospital for an X-ray, but the doctor said it was only mild concussion. Out for thirty seconds, by which time one of the green shirts had picked up the ball and scored a try, and the carthorses had passed the halfway line with their cheers and congratulations. He woke to a sea of voices - "Well done Kerry. He's all right. Well done Kerry, lad." - a sea of green and pink legs, mud splattered and bald - "Are you all right? Are you all right?" And he was all right, after he had grabbed the cold sponge and squeezed it down into his shorts.

When he had fully recovered and his mother allowed him back to school, Parry-Jones adopted him. There was first team potential there. He would need some coaching, of course. He would need to learn where the posts were, but what speed. He would have to stop smoking, but what stamina, what determination! Cardiff Arms Park and thousands singing 'Land of My Fathers' loomed on the horizon. There's potential! And there was the mountain race -

"Never heard of the mountain race, lad? Where have you been living for the last fifteen years?"

"Sir." Kerry remained still while Parry-Jones told him of the annual holiday when everyone used to go bilberry picking on the mountain, and when the strongest farmhands or quarrymen raced up there with cartwheels on their backs, rolling them off the top and into the lake.

"If you dived down into that water, you'd see hundreds of them. Hundreds of them, lad."

"Sir."

"Just a cross country race now, couldn't dump tyres in the lake, we'd have the conservationists on our backs."

"Sir."

"I was champion of the mountain, 1965 to 70, a record yet to be beaten. Of course, it's all foreigners now, never recognise any of the faces."

"Sir."

"About time a local lad won it, if you ask me. And it'll be good training for your rugby, nothing like it."

At the end of term his mother was pleased with his report.

"I never knew you liked rugby, Kerry? We'll have to think about a track suit for Christmas, won't we."

His mother's suggestion was keen, almost happy, as if she had seen for the first time that the valley was the only home they had and she better make the most of it. The new track suit was green and red, with a dragon motif on each arm. It had a hood, and a chest pocket which fastened with a zip. This was Rhiannon's home when Kerry ran on the mountain.

Parry-Jones ran with Kerry as far as the cwm, to show him the route. He pointed past the hawthorn and the lake, to the path which zig-zagged to the summit.

"That's the way, lad. Best get a few runs in before the snow comes."

Kerry watched the bristling hair bobbing in front of him and the green nylon socks slipping past Parry-Jones' balding calf muscles. And he saw for a moment the green and pink legs standing around him under the posts, and heard their voices - "Are you all right? Give him some water. Here, have some water." And then Parry-Jones' voice:

"How are you finding it, lad?"

"Sir."

"Tough, eh? Don't worry, you'll get used to it - easier than walking after a while." And Parry-Jones was right: easier than walking down Stryd Fawr, at any rate.

Through the Christmas holiday he ran every day: in the afternoon when the dark gathered around him, speeding him on past the beasts rising out of the brown crinkle bracken and black-green gorse, on past the hungry shadows that called him to stop. Sometimes the lake appeared like a black carpet waiting to take him to the summit, more often the cartwheels rolled, hundreds of them, under the surface - so no strongman could face the windblasted waves for long. Rhiannon, safe in her pocket, jogging against his chest: no need to talk, except when they were past the lake, past the ring of bilberries and by the cairn on the very top. Then the scream of the mountain made him call out - "Can you hear it, Rhiannon? Can you see it?" He took her out, cupping his hands to shelter her from the wind, and showed her the layers of hills and crags surfacing like whale backs from the ocean of hidden valleys, tossing occasional farms or forestry plantations in their primordial rising for air. He would shout over the wind, imagining each layer to be another world, another country - "Over there, Rhiannon, yes, that's France. And over there, right over there, America."

He took Rhiannon out even when the air became still and the mists closed, curling his hair with insidious beads. Then, with his finger to his mouth he whispered to Rhiannon - "Can you hear it, Rhiannon? Can you still hear it?"

Old broken thistles appeared out of nowhere, like prehistoric trees, brown and ragged in the mist but strangely permanent. They marked a path, of sorts; promising a break in the screaming grey silence. The descent was always a race against the ravenous shadows, as he chased the night down into the valley, Rhiannon zipped up safe, back in her pocket. No need to talk, not now, not even when they reached the edge of town, and the twilight owls screeched a welcome. It was enough to know Rhiannon was with him as he ran.

The new term started with a home game against Aber, and 'Potter' scrawled on the blackboard, joined by a heart and arrow to 'Mossy tits Blodwen, Miss Mountain Queen 1889'. Parry-Jones' protege was bound for Cardiff, the home of all homes, the throne of the greats - Gareth Edwards, Barry John, JPR and ... Kerry knew nothing about that, or about Blodwen, but so long as he wore his track suit he could run out of the house without "Kerry, where are you going?" ringing in his ears. He was even excused Sunday roast. Sundays were best of all because the Owen Glendower, together with the chapel, stripped the mountain bare.

It was on a Sunday, the last day in January, that he heard the shot echoing round the cwm like a ball bearing in a tin can. He ran down from the hawthorn, following the shortest sheep track to the lake, which sat with a sombre black cloud reflected in its glaze. He could smell an acrid burning as he approached the ruin, but found footprints and the bin bag first - inside, a pile of clothes topped by a blue woollen hat, a black false moustache and a pair of sunglasses. He took the moustache and was about to try it on his hairless face when the scream rose in his head. He caught a glimpse of the wet red splashes in the snow, and followed the yellow ribbons of her dress. A warm steam entered his nostrils and a groan crawled through the splattered snow towards him. The shotgun was wedged between two stones, its barrels pointing towards the cairn on top of the mountain. She was lying on her back on a granite slab, a hole blasted through her chest, rising through her shoulder, exposing splinters of bone on the blushing lichen and snow underneath. The scream sank to his throat and stomach, as he heard her groan. He retched, retched until he saw red in his vomit, crimson in the snow and the sky. He went to the lake and drank. Still groaning, he brought water to her in cupped hands but it dripped through his fingers onto her neck and down into the wound. The scream shook him each time he returned, so no water ever reached her lips. All he had was the scream, the scream growing louder, the scream growing inside.

On the way down she felt like a cartwheel, dripping as if she had been in the lake: warm on his hunched back but turning to ice on his thighs, like driven rain, plastering the track suit to his legs. Such a big wheel, he had to stop every few steps. At the hawthorn he stopped, by the torn shreds of a bin bag hanging limp around some scabby brown berries; the scream growing louder, so he tried to ask Rhiannon, tried to tell her; but it was all too loud; such a big wheel, a step at a time, screaming, staggering. Such a big wheel; at the road he stopped, not thinking to wait and stop a car. The scream was moving his legs, so he rested less, down, down into the valley; he raced the scream, raced the wheel, losing, rolling down, louder, he was losing to the scream. "Rhiannon. Are you ... Rhian ..." But a jet flew overhead, shearing the clouds with a climbing rasp. He stumbled on but had already lost.

Parry-Jones, returning from chapel, came across Kerry and his load by the school. He shook his head and removed his jacket before helping her down.

"What happened, lad?"

Kerry silent: no 'sir', no 'yes Mummy'.

"I'll phone, you wait with her." So, Kerry was left staring at her, a real body not a wheel, slumped against the railings; not seeing her, only hearing - no groans now, only the scream in his head mixing then and now with the other noises, only the scream and roar in his head, like a millstone and blasting siren combined, echoing around the old quarry pits, all around the Stryd Fawr pebble dash.

Parry-Jones assured the police he would take Kerry home. But how could he? His mother would die of fright. He decided to clean him up first. The sweat and blood on Kerry's back had congealed, so Parry-Jones had to tear the track suit off.

"Best get to the showers, lad, I've got a key to the gym."

He took Kerry inside and cut his rugby shirt off with the scissors from the first aid box. He threw it on the floor with the track suit and kicked them over towards the bin. He got a black track suit from his own locker and offered it to Kerry.

"What did the police say, lad?"

Did you see or hear anything or anyone after you heard the shot? Kerry silent, now in black. He had heard nothing since, nothing but the screaming. He asked his mother for an aspirin after the doctor left. She gave him two sedatives instead, so, as he lay in bed, he saw a hole in the ceiling, a hole in the sky - apart from the screaming, apart from the hole in her shoulder - but his eyes closed before he knew where the hole led.

Staring at the bathroom mirror the next morning, he remembered. Only a black baggy track suit, not his own, so he put his school uniform on and ran out of the house, not hearing his mother's shouts - "Kerry, you're not going to school today. Kerry! Kerry, come back!"

The school secretary told him Parry-Jones would be in after lunch. Some had heard and stared at Kerry across the dining room, looking for blood on his hands. He sipped his water and clicked the serrations of the plastic knife with his nail. No-one had seen him in the dining room before: where were his sandwiches? His mother would never think of looking for him there. The gym showers had been mopped, the bins emptied: nowhere left to search but Parry-Jones. Kerry accosted him as he strode across the playground for afternoon lessons:

"Where is she?" The words were spat out like missiles.

"Who? Oh, not good news I'm afraid, said she'd lost a lot of blood ... What are you doing here, lad? You shouldn't be here today, not after what you've ..."

"What have you done with her?"
"What, lad? I told you, she was in a bad way."
"In my track suit, in the pocket."
"Don't you worry about that, lad, I threw that away. You get on home to your mam. If you wait I'll see if someone can give you a lift."
Kerry pulled out the knife, the plastic knife from the dining room, and obeying the vow, he charged at Parry-Jones, who was too bewildered to take evasive action. The blade struck hard on the lapels of the herringbone tweed and snapped, so that Kerry's fists came down on the jacket, pummelling, shouting, screaming, punching, until silence finally drowned him and he fell to the floor.

To End ...
She took the yellow dress out of the wardrobe a week after *cariad* Mam's funeral. She tried it on and paraded in front of the wardrobe door mirror. Now, there's beautiful, she thought, there's a princess. And as she turned and twirled she caught a glimpse of another yellow, the wallpaper and its faded reds and yellows, the roses peeling all around her. There's no place for a princess, no place for a princess at all. She unzipped, took the gun and cartridges from the wardrobe, wrapped them in a bin bag with her yellow dress, a new pair of tights and her black patent shoes. With *cariad* Mam gone she had no place to go but home: to the farm, with her father, and his father before him. Some said she died in the ambulance, others said she died on Kerry's back. Most popular in Yscol yr Berwyn was the story of a lovers' pact with Potty Potter, the unfaithful coward.
They said Kerry underwent electroconvulsive therapy, 'ETC' Jones the Post Office called it, and when he returned they said he would be on valium for the rest of his life. Jones the Post Office said it was all to do with German blood. But the rumours didn't have time to take hold before the Hertz-Randles left the quarry manager's house.
When Kerry's mother had explained, Parry-Jones himself searched through the bin bags at the school:
"Funny thing for a lad of his age," he said, handing over the terracotta doll. "I shouldn't encourage it if I was you."
"No." said Kerry's mother, trying to fix Rhiannon's broken arm. "I've always thought it looks like an effigy, don't you think?"
His father had recognised Rhiannon in the hospital, as he held

Kerry's hand in his own swollen knuckles,

"About time we put a glaze on that isn't it?"

His mother's eyes brightened and she jumped up,

"Yes, that's what we'll do, we'll put a glaze on her, a bit of colour. That'll do her the world of good."

"No!" Kerry was lost; Rhiannon was his mother now. "No, no, no, no ..." he screamed as the nurse ushered his parents away. "No, no, you leave Rhiannon alone!"

Eventually the screams subsided, leaving only a blurred grey-crimson trace, a secret left over. He told Rhiannon. She was the only one who knew, because she could see it and hear it as well -

"Can you see it in the waves? Riding on those white caps, can you hear it? The sand shifting with the sea: Rhiannon, can you hear it? Grating, grinding - can you hear the roar?"

It was a few years later, after the quarry manager's house had become a quarry museum, that Jones the Post Office, on his annual day trip to the coast, saw Kerry's father sipping orange juice in a hotel bar. Jones reported back to the valley:

"They are living up that way now" and "They've bought a small hotel". In private he said to his wife, "Most probably on holiday - but I tell you what, I bet there were one or two whiskies in that juice."

As for Parry-Jones, his dream had gone: the attack with the plastic knife had thrust a realisation upon him. What hope was there in a town full of carthorses? His hair lost its sergeant-major bristle; scrums and mauls were of no interest to a runner, a champion runner such as himself. Jones the Post Office noticed a fortnightly decline, when Parry-Jones came in for his TV licence stamps, and consoled him sympathetically when a German runner broke the longstanding mountain race record. Jones turned to his wife and whispered when Parry-Jones was leaving the shop,

"Mark my words, he'll be off home to Cardiff before long. No doubt about it. It's a funny business that'll make a man like that turn inwards."

"A funny business, bach, a funny business indeed," said his wife, as she pulled down the end-of-day blinds, shutting out the coal black night and its orange streetlamp umbrella.

"No shelter for the wicked tonight, cariad," Jones observed, peeping out on the evening.

"Cariad! I'll give you cariad. It's a long time since I was your dear. Cariad, indeed. I'm more like your mam than your sweetheart." - and she waved her broom at him, threatening to sweep him out into the granite grey drizzle driving down from the mountain.

Dick McBride

Cwazy Man

In 1958, a mad-dog boy with short, bandy legs and a speech impediment slavered across the great plains in America, his fourteen year-old girlfriend, yelping beside him.

This is the way he was described by the police:

"Five feet five inches tall, 150 pounds. Scar over right eye. Green eyes. Dark red hair cut short on top, long on sides and back. Bowlegged and pigeon-toed, swaggers when he walks. Believed wearing blue jeans and black leather motorcycle jacket, black boots or cowboy boots. Sometimes has speech impediment, trouble pronouncing W's and R's."

He was Charlie Starkweather, age nineteen; she was Caril Fugate, fourteen. In eight days they killed ten or eleven people. They started their rampage in Lincoln, Nebraska, and were finally apprehended on a highway in Wyoming. Realizing the game was up the girl ran, leaving her boyfriend to face the music alone.

"He's killed a man!" she screamed to a deputy sheriff in the posse.

She always denied having anything to do with the murders, stating that she was a hostage.

After a time Charlie did not see it that way.

This is a statement he made with a borrowed pencil, writing on his cell wall in Gering, Nebraska: "Caril is the one who said to go to Washington state ... by the time any body will read this i will be dead for all the killings then they cannot give caril the chair to ... From Lincoln Nebraska they got us Jan 29, 1958. 1958 kill 11 persons ... Charles kill 9) all men ... Caril kill 2) all girls ... 11 ..."

But, while in prison, he also wrote to his father, asking that if Caril came back to Lincoln to be nice to her; that she had nothing to do with the killings. All they wanted to do, he wrote, was get out of town.

It will probably never be known who pulled the trigger or pushed in the knife. But it made good press for awhile.

Shrinks and do-gooders, preachers and reporters wrote about causes and motivations. Possibly no one understood. All that is really known is that eleven people were suddenly dead who might have been alive the next day were it not for Charlie Starkweather and Caril Fugate. But you never know ...

After seventeen years behind bars, Caril was released, wanting to become an "ordinary little dumpy housewife".

Charlie was not so lucky; he is now pushing up daisies.

*

In his last cell, before he was executed, Charlie was befriended by a guard, Mike Shimerda. Not long before he got the chair, Charlie gave Mike a picture he had drawn in prison of a little boy holding a teddy bear. The guard said, "I broke down and cried. Second time in my life."

"Don't wowee about me, Mike," Charlie is reported as having said. "I died the last time. They can't kill me again. Nobody wemembahs a cwazy man."

When he said these words he was smoking a cigarette. He did not take it from between his lips to talk. Smoke curled up in front of his strange eyes.

"I alweady knew Death a long time ago. Came to me at night. Sometimes I saw him on TV, talking on'y to me. Cwazy! He was big and haiwy, like a beah - half beah, half a man, know what I mean? On'y he didn't have no awms awe eahs. And no neck to speak of. Just a little fuwwy head in the middle of his showdahs. He had a gwuff voice but nice - kind - kind of nice. And he always ended up by saying, 'I'll be seein' you'."

Later, the same guard shouted at the journalists and other invited guests at Charlie's execution: "All right, you goddamn vultures. You're finally going to see what you came for."

"Hey, Charlie," they said on his last day. "How about givin' your eyes to a eye bank? You won't need them where you're going."

"What for?" Charlie asked. "Nobody evah gave me nothin'."

After a couple of delays and stays of execution they finally set the date: June 25, 1959.

Even so there was a last minute hitch. Thirty minutes before the execution was scheduled to start the doctor who was to pronounce Charlie dead dropped dead himself of a heart attack.

Then they came to get him. The usual gang: warden, chaplain, guards, doctor ... Just like in the movies.

"Come on, Charlie," they said. "Let's get this over with."

"What's the huwwy?" said Charlie.

This was supposed to be the last thing he said. It wasn't. Before they pulled the switch the final time, he said, "Shit! You call this hot?"

Charlie took a last bite of steak, a final deep drag on his death-fag, snarled like he had seen James Dean do in the movies and shuffled off. About a hundred yard stroll under the grey walls and high towers of prison into the main building, down to the basement, past the photographers and reporters and other invited guests (about forty in all), into the fry-shop. Charlie was wearing a blue chambray shirt and jeans. The top of his head and left leg had been shaved. It was a warm, summer night, still except for the weird noise the Nebraska wind makes.

Charlie did not have to wait long; he was the only customer that night. They strapped him in the chair, smeared grease on his left leg and top of head, attached the electrodes. Then everyone cleared out so that Charlie could be alone when he met his maker. And then they gave the signal.

An electrician from out of state - whose fee was $200 plus expenses - pulled the switch three times, each time sending 2,200 volts of electricity through the boy described by Robert Ruark (a popular syndicated journalist of the day) as: 'anything with a face like Starkweather's literally belongs in a bottle in a medical museum ...' Each time the switch was thrown it made a loud thumping sound. Charlie's legs jumped. The first shock stunned the boy, the second knocked him out, and (waiting until he came round) at the third jolt his heart stopped. He was pronounced dead at 12:04.

On the street in front of the prison a gang of fifty young people - boys in jeans and t-shirts; girls in shorts and summer blouses - cruised back and forth, drinking beer, their little radios going full blast. The boys all looked like James Dean; the girls resembled Natalie Wood. Maybe they were looking for a cause of some sort.

Police had to be called in to help clear the way so they could remove the corpse.

Panurge 22

Dick McBride, ex-City Lights Publishing, ex-distributor, ex-book trade on **Publishing Against The Grain.**

Terry Tinthoff

Pet Elephant

Lately he was inexplicably drawn to the mannikins in the windows of Saks Fifth Avenue. Every time he passed he saw a crowd of people staring hard at the store windows as if mesmerised. Then one by one they'd disappear inside. He resisted, focusing his Hasselblad on the display. As the shutter clicked he thought he saw one of the lascivious faces move. He lowered the camera and moved off, fast.

The cafe was so dark he walked into a chair. A couple sitting nearby turned and looked as he sat down uneasily two tables away.

"It's no good," he heard the frayed-looking man say to his woman companion. His hollow face held two piercing eyes. She blinked twice and picked up her milkshake. The waiter behind the cash register sent a puff of smoke out into the air. It hung over the counter, in which there were four flavors of candy lifesavers on display, each in its appropriately colored cardboard carton. The woman's hair was close to the color of the cherry lifesaver stripes. A radio played softly. The woman's foot kept silent time. She looked at the man with the camera, then at her feet.

"Thom McAn specials - only $14.99, on sale till November 15th, at only these four locations, 42nd and -"

"She has a remarkable memory," commented her friend, his sharp features focusing on the stranger.

"Everything should be remembered," explained the woman.

"Everything?"

She nodded. "My life has far more meaning now. Everything, I try to remember. This morning, I rode on subway car 4332. Yesterday I had 388 - um - seven I think. No, I'm not neurotic, I know that's what you're thinking. I remember the important things, too."

"So you're a computer."

"Correction - a human computer. A fully utilized brain. There's no reason why everyone can't be that way. It just takes practice. What's your name?"

"Plato," said the newcomer drily, preparing for the wisecracks. "Plato Platter."

The woman stared. "What a name!" She looked at her friend. "Ronny, isn't that a great name?" She turned back to Plato. "I've never met anyone named Plato before, though I once memorized the first chapter of 'The Republic'."

"I never wrote that," replied Plato unhappily as his coffee arrived.

The other man said, "This is Zum."

"Nice to meet you."

"Do you live here?" asked Zum, eyeing his camera on the table.

"Yup."

"What're you taking pictures of?"

"Those mannikins. I've never seen anything like it."

"Yeah," observed Ronny, "they take it all out of you."

Plato was relieved. He didn't have to explain.

"New York's always first with everything," laughed Zum.

"Do you have a theory?" said Plato.

"Mmmm. Ultrasonics...maybe," said Ronny.

"Yeah. There's only a few now but no doubt -"

"I think," Zum interrupted, "they think people aren't like consuming enough so they try to condition you like - like Pavlov's dog. It's very degrading." She shrugged. "But Ronny says he's conquered materialism."

Ronny stared into his coffee cup and rubbed his head. His arms were covered with tiny scratches.

"Do you have a headache?" asked Plato politely.

"Naw, it's her," he said, miserable now. Some cat had got out of the bag.

Zum giggled. "One time -"

"Can't you keep anything to yourself?" snapped Ronny. Zum looked crestfallen. To hide her feelings she picked up the milkshake. Plato noticed her lovely hands, and the shapely figure outlined in the black lurex top.

*

Plato walked in the evening rush hour, dodging business men and women. He reached Lexington and 72nd and turned east onto 72nd. At number 535 he rang the buzzer. A blurred sound came out of the speaker.

"It's the photographer," he said.

Up on the seventh floor a woman in her mid-forties opened her apartment door. "Come in, come in please." She stood aside with erect stature as he walked in. Before him he saw the skyline view. "You may take a few shots of those if you like," she said, adjusting her toga and piled-up hair before seating herself on a beige silk divan. Plato set up. He turned a floodlight on two enormous marble urns.

A bronze Cupid brooded behind the divan. The woman struck an arrogant pose.

He shot two rolls of assorted poses. Then he said, "Madam, can I talk you into something more somber? Do you have an electric fan?"

His client looked faintly amused. "Why?"

"We could put red cellophane over the light and have the wind blowing through your hair as if Rome were burning."

She laughed good-naturedly. "Don't you think it would be foolish of me to acknowledge any decline?"

Plato's face was impassive as he walked down the hallway. He had far stranger encounters than this one. He had learned the key to a successful portraiture career: indulge the client's fantasies. Among others he had done an Attila, a Jesus on the Cross (he was proud of the technical *trompe l'oeil* on that session and had even hung a big print of the best photo on the back of his bathroom door), and a woman impersonating Hitler.

He fell back heavily against the elevator wall and closed his eyes. Floor after floor wheeled by. The lobby was overheated and outside the cold air thrashed his face.

He passed the cafe where he had met Zum and Ronny. Glancing in, he saw another waiter with his arm propped on the counter staring off into space. He hesitated, and walked on. It was a quarter to seven. He didn't want to go home. It seemed there must be something that could distract him, sidetrack him, engage him, yet, for all it offered, Manhattan stretched into monotony, a giant circle of restaurants, clubs, work, and sleep. The only way to break it was to leave, and he had no desire to return to his native town, a small dot on the map of the North American continent: Russell, Kansas. Sometimes he missed the open skies, but he could never forget the landlocked plains, the utter lack of hills or curiosity. The only things he'd liked at school were art and geography. Sometimes he would lose himself in his father's oversized atlas, dated 1904, full of grand extinct countries. But flatness, except for his mother's high planes on her cheeks, was all he had known growing up.

As he came to, he realized that he had been looking at the needled cap of the Chrysler building.

*

ONE PET ELEPHANT: LOST began the ad. Plato smiled. He had ridden an elephant once. His parents had taken him to southern

California for summer vacation when he was nine and they'd gone to Jungle Land, an African theme park. The whole time they were on the elephant he felt as though he were about to fall off. Grateful for the return of a forgotten memory, he picked up the phone.

"Hello, I haven't seen your elephant, but I wouldn't mind taking a picture of the owner."

There was a moment of silence on the receiver.

"Hello?"

"Yes?"

"I said -"

"I heard you."

"Oh. You didn't sound like it."

"I didn't say anything," came the woman's voice.

"Do you have red hair?"

"Yes. Why?"

"Ah, nothing. Just thought I saw you walking your elephant in Central Park last summer." Help, he thought. "See, I do photographs of people... as they'd like to be. If you could be anything in the world, what would you be?"

A long musical laugh came down the telephone. "Boy, are you ever weird!"

"If you want your photo taken my name's Plato and the number is 224-4222, okay? Bye!" He hung up before she could say, "Excuse me, did you say your name was...?"

Maybe she'd call.

Next day Plato woke up feeling exasperated. A shred of a dream lingered as he got in the shower. He was in court by mistake. His lawyer wore an awful yellow suit, from which protruded cow's hoofs instead of hands. They rested on a pile of paper that kept growing as he talked.

Plato scrubbed his head furiously. His career disgusted him. His clients' shoddy fantasies disgusted him. And the poverty of his own dreams disgusted him.

He made himself think about the girl with the elephant instead. He was in love with her laughter. And he would like very much to be in love with her. He recalled times when his acquaintances would set him up to meet this or that girl, because they all seemed to think he 'needed one.' Well, he'd 'got one,' and a fat lot of good it had done him. Linda had come and gone in a year.

At one o'clock he delivered two sets of portraits. This was

always the worst part. The clients fussed over enlargements and duplicates. Which did he like best? He expressed enthusiasm but wearily took notes. The man tried to demonstrate his thanks demonstratively. Plato managed to ease himself away. As he left he felt the smile stuck to his face. He knew that smile well. It appeared whenever he felt nervous or afraid: for, apart from running, he knew no other defense.

Later, at home, the phone rang.

"Is this Plato? Is that right?"

"Yes."

"This is Layla, you know, you called about my ad?"

"Oh yes," he said, as casually as he could.

"Well, I've been thinking about what you said and I decided that I'd like you to take my picture."

"With or without the elephant?" He thrilled again to her beautiful laugh.

*

He met Layla in a cafe on East 12th Street. Sure enough, there sat a woman with short red hair who gave him a wave. But he immediately recognized her as Zum, the girl he'd met the previous week.

"Hi!"

"Hello."

"Don't you remember me?"

She looked blank. "No, I don't think so."

"You're the one with the perfect memory."

Her face grew alarmed as her slender fingers reached for the fake pearl necklace that lay between two shapely breasts.

"Cafe Chioroscuro? Thom McAn specials?"

Zum-Layla blushed. "Oh, it's... of course, I remember you now! And oh, that horrible Ronny!"

Seeing her discomfort, he left her an escape. "Why? What happened to Ronny?"

She leaned over and opened her eyes wide. "He O.D.'d a few days ago. He's in the hospital. And can you imagine - his parents didn't even know - I had to call them!"

"Was he a junkie?"

"Sort of. He'd just been doing it on and off for about a month, and then I guess he goofed."

"That's too bad."

She pouted. "He was mean to me a lot."

Plato wished he could make her laugh again. As he conjectured what she might secretly like to be he caught fragments of her conversation. "... just as I am... relate to me as a real person..." He sighed. The more she spoke, the more she faded into the ordinary.

"...can't run away from life, like Ronny."

"Did he?"

"Yeah, he cut himself off. Even from his friends."

"Maybe his friends let him down."

Zum looked doubtful. "No, he just wanted attention. I told him so, too. Then we had this big argument. I told him to get out. He'd been staying with me, and didn't have anywhere to go, but I didn't care by then. I was so furious."

"So where did he go?"

"I don't know. He turned up the next night and pleaded with me to let him stay. I said you can sleep on the sofa. I could tell he was coming on to something and sure enough next day he collapsed and that's when he was taken to the hospital." She spoke the word 'collapsed' with contempt, as though it had been in poor taste.

Plato picked up his coffee but only swirled it around. And now the wit of the ad receded to mere bait. He stared up over the rim and along the coffee table's shiny surface, then along to Zum's shiny nails. As soon as she got her photos she would be off. So who was she reciting all this for?

"Let's go visit Ronny."

"What for? He'd only get mad at me."

"Come on! He's probably bored stupid."

Zum looked stubborn.

"Which hospital is he in?"

"I don't know."

"You're not a good liar, you know."

She picked at a nail. "You don't know how it was between us."

"Do you like him or not?"

"What's that got to with it?"

"Do you *want* him to die?"

"No! I -"

"Well then, let's go. You can take him some flowers."

"Ronny hates Nature. He says it's completely artificial."

"Well then buy him a book or something, I dunno." He stood up. She remained seated.

"What about my photos?" she said. "When can you come take them?"

Plato summoned his courage. "I'm sorry. I can't."

"Why not?"

"Because I only take pictures of people I want to and I've changed my mind about you."

Zum looked up at him, critical now. "Let me guess. If I'd gone to see Ronny you'd have taken them, right?"

"Maybe. But mainly it's because you've got no imagination."

"What do you mean?"

"I mean...you wouldn't make a good subject for the camera. You'd never risk exposing yourself, or a pretend self, to anybody." Plato had never dared say such things before, but the caffeine gave him nerve. "You're not the only one, don't get me wrong. There's lots of people like you. You think you want to be something, but you can't because you don't know about yourself or anything. You can't understand why you should go visit a friend in the hospital. Okay maybe he's not such a great friend, but the point is he's sick. And maybe you'd help him feel better but you don't think you're capable of affecting anybody, one way or the other. I feel sorry for you."

Zum stood up. She was tall. "You're insane. Every single person I *meet* here is insane. All this time I was thinking, here's somebody normal at last! But no, you're like everyone else: hung up, and blaming other people for it. I swear, I'm going back to Wichita, I've had it with this place."

"You're - from Kansas?" said Plato.

"Yeah."

"So am I. I'm from Russell."

"So what? It's a big state."

Plato looked at his camera. "Yeah." He got out his wallet. "Yeah, it sure is." He slung the camera strap over his shoulder. "See you later." He put $2.00 on the table and went out into the low winter sun.

E. H. Solomon

At Sea

I didn't notice the old boy standing to one side of the painting and accidentally kicked the cane he held in an arthritic hand, clattering it to the floor. No complaint. The oldie bent down. I got to the cane first and pressed it into his hand.

I said, "Sorry, sir, clumsy of me. I trust you have come to no harm."

At the time I was fourteen and spoke a mannered English for effect.

He nodded to me curtly, sat on a polished wooden bench, propped his chin on the top of the round handle of the stick, and regarded me with more interest than rancour.

"Young feller," a pause. "Where the shit did you learn that archaic stuff?"

Shit and archaic are two words I don't expect in the same sentence, certainly not from a respectable old man, better heeled than I was ever likely to be. The round handle of the cane was some sort of stuff like amber, expensive.

"A Spanish lady is my English teacher," I said politely.

The technique works, makes folk curious.

"Don't account you quitting real American."

"She," I said, enunciating carefully, "is a very precise lady, very, very correct. Slang or slipshod speech is the best way to bad marks."

Nodding a balding head, he accepted my explanation. He was solid shouldered, and although crippled by arthritis looked energetic and alert.

"You got a funny accent," he said; something he couldn't cotton on to puzzling him. "You ain't no New Yorker. Where you from?"

"Wales."

I let him have the full length of a flat elongated 'a'. The chin lifted from the cane handle.

"The native woodnotes," he remarked.

"I beg your pardon."

"Professor Higgins at the Guild," he said.

"Pygmalion," I corrected.

"No matter."

He eyed me critically.

"That senorita, or maybe senora. Who is she, this special lady from Iberia, so concerned for the purity of the English language?"

Tapping the cane on the floor.

"Senorita Aranxa Saruya."

Full title; he wasn't impressed.

"And she's pretty."

That didn't impress him either.

"Why do you think this Castilian lady has so special interest in archaic English? American not good enough?"

He spoke floorwards, but it didn't need much nous to see he was interested.

"She studied in England, at Oxford University, vacations she's back there. Carries a torch, for the English. New Yorkers in her book are barbarians. Only barbarians, she says, would massacre a beautiful language."

"Well now," said the old guy.

He lifted his head to look at me.

He had, I decided, reservations about Senorita Saruya and the sanctity of the English language...

"Well now," he repeated, "she may be right at that. How come she don't teach Spanish? "

"She does," I said, "only the class is full, I have to learn French."

"How old are you?"

"Fourteen."

He looked at me enviously.

"One thing I don't get. You're Welsh. They speak English in Wales?"

"They do."

I pretended patience.

Then I put on the precise stuff, to see how he'd take it.

"Sir, being Welsh in New York is a problem for me. The Welsh are not English. They are Anglo-Saxon, we're Celts. The Romans fixed it so we'd stay that way. My family speaks English fluently, but to us it is a second language. We originate from Welsh-speaking Wales. At home we have little occasion to use English."

He seemed genuinely interested, so I went on.

"English is a bastard language, but useful. Spoken everywhere."

"The Empire," he interrupted

"Because of the Empire." I agreed. "But the Welsh consider English poor stuff. Our language is more ancient, more elegant and expressive, more musical, more beautiful."

"So?"

He meant, what's the problem?

"The school I attend, hardly anyone speaks English. Studying English, or rather how to speak it, is compulsory."

The old boy got slowly to his feet. With his cane he indicated the paintings, then pointed it at me.

"You like these paintings?"

"Very much."

"You wanna be an artist?"

"No, a writer."

I jiggled my feet, hinting a desire to be away. But he'd not done with me yet.

"Cafe hereabouts?"

"Yes."

"How about a cup of coffee and a Dutch?"

I was a bit wary. A few months ago a similar sort of guy had talked to me about the paintings, bought me some lunch, and offered to take me home in his car. When I was in the seat next to him, he opened his flies and wanted me to suck him off. I offered to bite a chunk off the end. He got me out of the car quicksticks.

I said he was a similar sort of guy. Not true. The other was thin and reedy, wore gold rimmed glasses and had a newspaper stuffed under his arm. And he was younger. Still, I wasn't about to take the chance again.

"Sir," I said, "my parents are averse from me accepting hospitality from strangers."

"Stuff," he waved the cane angrily, "tell you not to cross Fifth, do they?"

He had a point, and temptation in the way of food took some resisting.

"I agree with you, sir. I assure them I really do know how to take care of myself. You know with parents. They worry."

"Good," he said, "let's go. Coffee good here?"

"Coke'd suit me better," I said

"You do speak American."

"Some," I admitted.

After the coke and Dutch, manna and ambrosia for a slum kid, I told him I would have to go home; my mother would be expecting me. Ultra-cautious, I suppose, but you never know, do you? He made no effort to detain me. On the museum steps I thanked him and shook a dry, club-knuckled hand.

"Been a pleasure meeting you, sir," I said.

I couldn't keep it up.

"Thanks for the coke. The Dutch was great."

His craggy face unleashed a smile.

"Learn to write good American, kid. Ain't many can."

"I'll remember."

Then I got a shock. A big limo' pulled up in front of us, a cocky guy in uniform got out, opened the door and waited.

"Not mine," said the old boy. "I just hire it when I need. Give you a lift?"

I said I'd walk.

"O.K."

He got into the limo', waved at me, and the big, black bastard of a car occupied Fifth Avenue like an invading tank.

*

Traditional those days, if you were bright enough, to look forward to N.Y.U. or Columbia. If your parents hadn't the wherewithal, or even if they had, it was expected, obligatory in fact, to work at spare time jobs and earn enough, 'to work your way through college'. For me, after an indigent childhood climbing miles of stoops and stairways loaded down with glossy magazines, that hung like armour plate from one shoulder, and gave me the feeling of permanent lopsidedness, inclination to deform my body in exchange for an academic education changed to the conviction there must be an easier way.

Graduating High with goodish grades (I wasn't noted for hard work or over-enthusiasm) I landed a cub slot on a small circulation magazine. My journalistic teeth were broken on assignments dumb enough to test a stoic. Snide comments from the editor didn't help. A smartalicky Manhattan newsman, he treated me to contemptuous, mostly bad advice, and paid his staff, (I was the lowliest dogsbody) a miserable pittance; sufficient, if you were real careful, to starve to death on slowly.

"New series," he said.

His smile cuts in and out like a neon light.

"Famous at home."

"Like who?"

He rattled off a selection of has beens and no hopers.

My face reflected my opinion.

"Come on Taf," he said, knowing I had no choice, "we can't raise ante for big names. Agents cut us up in little pieces as it is."

Fanwise he shuffled a hand of photographs on the desk top.

"One of these, plus up to date print, and Taf, you cocksucker, you gets a by-line."

The smile clicked off. He was far too close to a promise for his liking.

"Afterwards," he qualified.

I picked up a print.

"Don't even look."

I looked.

"Listen, schmuck, don't ever give interviews. Sees from nobody. Number one you get throwed out first base. Two says ten bucks you don't lay a bunt."

"Who?"

"Cal Grover."

"Grover, the sculptor?"

"The Grover. Seventy three, last show back in Hoover time. Sells for a high average."

"The photo' ?"

"Archives. Fifteen years old, at least."

That's why I recognised the old bastard.

"Where's he now?

"You guess. Best I know he ain't been around for ten years. Forget it Taf. Fort Knox with a can opener is easier."

"Still putting that ten bucks on the line?"

He was immediately suspicious. But I had him by the crotch,. Besides, if anything came up on Grover it'd be worth a ten spot.

Taking the print, I left. Prospect of easy bucks cheered me no end. On an open top up Fifth I looked over the park muffled in mist, thick with snow. Along the kerb a parapet of dirty white broke at street corners to let people cross. Even in my padded coat, sheepskin collar pulled up, I froze. There may be colder places in winter than New York, but I don't want to visit them.

I was staking Grover'd be coming to the Met. If he could walk or crawl.

The woman in the office had a good line in non-cooperation.

"Yeah," she said, "I recognise the guy. Comes in now and again. Not much these days.. Walks bad. Told me he'd a hip done. Cal

Grover. Whaddya know. Never knew he was that famous. No, got no idea when he'll make it here again, if he does. No I don't really know nothing about him. (lying bitch) He's just another guy comes in. Keeps himself to himself. Don't like reporters."

The look she gave me. She wasn't dying of unrequited love of reporters. I'd get nothing from her.

I tried for an address or a phone number and came up with zilch. My ten bucks looked increasingly a lost cause. Perversely it wasn't the lettuce got to me, I really did want to see the old boy. So I camped on the steps, smoked cigarettes to keep warm, and froze my butt off.

I don't believe in God. He surprised me. Couple of days later, weather quit winter enough for rain to clear away the snow, and late one afternoon a limo' pulled up in front of where I was leaning against a column. Grover, older, obviously, but not mistakable, struggled out of the door, helped by the driver. Black man I noted, big, big guy.

Caution, Taf, I warned myself.

I needn't have worried. Using two sticks Grover hobbled to where I stood smoking my one thousandth cigarette.

"Changed a bit, young feller," he said

"Father time," I said, you got to the two stick stage."

He held one up as if to inspect it.

"A nuisance, but bearable. What happened to the Spanish lady?

"Sabbatical to England and didn't come back. Married a professor we was told. I left school long gone since."

"One stick ago, ain't so long," he said drily. "You been waiting for me?"

"You're worth ten bucks, maybe more."

"A newspaperman. Don't tell me. I guessed. Sorry, don't give interviews, never have."

I'd thrown crap. Always the optimist. Ten bucks down the john.

"Least you speak American," said Grover

"I learn fast."

I really was glad to see the old boy again.

"Coffee?"

"And a dutch?"

"I'm in credit."

"The museum?"

"Another time. Trust yourself in my apartment? You was wary as a skunk last time."

"I had my reasons."

"And now?"

"Big boy, speak good American, even I make it across Fifth."

Grover laughed, youthful, in spite of his seventy or so years. He signalled the black guy, who treats me like I could pinch-hit for Picasso, and opens the limo' door with a flourish. We headed downtown past Fourteenth and pulled up at a dump on East Twelfth, a warehouse, the ground floor packed with metal sculpture, Grover's speciality. He'd begun life as a shipyard riveter and for the hell of it still built up his impressive sculptures with mushroom headed rivets. I looked around and figured a few hundred thousand good dollars stashed in the cavernous workshop. We rode an elevator with doors wide enough for a truck a couple of floors and in to a fairly comfortable apartment filled with old fashioned furniture. Grover waved me to a chair, then sat in a stiff backed lounger.

"Watch this," he said

He picked up a copper cowbell and tinkled it. Almost immediately a young and very pretty black girl came in. She looked at me inquisitorially.

"Coffee and crullers, Aurelia. This young feller is grepsing his stomach's so empty."

"Pay no attention," said the girl. "Name's Addie. Be a minute."

She kicked the swing door open and went out. Grover sighed and relaxed.

"Pretty broad, huh. Cutest ass. I like her round just to see it move. Sassy. Mind of her own. Don't do nothing she don't wanna do."

"Manumitted or emancipated? There was a war you know."

"So they tell me. Gettysburg and all that. Don't remember being around. Nor you for that matter. No ante you get smart with me."

"No cracks. A deal. I need those crullers."

Grover sat up.

"How come I always get pestered by smartass comics?"

The girl came in with a tray. She set a plateful of crullers on a little table by my side and handed me the mug of coffee. She was making up her mind, weighing me up. I was on probation.

I watched her disappear through the door. She had a round lobed can and very good legs. Lucky old bastard, I thought. Guess he was still up to it.

Grover sipped his coffee. I ate two crullers.

"I could do with that ten bucks," I said.

"Don't give no interviews."

"Double negative, hopeful. Why have you invited me here?"

"I'm about to tell you a story and I want you to write it down for me."

"Sorry," I said firmly, "I don't ghost."

"Wait," said Grover. His eyes had brightened and he looked eager. "Here's the deal. You write the story, you get the interview and twenty."

"I need a photograph."

"You got it."

"For real?"

"For real. More coffee?"

I shook my head.

"Go ahead, smoke, you want. You look nervous."

I lit a Lucky and waited. Grover shifted about getting comfortable.

"You're a writer. Got a good way to start?"

"Once upon a time...." I began.

"The deal includes," said Grover, "you give up on smartass remarks."

The black girl came in and took away my mug and plate, but left Grover's. She gave me a mixed sort of look; I felt I had a long way to go to make the grade with her.

"The King gave a piece of good advice to Alice," I said. "Begin at the beginning, go on to the end, and stop. There ain't no more."

"O.K.," said Grover, "I get it." He looked at me defiantly. "Starts like this. I was sixteen."

He paused for a moment, covering the think time with another swallow of coffee."

"Sixteen is a pretty good age. You play ball?"

"Third, sometimes left field."

"Look as if you got a good arm. I started on the mound and stayed there. I'd a curve, a slider, a fair fast ball, and good control. Enough for any High School ball team. My special buddy was the catcher. His father worked on the ships, deck steward on the old Panama Pacific. During summer vacation he pulled strings and got us both signed on as bellhops. The company had a no relatives rule, so Vincent, the catcher, and I sailed on different ships.

I was sorry we was separated, but that's the way it was, and no use griping. I was up for some dough, wages and tips, and the voyage was only six weeks. I planned to buy a canoe and go camping up river

Sailing Day I was in the Pantry helping one of the chefs make sandwiches. I missed the passengers come aboard, didn't even get to see the ship cast off and sail down the Hudson. I was familiar with the Manhattan skyline from trips to Staten Island, so I was not too disappointed. The ship made it out to sea through the Narrows. Later I was taken to a cubby hole on one of the upper decks, just a small counter, a chair and a double row of indicators. My boss, the second cabin steward, a large man, substantial in the gut, and very bad tempered, looked at me in an unfriendly way.

'No sleeping on the job. One of these fuckers,' he indicated the rows of lights, 'blinks, you hot foot to the cabin and see the passengers gets anything he wants. Get me. Anything!'

'Anything?'

Just enough in my tone to make him regard me closely.

'Don't get smart with me, sonny boy. You heard. Do like I tell you, keep your nose clean. We get on good, just fine.'

He glared at me, jowly-faced and sweating.

'One more thing, half you make on tips is mine. Take liberties, baby face, you get trouble. Hold out on me I kick your ass, but good. Also you get dumped in the Pantry, whole trip. All the tips you make there, you keep.'

The canoe dream took a rap. But I didn't argue. He had the cards and I could tell he'd played them before, lots of times.

Morning after breakfast was a slack time. On deck I helped issue games equipment for deck tennis, quoits and such like. Later I served bouillon to passengers lying dozing on comfortable deckchairs. Vincent's old man, the deck steward, had a knack of wrapping up bodies in large plaid blankets so they'd some room to move but were sealed up against wind. He didn't offer to teach me, and I didn't ask. Pantryman brings up a tray with double-handled bowls of bouillon, and I walk along the deck offering them to the cocooned figures. A woman wearing dark tinted glasses and a colourful scarf, jerked her head at me.

'Take 'em off, kid,' she said, 'goddam steward's trussed me up like I'm a ringer for a chicken.'

I put down the tray and took off the sunglasses. The reward was a pair of eyes, luminous, perfectly blue. For a couple of seconds they regarded me with a certain amount of what I hoped might be interest.

'Feed it in kid. I can't make with the left, and the right's bust.'

Sitting at her side, I spooned the bouillon into a wide, lippy mouth, resting the bowl of the spoon on a pink tongue, turning it so the thin soup dripped slowly and gently. Her teeth were white and perfect. If her mouth hadn't been wide open when the spoon went in I'd have thought them false. The bowl empty I offered her more. She shook her head. I made a big production of wiping her lips with a soft napkin. She smiled at me, appreciative. 'Thanks, kid. Sorry, don't have nothing with me. Cabin number's 137. Come round when you can. I'll see you alright.'

'Ain't necessary, miss.'

I didn't actually mean to butter her up. I couldn't see her hands, so I couldn't tell if she was married or not. But she was pleased.

'Mrs,' she said, 'name's Canzoni, Mrs Canzoni.'

'O.K. Mrs Canzoni. A pleasure.'

'You can't make it to the cabin, don't worry. I'll look out for you tomorrow.'

Dazzled, I replaced the sunglasses, picked up the tray and went back to the buffet. She means it. It'd be my first tip. Also she was on top deck, first class, in an outside cabin. That meant dough, probably lots of it."

Canzoni, Canzoni? The name pushed a button in my mind.

Jesus, not that Canzoni!

Grover had got animated. He stopped talking.

"Tony Canzoni," I said. "Middle weight. Both titles, lightheavy and middle. Knifed in a brawl in San Francisco. Never got the guy who did it."

"In for a strike." said Grover. "I am impressed."

"Nothing," I disclaimed. "I write the sports column. In the archives. I got a good memory."

Grover shook his head.

"I still say impressive. You're right. She married that brainless gorilla. Won a hick beauty contest in the sticks and came to New York. Hoped for the big time, Broadway, the works. Canzoni saw her doing a song and dance number in a nightclub and made a play. She fell for him like she'd hit a truck. Found out after they were married how right she was."

"He beat her up."

"Only not her face. He loved her. Bastard jealous, went after anyone looks at her. Threw her down a stoop cause she smiled at a guy. An iceman, sixty years old. I ask you. An iceman, for Christ sake. Can you figure that one?"

"Rough customer, Canzoni. Great fighter."

"Say that again. He was in Frisco, in training for a tough fight, she on her way to be with him. Every morning she's in the deckchair wrapped tip to toe in the plaid blanket. Me, I spoon bouillon into that gorgeous mouth. Then my boss, the friendly second steward sees me at it. He is less than pleased. My career on deck came to a crash stop. After that I saw her only when the indicator flipped for 137."

Grover drank some more coffee. Storytelling looked like dry work for him.

"Guessing," I remarked, "that'd be like now and again. Only often."

"Don't anticipate," said Grover. "This is my story."

"I said nothing!" I said.

"No, no, you're right. She had trouble with that broken arm, stopped her doing lots of things, and she wasn't too backward yelling for help. On duty she special made a point of calling me; no Union those days, I could be on call twelve, fourteen hours. Lucky I had a good stomach and didn't get seasick. She was the same. Boy some healthy appetite. Those teeth could have chewed up a horse. Being first class, expensive cabin, bathroom attached, everything laid on, she didn't go to the dining saloon. Had her meals sent in."

Again Grover broke off. He seemed to be searching his memory for details, bills of fare and so on.

"I don't have to guess who gets to take in the tray."

"I told you. Don't butt in. Who's telling this story?"

I held up both hands, palms forward, then put a finger to my lips.

"Son of a bitch second steward don't like it, takes a real poor view. He details a stewardess, special to look after her. He figured to put my nose out of joint, but he didn't know Mrs Canzoni. She took shit from no one except Canzoni himself, and was very used to getting her own way. She raises cain, then slips a ten spot, the first of many. He decides right then and there I ain't so important, eats bread out of her hand. Situation as before, only with me he's even more obnoxious. Crummy bastard even brings out the wise uncle routine.

'Listen, kid,' he says, and smiles like I was a chick he had to save from a fate worse than death. 'For your own good I tell you. Deep with that broad don't get. You ain't too young for a bad accident. You ever see Canzoni in the ring? A killer! Strong as a two hundred pound chimp, and take it from me, twice as nasty. You got ambition for your face in a sling forever, you're on track. Frisco is ten days ahead. Some little bird is gonna sing Canzoni a big nasty secret. You wind up in hospital. Maybe he break only one bone. Your backbone.'

I couldn't help butting in again, in spite of Grover's warning.

"Good advice." I said, "figuring he was gonna be the canary."

"Yeah." Grover was thoughtful, he clicked his tongue. "Yeah. But who ever listens to good advice. Ten days is a long time when you're sixteen."

He closed his eyes, silent for so long I thought he had dozed off. Then, as if he had been reliving the event for my benefit and wanted to get things right, he opened his eyes and went on.

"I guess nothing much would have happened if it hadn't been for the sunburn. I took in her meals and mixed highballs. She kept shovelling them down like there was no tomorrow. Didn't seem to affect her at all. Never even got slurry. She had me cut up the food and feed it into that mouth with a spoon. I'm sure as I goddam can be she was able to use her left hand, but it pleased her to keep me with her long as possible. She ate like I said, real good, especially desserts. Favourite was chocolate ice-cream loaded with dark chocolate sauce and whipped cream. Jesus, my mouth went into top gear watering. She cottoned on, made me bring in a double portion so's I could match her spoon for spoon. Oh what a baby!"

"The sunburn?" I said. I couldn't help myself. "The sunburn?"

I wondered if I'd heard aright. Sunburn?

"We hove-to, waiting to go through the canal. Purser put up a notice about it was dangerous to get too much tropical sun. Mrs Canzoni hadn't been up to sunbathing, but she went ashore in Panama in an off the shoulder dress, said she needed to buy a few things and get her feet on something solid for a change. Came aboard well scorched to a very low neckline. That night she rang me. I knocked on the door. She calls 'Come in.' I go in but the cabin is empty. I wait a couple of minutes. She comes out of the bathroom dressed in a large white bathtowel tied up under the armpits; top of that bright red, painful looking.

'Son of a bitch,' she says. 'Serves me right, I should done like the notice said. Feel like I'm on fire. You got anything for sunburn?'

'You wanna see the doc?' I asked. 'I could get him come have a look.'

'Him I could do without. Sunburn ain't that fatal, least I hope not.'

The ship's doctor was a redheaded Scot, heavy on the bottle. He gave me some Unguentine and a few pads of lint.

'Gentle massage with this - often. Bad?'

'Pretty.'

'Take a couple of days to ease off .

I explained to the stewardess. She was less than enthusiastic.

'That one,' she said, all sourpuss, 'can fry all I care.'

But she took the ointment and went off to 137.

About fifteen minutes later the indicator flipped. I was half expecting. The stewardess went past me in the gangway rattling like a thundercloud. She gave me a dirty look, but kept her lips buttoned together. Mrs Canzoni was at the cabin door, eyes flashing warning lights.

'A fifth of Scotch an' a pitcher ice. And tell that fat assed stewardess to keep out of my hair.'

I got the Scotch and ice. Mrs Canzoni was lying face down on the bed, her long white legs sticking out the bottom end of the bathrobe.

'Mix me a slug,' she said. 'Four fingers and easy on the ice.'

Her voice was muffled in the pillow. My hands were trembling, the ice chinked in the glass. She rolled over, eyes full of tears, grabbed the glass and knocked off two fingers.

'What you send in that battle-axe for?' she asked plaintively. 'She hates my guts. My shoulders hurt worse'n before. I gotta have a massage, you gotta do it. Only take it easy kid, I feel like I been on a barbecue.'

For half an hour I slid oily fingers along her sunburnt shoulders and arm, pausing only to make another drink, and then another one. Finally she sighed.

'Jeez, that's a whole lot improved. I like your touch, kid, fingers real gentle. Them stewardess's pinch-hit for files. I thought the fat cow was taking my skin off.'

She took another slug and drained the glass.

'Gonna get some sleep,' she said dreamily. 'Come back later an' do it again, give me another going over.'

'I'm off duty soon,' I said.

'What the hell.' She looked at me with those eyes. 'Come when you ain't on duty.'

I just about melted on the carpet, and must have looked doubtful, for she grabbed her bag and brought out a roll of bills.

'No, Mrs Canzoni,' I stalled her, 'I'll come. That ain't necessary. I'll come O.K., soon's I can.'

The blue eyes were grateful.

'Sorry, kid. I didn't mean. Hell, you know what I mean.'

Next day a storm warning came down from the bridge. Glass was falling too fast for comfort. Cabin and deck stewards got ready for the blow. I helped strain ropes along gangways and in the dining saloon, and fixed up the side pieces on the tables so's the soup don't get dumped in diner's laps. I had no time for station in the cubby hole; if 137 indicator flipped or not I was too busy to worry.

The sea roughened; the ship swung like a pendulum. Each roll her nose dug under: the hull shuddered: waves stood up over the bridge, crashing on the foc'sle head. Seconds the massive weight of water held the ship in a vice, then the prow reared, jerking into the air. Streams of water raced to the scuppers, tossing about everything moveable on the decks. A lot of passengers puked all over the place; I had a nightmare time attending to vomiting and suicidally depressed passengers convinced we were about to founder. The sour smell in the cabins, portholes jammed tight, made me queasy. At the end of the watch, my replacement, red faced with effort, gave me a solid wink.

'Just went past 137. That Mrs Canzoni. What a dame! Asked if you was on yet. I told her I was on my way to relieve you, an' she said have him bring a bucket of ice. Got a splitting headache. Hitting the bottle hard, by the looks of her. All yours, buddy.'

I filled an ice-bucket from the Pantry freezer, negotiated the companion and gangways and knocked on the door.

'Come in.'

Throaty voice, alcohol thick. Mrs Canzoni lay on the carpet, head propped on a cushion, a full tumbler of whisky in her outstretched left hand, the plaster cast tucked to her side. Her eyes were closed. I filled an ice-bag and put it to her forehead. She rolled her head away.

'Forget it, kid. I'm O.K. Help me up. I need company. Get it?

She was wearing a loose silk kimono and, as far as I could make out, nothing else.

The storm hit peak. The steel cage of the ship groaned like an animal in pain. I helped Mrs Canzoni to her feet. She clutched at my shoulder so's not to fall, and in doing so presses against me, holding on just too long, lengthening the contact, like intimate. I got her to the bed. I had to say something but my throat glued up.

'How's the burn?' I got out.

'She pulled the robe from one shoulder. Pink but no longer angry.

'Massage did the trick. You got good hands, kid. Anybody tell you? Wanna drink?'

Before I could reply the ship dug in its nose, real deep. I pitched forward on one knee. Mrs Canzoni held on to my shoulder. For some moments we rode with the ship as it pulled its prow clear. I got up trembling.

'Better go,' I managed.

Mrs Canzoni looked at me so hard I wasn't sure she couldn'ta have hypnotised me.

'Listen, kid,' she said. 'I'm nervous like a new kitten. Jesus, what a trip. You gonna leave me alone? What for? Stay with me and see out this goddam storm. I mean it.'

The expression on my face amused her.

'You got it, kid, in spades. That's exactly what I had in mind.'

She spoke very, very slowly. I tried to misread her blue eyes, more luminous than ever. Unmistakable.

'Exactly.'

Some things are unbelievable. I didn't believe what was happening. But I stayed.

Dawn. Storm blown out. I left the cabin, exhausted, my thoughts in a screwed up tangle, my nerves at peace.

After that I only remember the nights. Days didn't count.

They did, of course.

The deck steward said, 'Diego, manana. Put in for leave you wanna go ashore.'

San Diego. First port of call in California.

Feeding Mrs Canzoni her bouillon, dazed, I heard her whisper.

'Purser's given me a wire. Canzoni's meeting me at San Diego. We gonna motor up to his training camp.'

I was dismayed, panicked.

'Better keep out of your way,' I said.

'I guess so. Tomorrow for sure.'

She looked at me with a wild expression, grabbed my arm, kissed me and hung on..

'Just don't leave me by myself tonight.'

I'm gonna get killed, I thought.

What amazes me was I didn't care.

Next morning the ship docks early. I am on deck and have a good chance to observe Canzoni as he came up the gangplank and onto the deck. He wore lightweights, linen suit, pale blue, a cream silk shirt, two tone shoes, spotless Panama. Massive shoulders bulged the jacket; long arms poked from the sleeves, huge hands like bunches of bananas. He had a habit of clenching the fingers into club hammer fists.

My luck was shot. I was on duty. Frustrated I saw Mrs Canzoni embrace the brute, throwing her good arm about his thick neck, kissing his lips with extravagant enthusiasm. The second steward came to my shoulder. He put a slobby mouth to my ear and whispered suggestively.

'Maybe he don't find out, babyface, maybe nobody give him a little song. Maybe!'

I felt condemned, a man on the way to the chair, without even breakfast or a last wish. The Canzonis went below. In the cubby hole, only half watching the discs, I thought, I can hide in the engine room. The usually sour pussed stewardess went by carrying a large tray. Looking at me triumphantly, she beamed all over her fat face

'Special breakfast for two in 137.'

Coupla minutes later she came back even more triumphant.

I wished I'd been nicer to her. Got on her good side.

Did she have one? Doubtful.

'Piper Heidseck, ice bucket. They got glasses. And hop it.'

She leered at me very nastily.

I took in the champagne. Outwardly I managed calm, inwardly my stomach was quivering. Canzoni lay on the bed, the soles of his two tone shoes pointed at me. His face seemed none too pleased. I thought he gave me a dirty look. Mrs Canzoni came from the bathroom with two champagne glasses. She looked through me like I didn't exist. I made believe I didn't know her, just filled the two glasses. She opened her purse and slipped me a five spot. I had to take it, the meaning in her eyes was too obvious. Clutching the bill, hardly daring to breathe, I managed to get out of the door. Half hour later the deck steward gives me a call to help him get the Canzoni baggage from the hold. We carried the expensive trunk and leather suitcases to the dockside and left them for shore porters to handle. The Canzonis hadn't materialised. The second steward whistling La Paloma waited for me by the cubbyhole. The bastard!

'Mr Canzoni, he looka for you,' he mimicked. 'He no lika babyface do things fora hees wife. Special he no like you jig-a-jig with her. Remember, I tella you good. You no listen.'

He pushed a large bundle of flowers wrapped in cellophane into my hand.

'O.K. babyface, you get to deliver. Compliments of Captain and crew. You see Canzoni, he see you.'

And the son of a bitch laughs like a flushed toilet bowl.

I saw myself in hospital, nose pulped, toothless, arms broken, jaw swollen, lips split. With that kind of vision I had to force my footsteps to the door of 137. A quick prayer for divine intercession. I knock. My knuckles are numb. The flowers stink sweet.

Canzoni, naked to the waist, a black curly rug on his chest, opens the door.

'Mrs Canzoni. Compliments Captain Mayo and crew.'

My voice is strange and falsely bright.

'She ain't here. Put 'em on the chair.'

I make a pretence of placing them to best advantage. I can feel Canzoni's eyes boring into my back. When I turn he is by the door, facing me. There is no way around him. I look at the porthole. No chance. I struggle with my tongue and stare at the wiry glistening hair on Canzoni's chest.

'Mrs Canzoni.' My voice seems far away. 'Please say good-bye to her for me. Been a pleasure to have her aboard.'

Canzoni scowls. He grips my arm.

'Listen, kid, I heard about you and Connie.'

Her first name! She'd never even told me.

'Mr Canzoni,' I said and stopped.

I was for the high jump. So be it. Maybe I'd get out in one piece.

'Yeah, you took good care of her.'

He looks at me accusingly.

Suddenly, in the silence that follows, I realise no real hostility emanates from him.

The frown, the accusing look?

The man is embarrassed. He drops his eyes and stares at my polished shoes.

'Connie says you done lotsa things for her, more'n you was entitled. But she don't like you to feel she thinks you on'y did 'em to squeeze a good tip. I guess you didn't at that. Still I gotta tell you I appreciate everything you done for her.'

He presses a century into my nerveless palm.
'Just to please me.'
'Jeez, no Mr Canzoni, I can't accept this.'
'A favour to me, kiddo, You looked after Mrs Canzoni good. I wanna thank you.'
He grips my arm again. The fingers are like clamps.
'You mind I give you a piece of advice?'
'No,' I mumble, 'I'll be glad.'
'Spread the dough on me for the fight. That stumble bum drops in five. He ain't worth no longer. His mother don't know him.'
He puts a long, powerful arm about my shoulders and gives me a friendly hug.
'So long, kid. Do like I tell you with the C, an' don't take no plugged nickels.'
I shut the door behind me. One hundred bucks and a chance to double it. The canoe graduates to a sixteen foot cedar full of camp equipment. I am outwardly calm, the efficient bell-hop, but mentally I do a war dance all the way back to the cubby hole."
Grover stopped at this point, practically to get his breath. The black girl put her head in at the door. She looked at Grover, then at me, disapprovingly.
"I'm off out to the store. We need things or we don't eat."
She gave me a hard look which said 'he invites you, say no.'
I got the message.
When she'd gone Grover turned to me.
"About the story. Ain't no more. Except I won a hundred at evens."
"You ever see her again?" I asked. "Canzoni got his a couple of years after that fight, if I remember."
"Your memory's O.K. No, I never did see either of them again. Least not in the flesh."
He saw I was puzzled and hurried to explain.
"Damnedest thing. Canzoni's bumped off, she vanishes, changes her name, gets a bit part in an M.G.M movie. Before you know it she's starring, and makes it big. Being a stunner and able to act as well she couldn't miss. Big, big star. Now and again they show her old movies on television. I got copies all could get."
He let his chin droop to his chest. He looked worn and very tired.
"In the dark," he went on almost inaudibly, "in the dark I see the image of a beautiful woman. She's dead some time, but I tell you

she's alive and real to me as on that five week trip to Frisco. When the film dies into credits, I have my own vision I don't share with anyone, of her on the night of the storm, face down on the bed, the ship pitching and tossing like a mad thing. She has her curved chin resting on the white plaster of the cast on her right arm. Her beautiful lips are wide, smiling, happy. And those eyes, blue, intense, dragging the heart in my chest. I see, I remember. A man should know perfection at least once so's he can die knowing he's lived. I cannot see myself, yet I am there, that flawless body moves under my hands. I thrust with the wave. I beg the gods of paradise. That that moment is forever. That the ship dig in too deep, sink deep, deeper, into nothingness and silence.

Grover drew in a painful sounding breath and exhaled slowly

"Write it down for me," he said. "When I'm gone it's yours."

We talked for a while. Then he fell asleep, snoring gently.

Aurelia, Addy, came back from the store and found the two of us. I hadn't wanted to leave without saying good-bye.

"You better go now," she said. "He'll sleep for a while."

She saw me down the huge elevator and into the street. I could see by her frown and the tight set of her lips she was thinking how I could be got rid of. I had no intention of falling in with her plans.

"I'll call around in a couple of weeks with the draft."

"What draft?"

"The story he wants me to ghost for him."

She thought for s few moments.

"You do that." She didn't smile

Well she knew, of course. When I called the place was all locked up. I questioned around and found Grover had gone to the Virgins. He owned a house there. I waited, tried again, then again. Finally I gave up. He never did come back

Some months later the paper folded. I made it on to a couple of rags but didn't last long. I had the bright idea of going free-lance. For a time it worked. I sold a few articles and a couple of stories; not enough to make a living. I had a few hundred dollars in the bank left to me when my mother died. The old man had preceded her. With that and a few bucks from odd jobs like working in a bar washing glasses and sweeping out I managed to get by. It was poverty, sure. But I had my freedom, I was ambitious. I believed in my luck.

Couple of years after the Grover incident, I got a letter from Addy. Wasn't much of a letter, pretty unfriendly. Said she'd had a helluva job tracking me down and would I call her .

On the phone she was even less friendly.

"Grover's dead," she announced without preamble.

"I read the obits," I said.

"He left a load of dough," she said.

"So?"

"You don't score." she said.

"But you do get a piece of sculpture," she added.

Telling me seemed to bug her.

"What is it?"

"I'll bring it round. I got the address. When'll be good?"

Wasn't that big then. I was curious.

"Anytime. I'm mostly in."

She came in followed by the hunk of chauffeur. He was carrying a box, large enough to go under his chin, just. He unwrapped the sculpture and looked for a place to put it down. I took away my typewriter and made room on the table. Addy was checking out my room. I could figure her saying, What kind of a dump is this? I didn't like it more'n she did, but I had no choice.

The sculpture was something else. Not a bolt near it. Just a beautiful construction in stainless steel, blued here and there by a torch. I looked at it and forgot all about Addy and the driver. I had never owned anything beautiful. Jesus! Grover, you done me proud. He'd remembered me. And I'd never been able to show him the draft of that story. Now he'd gone I was maybe like the only person to know about that sea trip. The love affair that had haunted him all his life.

Addie interrupted me

"You like it?"

I nodded.

"Worth bucks."

"Must be."

"Wanna sell?"

"How much?"

She looked at me with contempt, knowing she'd sized me up. Her book put me down cheap.

"Four, maybe five grand. Depends."

She looked round the crummy, untidy room. Hole in the wall she'd be thinking.

"Well?" she asked.

She was anxious to go. So was the big guy, even though he smiled at me.

"No dice," I said.

"Five thousand bucks," I said. "I can do without. I don't need money that bad."

She wasn't about to waste time on a no hoper. She walked to the door. The driver followed her but she let him go through first.

"You sure you don't wanna change your mind?"

I shook my head.

Then cause she knew she'd sized me up right, she gave me a mouthful of white teeth.

She said, "You will, buddy, you will."

I don't blame her for thinking. So far she's wrong. Five thousand bucks I could use bad. I'm not tempted. The sculpture, my Grover, better'n anything I've got. Or am ever likely to have.

Geoffrey Heptonstall

Yawning Stories?

On the airwaves every programme must work to establish itself. The vague and directionless fade into the background of something half-heard amid the distractions which often accompany radio listening. The mind, if not the hand, turns the dial. Print on the page has the advantage of an immediate authority, even if it proves illusory on closer inspection; whereas the memorable phrase may be lost in conversation.

Three of the BBC's five networks in radio regularly accept the challenge by broadcasting, among other aspects of culture, short stories. The tradition of doing so is as old as the medium. One of the earliest demonstrations of the power of the microphone was a story by Ronald Knox in the Twenties, which created a sensation and considerable panic.

Less sensationally, the BBC invests precious air time every week-day on its main radio channel where it broadcasts a fifteen minute story between the arts review and the five o'clock news hour. For radio this is prime time, catching the first of the commuters as they drive, and the people at home making tea. The moment between day and evening allows a brief pause in the thread of news and information which is the mainstay of the speech channel.

Listeners tend to be loyal to what they know. Those who can and do listen to the short story do so regularly. They are accustomed to the change of rhythm which the additional concentration brings. This is certain to foster a habit which may compromise the critical ear, but which will act as a guarantor of a generally intelligent audience.

This may need stressing. As I draft this my attention has been drawn to a considered plea by the novelist Kate Saunders for literary radio which seems to be losing the prestige of past times. The radio story could disappear, along with other aspects of imaginative programming. An observer cannot have an insider's knowledge and sympathy. Such a decline would beggar belief. But innocent ambition for the development of radio fiction - with precedents in Britain and overseas - may founder in the labyrinth of media politics.

It is timely to speak of the BBC's traditional role as patron of writing, with a particular regard for the promising tyros. Attention is more usually focused on dramatists, but it should be said that the number of novelists who found early and crucial encouragement at Broadcasting House is legion.

Beyond these pragmatic concerns, valid as they are, is the aesthetic of the genre. An oral tradition of story-telling is older than any written culture. It is the foundation of much Classical literature. By chance, the tales of Scheherazade are currently in the broadcast schedules.

In the radio story there are two voices - the author's and the speaker's, even if they are the same person. Edna O'Brien possesses one of the most compelling narrative voices in the world, yet that is not the voice I heard when I read her work. However much we may value an oral literature, we are not a pre-literate culture.

Listening, we forego our literacy and are beholden to another's tongue. It is an unsophisticated act, as irrational as falling in love. It connects us to our childhoods and to ancestral memories of our tribes. Oral literature strips away the civilisation about us. A lightness of touch sustains interest, while the communication is deeply intuitive. A world without story-telling would be a world where no-one knew how to dream.

*

'When the circus came to town and Lizzie saw the tiger they were living in Ferry Street in a very poor way.' So begins Angela Carter's 'Lizzie's Tiger', one of her last. It is a model of how a story written for broadcasting should begin. Situation, character and mood reveal themselves with the least intricacies of description and plot. This, for Duncan Minshull - BBC Stories Editor - is essential to the genre. What is true of all short fiction takes on an intensity when there is no opportunity to turn back the page. The sense of acts and responses must be caught at first hearing.

These economies and their attendant demands are for many writers a useful discipline. There is the challenge to hone down the narrative to classical perfection. A short story is not a compressed novel, nor a chapter of a larger work.

Some writers complain that the economy of broadcast fiction has the deadliness of writing to a formula. I put the point to Duncan Minshull who had no difficulty in agreeing that the 15 minute format could be a limitation, adding that Radio 3 did allow more time - though less regularly - and more intricacy of language and plot.

Brevity and crystalline clarity are not necessarily virtues. It may be possible at some time in the future for radio to think in more flexible terms. The imaginative and experimental possibilities of radio are not yet exhausted. Tellingly, Minshull's collections of reprinted stories from the air find much of the material from Radio 3.

Whatever the future, it should be said that these collections are part of what is evidently a renewal of radio literature. The change from the doldrums of mid-morning was but one indication of a marshalling of spirit - in fiction and drama. The primacy of the script began to re-assert itself even against the possible tides. The term 'a writer's medium' regained the currency it once had in the days of Louis MacNeice and D.G. Bridson, romantics whose administrative gifts were secondary to their imaginative concerns. This takes us beyond the short story, of course. But broadcasting genres find their place in a broader pattern of listening. The radio story would not survive were the future, for some reason or unreason, to be indifferent to literature as a whole.

*

The short story in Britain never did have - at least, not in the last fifty years - the prestige it has maintained in Ireland, France and the United States. Those are three different societies with nothing in common, as far as I can see, which might account for the prestige of a particular fictive form. As nations they have a revolutionary foundation which Britain singularly has not. But that cannot be the answer. All one can say is that something in British culture - specifically the culture of the metropolis - is indifferent to the short story. Habits don't establish themselves easily. Attempts to follow 'The New Yorker' or 'The Irish Press' have failed repeatedly.

A clue may be found in the English sense of reserve. Strangers on a train rarely talk. A journey by bus through Connemara or Trinidad is an opportunity to learn the life and opinions of a chance companion. Almost all social life in France is conducted at the café; friends rarely visit one another's homes. Whereas the English middle classes are both more formal and less spontaneous. This may have built traditions of humane conduct and stable administration, but is scarcely conducive to a spirit of carnival. Indeed, a lexicon of prevention exists to inhibit the unorthodox.

To put it another way, there is something unseemly about fiction - which is usually concerned with improper feelings - being found in newspapers which one might be found reading in public. To the English middle-class fiction is a private pleasure, something to hear in the car or the kitchen. It becomes something we couldn't help but overhear, like a piece of tittle-tattle which shocks and amuses in the same breath. The airwaves may be the only way many people are likely to receive the short story. Since the audience figures far outweigh the sales of story collections the point establishes itself, for whatever reason, readily enough.

*

The term 'radio novel' arose in American broadcasting some time in the Forties. Sandra Michael is one progenitor. Another is the Nobel Laureate Pearl S. Buck. Like Darwin and Wallace working on theories of Evolution, Michael and Buck separately and more or less simultaneously considered uncharted reaches of creative radio. Both writers had considerable experience of broadcasting. Despite some hostility, the idea of the radio novel did gains its adherents for whom it was a natural development in broadcasting. This was at a time when the creative possibilities in American radio had not succumbed to commercial pressures. The names at work make one gasp - Arthur Miller, Joseph Losey, John Houseman, Charles Laughton and so forth. The ambition and need were to create a new form of narrative fiction, arising from the short story, the novel and the play, but developed within the aesthetic of broadcast sound. In the early Fifties Tyrone Power turned down a lucrative Hollywood contract to participate in one of these sound narratives.

Of course there were similar ambitions at work in London and elsewhere. The ambition was less stated, although it was clearly there in, for example, Bridson's 'March of the '45' whose international audience was countless, like a movie. 'Under Milk Wood' is as close to a realisation of the radio novel as anything so far. That it is a transcription of a dream is significant. Equally significant is the evolution of Thomas's final script from fragments previously broadcast, stories and narrative feature material, capable of development well beyond something caught on the radio.

Whether the ambition of half a century past can continue to stimulate creative radio is a matter of reasonable doubt. On the other hand, there is no serious argument for intentionally diminishing its imaginative scope and purpose. The staple diet of good stories should not need defending. Nor should the projection of what might be.

*

A Sample Week

I took a week at random in late July, 1993. I listened to all the short stories broadcast on the BBC radio networks in what is as near to a typical week as there can be.

That first weekend there was nothing to be heard. At a time when people might be in their most receptive mood for a short story, a Saturday or Sunday afternoon, there is some drama on Radio 4, and there are some documentaries - mainly political or strongly factual.

The first story appears on Monday afternoon (Radio 4). It is by Chekhov and is called 'Tears the World Does Not See'. Expectations for this were dashed at once by such an obtuse reading. Emotional variety was registered in mumbles or growls, the reader apparently chewing his way through his ordeal. I lost interest within a few minutes.

Also on Monday Radio 5 had a Cumbrian tale originally published in a collection for children. One of 5's strengths has been its attempt to revive radio for a younger audience, but Berley Docherty's 'The Dragonosaurus' seemed to be written down, lacking the vitality and grace notes of a good story. The lively reading by Jane Hazelgrove compensated, but she was carrying her material. There wasn't enough for her to work on.

Tuesday on Radio 4 had what I presume to be an original radio piece, 'Touch and Go' by Brian Thompson, a new name to me, but one to watch. A lightness of touch sustained this telling story of life among the culturati. The production was by Gillian Hush, always a favourable sign.

Wednesday was a different matter. Radio 4 had a translated tale from the Spanish by one Antonio Munoz Molina. It was such a ramble with far too many characters, too much detail and endless asides. On paper this may work, but listening I was lost.

Later in the evening 5 broadcast the first of three parts of another tale for young people, 'Louis' by Julius Lester. Lester's strength is the sense of restraint in his narrative of slavery, letting the humanity come through where there might be hatred. His story of Louis a runaway slave had me hooked, but it was over much too soon. Each instalment needed half an hour. I know that 'Always leave 'em wanting more' is the watchword. On the other hand, timing is the secret of a good yarn.

'Louis' was read in, of all things, a cockney accent. Apart from being inapt it was also inept, an endless procession of glottal stops. A few years ago Charlie Chester read some W.W. Jacobs stories in Chester's authentic East End voice, with not a glottal stop in earshot.

His diction was perfect, as a music-hall veteran's is, and that is the standard to aim for.

I avoided further readings of 'Louis' on the two successive nights, but I did hear Gwyn Thomas's 'Good Night, Julius' on Radio 4. It was an accomplished piece of Welsh story-telling, touchingly evocative of the valleys and chapels. It had that sly humour, indelibly Celtic, most memorably associated with Frank O'Connor.

Benjamin Dean is another unfamiliar name to me. He is very clever, and I suspect he is an American of the New Yorker school. 'A Letter to Andrei' (Friday, Radio 4) was an affectionate pastiche of Chekhov. Clearly read, the prose had the cadence of an urbane, ironic narrative. The twist in the tale arose naturally from the emotional development of the characters, the only convincing way to surprise an audience.

That brings us to the weekend again. Where, you may ask, is Radio 3? Well, there was some drama - Seamus Heaney, after Sophocles - but the sole piece of fiction was a Radio Scotland production by the up and coming Glaswegian writer, Dilys Rose. 'A Little Bit of Trust' previously won a competition though not one sponsored by the BBC. (It must be years since they have bothered to seek out talent in this way, as far as prose fiction is concerned.) Encouragement is always welcome, not least for something which breaks through the fifteen minute barrier, or the Warhol Line. 'A Little Bit of Trust' was well worth the investment. It conveyed so much in so few words. The sense of place - it was set in Morocco - carried the spice, the dust, the exotic to western eyes. Two narratives were contrasted, a woman's and a man's, ironically presenting the nearness and the distance of their connected experience. Intricacies of plot were skilfully choreographed to its bittersweet bitter conclusion. The present tense gave an immediacy to the proceedings. So much life distilled into a few thousand well-chosen words. Above everything, it was the work of a truly original voice. Dilys Rose has something to say about life. Radio 3 has every right to be proud of giving her this early lift.

As ever, there was no fiction on Sundays. Now it is Monday. Later this afternoon Beryl Bainbridge will be reading one of her own stories. Mid-week there will be Sorcha Cusack reading a story by Tatyana Tolstoya. And so on. How typical is any given week?

Generally I hear one, perhaps two stories a week on radio. I never listen to Radio 5 as a rule, for reasons given above. Like many people, I find 3 inhibits me from listening by its dryness of presentation. Radio 4 has become too journalistic. There isn't enough talk about life in general, though there are enough such talkers around. Compare this with RTE.

Listening day by day and to a purpose I drew some conclusions which previously had drifted about nebulously. I had never realised fully before the contrasts in presentation on the networks. Second-guessing the audience in this way is patronising. A few years ago I made a programme with Clancy Sigal who talked about his childhood listening in wartime Chicago. 'Everyone listened to everything' he said with his engagingly perceptive enthusiasm for the means to a better life. Enthusiasm depends on confidence. All the restructuring of society in the last decade or so may be good accountancy, but it has left people, including broadcasters, exhausted. Confidence depends on stability. Stability depends on good will which arises from sensitivity in harmony with intelligence. That is where literature comes in ...

Of the stories I heard there was a healthy variety in sources, themes and voices. But the elements generally failed to combine with total success. Given the context hinted at above, this may be understandable. All one can say is that a marshalling of resources, even against the odds, is still a priority. The rest is another story.

Submissions to Panurge

All fiction is **unsolicited** and is considered all the year round. Do not be embarrassed about keeping on trying; it is the only way to get anywhere, as 'successful' writers will testify!

Stories are usually turned round within a week and all writers are replied to individually. No one ever gets a form rejection slip. At present we are getting about fifty stories a week for consideration.

Margaret Dunglinson

Of A Kind Unknown

Jan was musing and wished once more that he knew the name of that tree. It would be reasonable for his patients to suppose that after fifteen years he knew. But he did not. He had always been on the point of asking one or other of them what kind of tree it was, always on the point. But he never had.

It was a November day, quite bright and he had noticed, on his short walk to his surgery, that the sun was making every effort to dry up the pavement and freshen the air. Until today it had been foggy and depressing: Jan had felt the year to be as old and as heavy as himself.

A shaft of sunlight came slanting through that half of his surgery window which was not frosted glass and it glinted on his polished instrument cases. Jan turned to admire it, slapped his thigh as a gesture towards getting up from his stool, then ran his tongue over his carious teeth. He knew it was strange to his patients that a dentist should have carious teeth and bad breath. He had given the reason to one of them: Jan Spjnerre had been in a camp during the war but had talked about it only once since then, when he told his patient, Imogen Redfern, that part of his history. He did not, however, regret telling her; indeed he felt he had to. He could not at that moment think why.

After the liberation he had come via New Zealand, where he completed his degrees in dentistry, to Manchester, and had set up a considerable practice.

He did not get up, but returned his gaze to the upper half of his surgery window.

The tree stood in a small square of overgrown grass and weeds; Jan never tended the patch, there was no way of entering it, and in any case he was no gardener. It was bordered by a high wattle fence which had no door, and beyond it was a large shed which was not his. No-one but he and his patients could see the tree.

He ought, he considered, to be doing something, as Imogen Redfern was due at ten to have her wisdom teeth incised, then he remembered he had done everything; the instruments necessary for the operation were in the steriliser, he had laid out towels and his gown and mask. There was nothing else to do. Suddenly he felt quite hopeless so he stood up and began to walk about. The floor of the surgery was tiled and clean but he imagined it otherwise; it was befouled by human ordure and the air stank with all the rotting, but living, jaws he had seen. Pressing his hand to his paunchy belly he thought he might be sick. Then he looked at the tree and felt better; the tree was almost like a tooth, its branches having been cleaned and bleached by the coming of winter. It had not yet started to rot.

He paced about for several minutes, set his cupboards in order, and moodily prepared some amalgam, thinking absently that he might also fill a couple of Miss Redfern's teeth. On consideration however, he could not; it was of course enough to free the wisdom teeth. He was getting much too old.

Imogen Redfern came directly into the surgery at five minutes to ten, thinking she was late.

Jan looked up and pushed the mortar aside - Good morning, he began, sit down. I am going to free your left side wisdom teeth.

Imogen, who had forced a smile, faltered and began to protest. - But Mr. Spinner, she pleaded, I would rather you did it next week, please do it then. I had no idea, she continued desperately, that you would do it this morning. - So, Jan shrugged sympathetically, why do I give you the penicillin? Imogen looked at him hopelessly - I did wonder, she began, then her voice trailed off and she set down her battered shopping bag and stood awkwardly by Jan's small desk which was littered with papers for the Dental Estimates Board and the Executive Council.

- There now, Jan said, come and sit. An injection and you feel nothing, nothing at all.

Imogen, shaking, sat in the dental chair. Jan went to the door of the surgery and opened it wide. Imogen heard the door creak and was frightened. The surgery shared the building with some sort of agents, anyone might come in and hear her scream: she would be so ashamed.

Jan put on his gown and prepared the injection. As he leant over Imogen she felt his warmth and bulk upon her forearm. It was comfortable and after the injection she felt tired. Jan saw her face relax a little and smiled: Imogen was like so many he had seen in the camp; she had the look of hurt desperation he had known so well then, like an animal in a trap which will, in its struggle to be free, tear off a limb. He knew he must be gentle with her.

He had treated her first of all at the mental hospital; Imogen's had been that small, frightened face amidst the smiling blankness of the insane; Imogen's had been that hard, protesting, menstruous stench amidst the sweetness, the unbearable sweetness that made him sniff up so greedily the evidence of dogs by damp lampposts as he went home after his hospital duty.

Now Imogen was discharged and working in a shop: she had been cured and had taken up her rickety place in the world.

- You can get up, Jan said, and sit on the chair by the desk until the injection is taking full effect.

Imogen was still frightened, even more so now that the warm comforting bulk of Mr. Spinner had been removed from her forearm and she wondered if ever she would be able to get his name right. He was always called Mr. Spinner at the hospital but she knew that it was not correct. She got up unsteadily, balancing herself by the arms of the dental chair and went to sit by the desk: she was glad to be upright after tilting so giddily backwards. Jan got up on his white topped stool by the window.

Imogen tried to make sense of the words on the paper headed Dental Estimates Board but could not and thought she might fall asleep. The realisation of the operation ahead, however, jerked her back to consciousness. She felt that now she must never sleep; there was something in sleep which made her afraid and she dare not yield to it. Night after night she stayed awake, telling herself that she must on no account fall asleep. But what puzzled the doctors was the fact that this had all started before the intruder had forced himself with all the finesse of a ramrod into her twelve year -.old body. The time had been just before dawn. She had in fact slept since, although she did not realise it; she could remember only the times when she was awake.

Jan again reflected on the tree outside the window and considered that in another ten minutes Imogen would be ready for the operation. He knew that she was menstruating; he had smelt the stench. He thought about her record card upon which he had noted the drugs the hospital were using to control her: amongst them was tryptophan forte and he knew her to have been very ill. He thought he might ask her the name of the tree to break up the silence, but for some reason he felt that now he ought not to know. He could not explain why.

*

- Happy at the shop? he enquired eventually. Imogen, who, to keep herself awake had been staring hard at the back of him said briefly: -Yes, and she folded her hands neatly on her lap. - I think you are glad to be out, no? Jan enquired further and turned. - Yes,

Imogen replied. For a twenty year old, Jan thought, it was terrible that she had so little to say, and he looked hard at her intense white face. - It is good to be out, he went on in desperation, good to feel this November sun is it not? - Yes, Imogen responded. Jan could feel his words vibrate on the walls of the surgery and in the corridor outside; the corridor and stairs were quiet for it was a Saturday morning, the agents did not work on a Saturday.

Imogen did not know how to reply: brushing back her long hair she took out a grip from it and pinned it more firmly to the side of her head; being tilted back in the chair had made it all loose.

Jan, dropping his gaze to the floor, thought her a pretty child; at least she had the possibility of being pretty, for she had large luminous eyes and long black eyelashes. Her eyes were made larger and more luminous by the complete absence of colour from her cheeks. It was one of those things which made the starving become so frightful.

Imogen felt that her mouth was beginning to twist and feel lumpy; the injection was beginning to work. It came as a sort of relief to feel that her mouth did not belong to her, was lumpy but fleshless and could feel no pain. Then she knew that she needed to go the lavatory and twisted in her seat. - Mr. Spinner, she began, will you excuse me? - Please, Jan responded and waved his hand vaguely in her direction. Imogen got up and went out; she was overflowing and felt dirty and sticky. As she walked she felt as if her whole being was draining away. When she got to the door of the lavatory, which was shared by the dentist and the agent, she felt the flow stop; it was because she had been sitting which made it gush so.

Jan stared at the tree and planned out the operation to come moment by moment, although he could do it with his eyes closed; when she came back she would be ready; her mouth would be impervious to pain. It was the mind, he concluded, which could not be made so and he was angry: with whom he did not know.

Imogen came slowly back into the surgery and looked bleakly at him as he got up and smiled. - Yes, Jan enquired, you are ready? - Yes, Imogen responded as best she could for her mouth was now fully anaesthetised. Jan motioned her to the dental chair and she sat and gazed up at him. He put on the lamp and asked her to look at the point below its shade. She did not; instead she gazed up at him. Then he put towels about her.

Jan had started before he realised that he did not have on his mask. He dropped the probe with a gesture onto the round instrument table and turned to put the oblong of cotton over his mouth. Now he was fully prepared.

Once more Imogen felt his warm bulk as he leant gainst her then realised that she should not be comforted, she dared not be. Two large tears began to emerge from her eyes. Jan, taking up a gauze swab, wiped them away and tossed the swab into the pedal bin.

-You are afraid? he asked, no: we make you better. You will say if this hurts? Imogen shook her head and disturbed the padding he had just put inside her mouth. Jan, taking the probe up, packed it back into position carefully. Imogen's eyes were full upon him and he felt perspiration begin to form on his brow. If only she would not stare.

He began on the first impacted tooth and made an incision; the blood began to trickle onto the padding and he saw the white gleam of tooth; it was a big, perfect one. Imogen had the most perfectly white teeth he had ever seen. And he was to make her mouth one of the most beautiful; he knew that he would spare no effort, she was so worthwhile. Not even with his private patients would he expend such effort. He made another incision and the square of flesh was loose. Taking up his forceps he picked it out. The sleeves on his gown were short and the blood trickled up his arm. - You see, he said, waving the scrap of flesh at Imogen in order to interrupt her gaze. She saw and shuddered,then looked full at the lamp in order that she might not see what he did with the piece of flesh.

The tooth was still not free enough to push its way out and Jan cut into the flesh again: the blood came freely, Jan liked its brightness. Once again he held the loosened piece up for her to see and then he wiped his arms and her cheeks with a swab. It was such a pity, he thought, that he should have to remove the blood from her cheeks; it gave her that necessary colour.

Imogen was totally afraid; most of all because she had given in to the comforting warmth of Mr. Spinner's body soft against her, most of all because she had wanted to reach out and hold onto him and talk to him. To do so she knew would be fatal. She stared at him in continuous horror and watched the perspiration drip into his cotton mask.

Jan paused: - You look, he said desperately, at the tree. You see, he went on indicating, its branches are waving outside the window.

Then, with a gesture of despair he added: I do not know what kind it is. Imogen looked at him wildly and then at the tree of which from her angle she could see only the top couple of feet of its branches. Jan could see that he had upset her and wiped up the tears that came from her eyes. She looked at him once more.

He began the operation again, tidying the flesh neatly around the exposed tooth. He had made a precise job of it. - We had such a tree at the camp, he said, as he crossed to the sterilizer and started to pick out fresh instruments. There it was a magnolia that never bloomed, he went on. Imogen watched the steam from the sterilizer arise about him and could not respond. Her whole being felt sticky; she eased herself in the seat and felt a strong gush outwards; she knew that something horrible would occur as a result of the operation taking place.

- Nothing, Jan went on, ever bloomed at the camp. Holding up a dripping scalpel he turned and said - You understand? Imogen nodded, her eyes wide upon him; she was afraid that he might put the red hot instruments straight into her mouth, but realised that if he did, she would not feel them.

Jan was glad to be able to turn back to the sterilizer and away again from the direct gaze of those large eyes and he watched the water boil with relief. He ceased to sweat and became calm, passing his tongue reflectively over his dying teeth: his breath was specially bad this morning, but this patient hardly ever seemed to notice.

Imogen watched the broad back busy at the white bench and studied the many creases in the long white gown; it was tied with two tapes and she could see a pullover through the gaps. It seemed that that was the one relevant scene of her life, a figure in a long white gown hatched around with the raw stench of antiseptic. The stench of antiseptic made Imogen constantly sick and in the hospital the nurses refused to believe her: they said she made herself sick on purpose. She tried desperately to take her eyes off the broad back but could not.

He had of course done his best in the camp, Jan considered to himself. The water before him heaved gently and the instruments at the bottom of the sterilizer shone up at him. It was those eyes, those eyes and the desperation of not knowing whether he preferred them open or shut. He looked over his shoulder and met Imogen's gaze: turning abruptly he looked once more into the sterilizer. So, he mused on, she was a patient, they were only patients. He was a young man in the camp, already at his apprenticeship in his chosen profession. He had helped where he was able, he had been as gentle as he could. The rotting jaws came afterwards, as a result of the filthy made-up instruments and inhuman conditions. It was best forgotten, indeed it had been, until he encountered Imogen Redfern. She had hauled the whole frightful scene back into his brain: he knew her eyes were still upon his back. It was the little bits of extras he gained as a result of his services to his fellows which made him ache most of all; those pitiful extras made to look obscene by a world returned to normal: the minute opportunity they gave to feel hope somewhere within his being. And he had done his best for those who were mostly not his countrymen. Pursing his lips he shrugged to himself and stared hard at the tiled wall.

Imogen now felt very cold; the wide open door of the surgery let in a draught of the chilling November air and the staircase outside was very still. She felt she ought to run away, but remembered the packing within her mouth; it tasted pungently of cloves and she could not bring her lips properly together. Putting her hand up she felt them and flicked them: they were rubbery and nerveless. She tried to bring her tongue around to feel the incised tooth, but could not manipulate it for the packing. She thought that on going back to her room she would make a good cup of tea: she was very dry. The hospital had found her a nice room in the front of a terrace house: there were four other tenants in the place but they did not bother with each other: it was so much easier to let each other alone. What pleased her most of all was the key she had to the room; it was delightful to be able to get inside and lock the door then pull the curtain across and look around at all the emptiness. But sometimes it frightened her, it frightened her deeply; there were times when she wished to be alone and times when she did not; there were times when she wished that she were tied to something more than that episode just before dawn. She had felt it in this surgery, that desire to be part of something, to be relevant, somewhere to matter and not be used. But, she concluded, she was just another patient to be pushed around and told to look at trees. She looked at the tree outside the surgery window, but knew that she ought to be watching the back of Mr. Spinner. The tears welled up in her eyes and she dabbed them with the towel which Mr. Spinner had draped around her neck.

Jan let his body relax and knew that the gaze had ceased to bore into his body. He guessed that Imogen would be looking at the tree and he hoped that she received comfort from it. He had thought at one time, when considering the layout of his surgery, that he would have the whole window pane of frosted glass. He was glad now that he had not. Somehow the tree needed somebody to look at it, to know that it was there, even if the kind were unknown. He now had the instruments ready for the second half of the operation.

As he came to place them on the instrument table above her, Imogen did not remove her gaze from the tree.

Jan dropped the instruments one by one onto the enamel surface; they rang coldly and efficiently but still did not disturb Imogen. She had given up being disturbed; she was just another patient to be pushed around and told to look at trees.

Jan was distressed. Was it worse to have those eyes upon him or away from him?

- Open your mouth, he said thickly and bent over Imogen. Imogen opened her mouth obediently and thought about her rubber lips. Then she closed her eyes tightly.

Jan adjusted the arc lamp and shuddered.

The lower tooth was going to be quite a challenge; it was growing out at an angle from the jaw: eventually it would have to be sawn from the jaw bone. He made the first incision deftly and neatly and paused for the blood to flow out. It did so quickly and efficiently always as though it had read how to do it from a text book. He made the next incision and the flesh was loose. He picked it out with the forceps, stood back from the chair and held it up. A trickle of blood again made its way up his arm. - There you see, he began. But Imogen kept her eyes tightly closed. - Open your eyes, he commanded. Imogen did not respond. - Please, he pleaded, you open your eyes. Imogen did not respond. He disposed of the small piece of flesh and felt tears come up his eyes; he bit his lip and made a gesture of despair, sighing. His breath was cold about him and echoed in the tiled surgery. The front of his gown was now blood streaked; he wiped his forearm and then gently took a swab and brushed Imogen's cheek. She kept her eyes closed. One more piece of flesh and the operation would be over.

Imogen was not asleep; she merely did not wish to look. She conjured the tree up in her mind and thought determinedly, oak, ash, sycamore, rowan, magnolia. That struck a chord. It was Mr. Spinner who had told her about a magnolia; she had never seen one, neither had she seen a camp. Then there was lilac, beech, birch, laburnum; perhaps he had been right, it was so comforting to think of trees; and there were more; fir, pine, apple, pear, gum, eucalyptus, magnolia. No, she had already thought of that one. Cedar, balsa, cherry, almond, tulip, pepul, monkey puzzle, maple. Her mind was exhausted; she did not wish to think anymore; she longed for the drugs that would take away the damage to her consciousness. But she did not wish to open her eyes.

Jan took up his probe and determined on the dimensions of the incision which could complete the operation; it was the most precise he had ever performed, the most perfect. He then laid down the probe on the round instrument table and took up the scalpel. Soon, reflecting in the small precise blade, the tooth began to gleam. He had freed it and he was glad. Taking a swab, he cleaned up the area and then began to take out the packing.

Suddenly Imogen opened her eyes and looked at him. He was unprepared and stepped quickly back, his heart thumping: he realised now that it was the gaze he had hated. - So, he stammered, you are awake, yes? Imogen stared at him: - I, she said, have not been asleep.

He took off the towels which he had draped around her neck and held them up. - You look, he said, half smiling, as if you have been butchered. Imogen looked at the towels and then at the operating gown; what Mr. Spinner had said might be true - everything was streaked with blood. - You wash out now, Jan stated, regaining his composure and indicating the little hissing sink and the glass of pink liquid by her side. Imogen did so, noting the blood-tainted mess that was coming out of her mouth and oozing over the chromium rim of the drain.

Jan went over to the handbasin and washed his hands thoroughly then dried them on the clean towel hanging from the rail. Then he thought he might pack her mouth again with swabs to make it more comfortable.

Imogen was watching the back of him and wondering whether or not she ought to get out of the chair. Eventually she decided that she must, and made to get up.

Jan adjusted the towel on the rail neatly. - No, he announced turning, some packing and then we are finished.

Imogen flopped obediently back into the chair; the motion had made her gush again and she thought she might be going to overflow entirely.

Walnut, she thought, closing her eyes, orange, plum, pineapple - no, that was not a tree; Christmas, cypress, poplar: the names of trees seemed endless. Then quite by accident, they began to get muddled: cylar, sycoakpress, nastursium and they seemed to dance about in her brain.

Jan had got the swabs comfortably into position when his patient's head flopped sideways and she emitted a long sigh. Her mouth closed gently but her lips did not meet. Once more he swabbed her cheek and took away the necessary colour.

Jan had no further appointments and went to sit on the stool by the window; he ought to put the instruments back into the sterilizer, but was exhausted by the operation and needed to rest. He ran his tongue over his carious teeth and knew that he would take them to his grave. Just before the camp was liberated sentence of death had been passed on him. His meagre food supply had already been terminated: he remembered exactly the terrifying visions which become the lot of the starving, the awesome clarity of mind, when blood becomes twice the colour it is, life twice times its size: a starved brain being always the most active brain. He remembered that the magnolia tree had seemed bigger and its imagined blossoms twice as pink. He had been unable to convince himself at that time that a magnolia blossom is the most gentle of shades. The blossoms he imagined to be great gobbets of blinding light, like some unearthly Christmas tree. But the magnolia never blossomed in the compound and it had remained decidedly leafless.

He remembered the footsteps trudged out in the mud of the compound become gigantic, as if imprinted by a mammoth, as if the whole human race had made one massive mark. The rain drops on the window of the hut had become bigger and mirrored him perfectly, a white, shaven, starving man, twisting and tumbling down a large pane of glass. His bunk had become bigger, it was like a whole ocean and he in it, lumbering like a whale. The eyes of those about him had enlarged and blinded him whenever he looked into them and no-one could speak; the camp was too small to have contained their words, The jaws became more stinking and more rotten, but what they could utter became more massive. And the amount of air they could foul was not sufficient in the whole of the earth.

He pressed his hand to his forehead and turning saw Imogen mutter and stir. He then looked up at the leafless branches of the tree outside his window; it was not moving, it was quite still, it was quiet. He had seen it leaf and fall for fifteen years but what kind of tree it was still remained unknown. So it was better not to know. Trees were not the same as people; to know a person's name was to know a little about them - but trees were not like that; one could never know a tree.

Imogen slept on peacefully; the trees had become a joyful muddle about which she danced happily; indeed the girl who was dancing so happily had no idea why she had been so sad and looked up at the dream branches occasionally, puzzled.

Jan looked at her once more, smiling gently; he would make sure that she had the most perfect mouth that his skill could produce; he felt inexplicably that he owed her more than the usual patient-dentist relationship; Imogen was more than a mouth.

Imogen jumped suddenly, gave a little cry, then gaped around vacantly at the surgery. - I, she began, looking at Jan, then she tailed off and fear coloured her face. She grasped around at her coat and made to get up out of the chair. - Miss Redfern, Jan began, do not be afraid, and he motioned her to sit again. I am an old man.

Imogen looked deeply at him, at her unruffled coat, then seemed to come to some decision. - All right, she said smiling happily, may I sleep some more? - Please, Jan responded, you are very tired.

Imogen relaxed back in the chair: she noted that there had been no blood flow and went directly into a brief sleep.

Jan stirred on his stool and looked out at the tree: a slight breeze touched the branches, but since all its leaves were gone it made no sound, no sound at all.

Not A Pushover Quiz

Answer to Panurge 20 Quiz. It was Emilia Pardo Bazan(Penguin Classic) who wrote *The House of Ulloa* (as seen on Channel 4 at dawn). The winner was **Michael Eaude** of Barcelona who got a £20 Book Token.

Panurge 21 Quiz. Only one question. Who wrote 'The Confessions of Dan Yack'? Clue: the author only had one arm. First correct answer wins a £20 Book Token. Deadline 5.11.94.

Rhys H. Hughes

The Man Who Mistook His Wife's Hat For The Mad Hatter's Wife

1. They live in a house shaped like a hat. Music is in their blood, but they have different groups. In the evenings, they play backgammon by the light of a single candle. It is difficult to determine, with any degree of accuracy, whether they are inspired romantics or simply trying to save money. The dice crack on the baize like knuckles. They play with chocolate-covered mints, plain and milk, and eat as they bear off.

One day, the house blows away in a strong gale and lands on a hill. The view is terrific. The man, frilly shirt open at the collar, carries a saxophone out onto the verandah and takes revenge on the storm. The clouds pour hail down the mouth of his instrument and then part. He serenades the ideal stars.

A frosty rime glitters on his lips. His wife comes out to join him and they embrace. Her hair is a hundred shades of the darkest red.

2. The Mad Hatter is writing out invitations with a pen made from the leg of a spider. He is much happier now. He has bought a new suit and shaved his whiskers. Alice has finally consented to marry him. She is very young, but he is confident.

He pokes out his tongue as he forms the words. He wants only eccentrics to attend his wedding-reception. He has heard about a couple who live in a house shaped like a hat. The notion tickles him. He is thoroughly tickled. When he has finished, he drops the invitation into the mouth of a winged cat which flaps up the chimney and soars away over the rooftops.

My invitation has already arrived. I am the last existentialist. This is eccentric enough for the Mad Hatter. As a writer with no imagination, I look forward to the party. I will meet many characters there whom I shall be able to use. I pack my notebook, a piece of cheese, an apple and set off on my way.

3. Desire is not difficult to maintain. The couple in the hat on the hill are kissing. They are making love in front of a fire piled high with green wood. The wood spits as they suck and smokes as they blow. Each freckle between her breasts needs to be kissed. A constellation of incomparable delight.

Afterwards, they help each other to the bed and fall asleep under the heavy duvet. The clouds have returned and it starts to snow. As the snow settles, the preternatural landscape grows brighter. The snow dusts my coat and I turn up the collar. I pass the hill and gaze up at the house. Something small and dark has just landed on the brim. It scratches at a window and forces entry. I am reconciled.

As I walk, the unknown creature disappears inside. When the sun comes up, I sit on a hedge and chew at my apple. The couple awake and find a cat curled up between them.

4. Alice is playing the harpsichord, to calm her nerves. Her fingers fly over the keys, building up a dress of notes which cling to her naked body. These notes will shimmer and tinkle when she moves. These notes, semi-quavers and minims, glisten like ice. The piece she has chosen is old and cold and firm to the touch on the stave of her belly. As her arms are encrusted and grow heavy, her tempo decreases.

I have arrived at the designated spot. In a clearing in a wildwood stands the shell of a church. I am the first. I explore the crumbs of rock with a dispassionate eye. The spiral staircase to the belfry has collapsed.

Alice is ready and is on her way. The coda was the veil. Her bare feet make blue impressions on the mossy carpet of the forest floor.

5. The couple are also dressing for the occasion. The man has selected a frilly shirt of a different hue and a saxophone of black wood trimmed with silver. The woman has selected a hat in the shape of a young girl. The cat will guide them, like a kite on a string as long as a river.

Ribbons rustle, silk and crinoline fold and unfold into a meaningless tangram. And you and I? We know how to cling to ourselves, but not yet to each other. It is not true that no man is an island. We are all islands, misty islands, connected only by an irregular ferry service. Like form to its matter.

While they prepare themselves, I am joined by the caterers, the Husher, Father Phigga, a few guests. Tables and chairs are laid out. Prebendary Garlic has written a speech as creamy and corpulent as his own aspirations.

The Mad Hatter arrives and fills his mouth with his fists.

6. The cat lands in the belfry and the couple emerge into the clearing. There is a great deal of aimless chatter. More guests appear. Hands are shaken; large knotty hands, thin reedy ones. Father Phigga takes his place at the ruined altar of the abandoned church. When Alice breaks through the dense foliage, the musicians strike up on their bone xylophones. The long and the short of it is that there is a wedding, the wrists of Alice and the Mad Hatter symbolically bound with a braided cord.

And then it is time for the guests to kiss the bride. The man who lives in a hat takes rather longer over this than his wife would like. While she watches her husband with a frown, I watch her with a pounding heart. Prebendary Garlic is watching me. Observing the observer of the observer.

7. Soon, very soon, the guests sit down to the banquet. The cat wanders off into the forest and falls asleep in the hollow of an oak-tree, snuggled up tight with a large owl. There are three tables arranged in parallel lines, each table with only one side in this dimension, and the guests are seated as follows:

Humpty Dumpty	A White Rabbit	Edgar Allen Poe
A Glass Of Water	Bram Stoker	Dante Alighieri
Baruch Spinoza	Tweedledee	A Velocity Orange
The Hat Couple	Boris Vian	Achilles' Tortoise
A Sea-Horse	Guy de Maupassant	D.F. Lewis
Tweedledum	The Holy Grail	Grace Under Pressure
The 600th Orgasm	A Volcano	A Traitor's Gate
Caliban	Camille-Gabrielle	A Bloody Mary
A Wild Goose Chase	Soren Kierkegaard	The Narrator

The caterers mill and cough over the cutlery, wiping it clean with dirty handkerchiefs, while the Husher, Father Phigga and Prebendary Garlic stand at the head of each table declaiming avant-garde poetry. They are not guests and therefore not entitled to food.

We drink celery wine and toast the bride and groom. The caterers serve the meal. There are olives and mango slices for harlots d'oeuvre; toenail soup for starters; red onion bunions with pillow rice as the main course. For dessert we gorge ourselves on strawberry fool and raspberry idiot. The man who lives in a hat is staring at

Alice.

Anticipating disaster, I take out my notebook.

8. There will never be a past as remote as the one which is now the present. Everything seems asleep and vague, outlines of events thrown onto a paper screen in a magic-lantern show. Even as they happen I feel nostalgia for such events. As the remnants of the meal are cleared away, I am already regretting a lost chance I have not yet had. Fires have been lit and dancing is in stately progress. I boost my courage with more celery wine and approach the woman who lives in a hat.

Suddenly, my nerve unravels and I merely nod at her and walk past. I continue through the fence of trees that rings the clearing. She is far too beautiful to make any attempt at contact. As I gaze up at the highest elms, I stumble over the supine bodies of Alice and the man who lives in a hat.

It is obvious that they have slipped away during the dance to consummate an illicit passion. They are entwined together, crumpled, oblivious of all else. I race back to the clearing, my teeth shining brightly. I fall at the feet of the wife and babble everything. In the same static moment I see that the real Alice is dancing with a White Rabbit...

9. Relationships sometimes end for good reasons as well as bad. I should have been pleased that the hat was in the shape of a girl. I should have blessed the fate that directed the wife to leave her hat on the table and the man to mistakenly carry it off into the forest. But it avails me little. I have the story and nothing more.

The Mad Hatter and Alice fly off on a magic carpet, tins clinking on lengths of old string behind them. I am ignored. The couple who live in a hat become separated forever. She leaves him dumbfounded and when he returns to the hill he discovers that he is now homeless.

Hats, it appears, have gone out of fashion.

Philip Sidney Jennings

The Widow's Legacy

After Dad died and my ugly sisters ran away to breed with strange men in towns far away from our little bungalow just outside Eastbourne, I stayed at home with Mum.

I wasn't unhappy with her. In many ways I substituted for Dad. In the evening I ate a hot cooked meal and all I had to say to make Mum's eyes glow with pleasure, was: "Mum, Mum, that was really good." It wasn't hard to muster enthusiasm for food I was used to. Sometimes if I belched after a meal and Mum was in a good mood, she'd say: "Showing appreciation are we!" Then I'd grin. Sometimes if I belched like a donkey braying, which I do unaccountably sometimes, her small pretty face would become smaller and she'd say, fairly mildly: "Oh Bob, you're not sick are you?" She dreaded sickness as much as bad manners, perhaps even more.

"Sorry Mum," I'd say, "it just came out."

"Well put it back where it came from."

I tried to imagine putting a jet of stale exhaled air back in the place it came from. I laughed. Mum was grimly pleased that I was laughing at her joke. Actually I wasn't. I was laughing at myself but I would never be able to explain that to Mum, so I didn't try.

Sometimes, like Dad, I offered to wash up and make tea after the evening meal, but Mum wouldn't hear of it.

"No, that's all right Bob, I appreciate your asking."

I knew then she was praising my good manners. I thanked her and went in to our tiny neat lounge and switched on the huge colour television. By and by Mum would come in and with a few quick nervous glances around the room, she would seat herself in front of the screen and bring out her knitting.

She knitted sweaters and jumpers and pull-overs for me and because I had so many and because I was loyal to her I wore one of them every day of the year whatever the weather. I knew this pleased her and I wanted to please her. It made me sad to see her face grow older and smaller. I was thirty and looked twenty. I didn't have a care in the world.

In the years Mum and I lived together I learnt her likes and dislikes through watching television. If girls in strange dresses came on the screen and did high kicks with long legs so that just a small piece of glittering sequined material was visible between their legs, Mum yawned and said: "Isn't there anything else on Bob?"

Immediately I got up and found new channels. Sometimes a drama. Unfortunately these dramas did not often please her because so often the protagonists would kiss and suggest going to bed with each other. This made us both very uncomfortable. I had the odd feeling that Mum was looking at me out of the corner of her eye. She probably wasn't but I felt she might be. I rubbed my hands over my smooth pink face and peered at her, unseen, through my tent of fingers. Her face changed visibly. Lines were more clearly defined. She crashed through gears until she flew in fourth:

"That's it, that's it. That's all they think about. Sex! I don't know what the world's coming to. They've got one thing on their mind. Filth! They've hardly got their nappies off and..."

I won't go on from here to repeat everything she said because she so often repeated herself and like a great public orator she could talk non-stop, drawing energy from her first sentence to build her second and from her second to dart to her third and from her third to her fourth... I felt innocent and safe because I was sitting in the armchair with my slippers on and certainly I wasn't kissing anyone or making wanton suggestions. I got up and found another channel while Mum's words raced on and on with an undeniable vigour. It wasn't her night. A pretty blond girl with pouting lips was advertising a clean white bra while a choir sang songs of the ecstasy of angels. I was almost touched in some strange way but a glance at Mum and I was myself again. Her little face was pulled as tight as a single knot. Could I unpick it with a kiss on her paper cheek? I knew I couldn't. Sometimes my heart raced and thumped and I saw hands beyond my own, hands that picked and pulled at her until her face was back in shape and she was giggling like a tickled girl. She was sensitive. Often she noticed my invisible hands.

"Are you all right Bob?"

I nodded.

"Just a bit tired. On my feet all day. Seems like people think it's Christmas already."

I'd worked on the meat counter at Sainsbury's for the last eight years. I enjoyed the work, the smell of salami, the efficient hiss of the bacon slicer, the feeling that I was at the centre of our small commercial plaza.

"Well, you get an early night. I'll put a bottle in your bed. I'll make a cup of tea."

Often she'd insist on making a cup of tea just as her favourite programme, *Coronation Street*, was about to start. I'd plead with her not to, but to no avail.

"I'm sick of all these scroungers," she said, "never done a day's work in their lives."

I wasn't quite sure who she meant but it was enough to know it wasn't me and that I did a day's work six days a week.

Over the years I learnt that Mum's favourite programme was really the news and not *Coronation Street*. At nine or ten or whenever it came on, she sat bolt upright and I waited for her character to bloom. It always did. I was never once disappointed. Sometimes I was a little afraid. Mum was so convincing I thought the world might end there and then in the little lounge. Sometimes I even thought the news was in some way I couldn't explain, tailor-made for her. Often there was a strike: miners, steel workers, factory workers ...

"They don't want to bloody work!"

"Mum," I said, referring as she knew to her expletive, bloody. She excused herself quickly.

"It makes you sick. No wonder the country's in the state it is. What would happen if we all went on strike?"

My mind stopped as I suddenly contemplated this incredible concept. I saw invisible hands in front of me grasping for an answer. I saw headlines in newspapers and on T.V. "The World is on strike. There is nothing to say tonight." But that couldn't be right because the papers and T.V. would be on strike. In fact would we know if there was a strike or not? Perhaps people would even stop speaking to each other. Silence and inertia would reign supreme. Mum's knitting needles clicked and brought me back to our world. Then she was on her feet with a sudden cry:

"Bring back the birch!"

I glanced at her, then back to the screen. It showed the shaven head of an old woman who'd been attacked and beaten by two teenagers. The woman's head was stitched and sewn up like a football. It was a truly ugly sight. Mum said the world was coming to an end.

"Birched! These things never used to happen. Animals. They're animals. Look at that! And, my God, would you believe it, they got two pounds and thirty pence from her pension. I'm glad I'm not young any more. If they knew they'd get birched ..."

Mum went on and on even after Val Doonican was crooning a sweet song into the room. He smiled like a flower from the roots of his polo-neck sweater.

"We can't just let the Russians walk up to our doorsteps ..."

Perhaps I'd fallen asleep. The news was on again. Smartly dressed men were escorting long pointed missiles on a walk somewhere.

"Communists! Red blighters. They'll never get me. Look at the world!"

I did and I was amazed. When Mum said 'communists' I thought of Kermit the Frog, Mickey the Mouse and Donald the Duck and if we didn't watch it in some way we'd be Broody the Bear, Ivan the Eagle or a bulldog or lion or something. I realized we all had to be careful.

November became December and I couldn't help but notice that all the tragedies in the world happen in this Christmas month. Planes crash, ships sink, little innocent children develop strange incurable diseases, floods roar and sweep away distant villages, volcanoes dormant all the year choose this time to shrug their shoulders and rage with fire ...

'Her head had been removed and was found with her hands fifty yards away in a septic tank. It is believed her attacker ...'

"Bring back the birch! These animals don't like it when they get a taste of their own medicine. If they knew what they were going to get, they'd think twice. These Arabs have got the right idea, cut their hands off..."

Mum was off again, racing round and round a track of words. Sometimes I tried to keep up with what she was saying but she was too fast for me. In my armchair I suddenly felt sick and giddy as though without moving I was being propelled at an incredible rate. I never could stand fairground cars and fast sorts of things, things that go round and round, faster and faster, until all is lost in speed and vortex and you somehow don't exist or you're completely different, maybe even a communist.

She shook her little knotted head at an earthquake and spoke sadly:

"Well Bob, there's so many people over there. It's Mother Nature's way of keeping the population down... oh my God, would you believe that, robbed and beaten in his wheelchair..."

I looked across at Mum and suddenly I saw her tied up in an armchair about to be tortured by two youths. I come through the door with my arms innocently full of groceries. I've just put in another hard day's work at the shop. Wham! The ugly youth knocks me to the floor. He stoops to pick me and I stove in the part of his head above the eyebrow with a family-size tin of baked beans. The other youth, also ugly, tries to jump on my face, but quick as a flash I roll over, up-end him with a hard salami and before he can get up I give him the same treatment his friend got, though this time I use a tin of tomatoes. I turn to Mum and release her from her bondage. Gently I massage the circulation back into her old wrists. She smiles at me with all the love in the world.

"I'll make us a nice cup of tea now. I expect we can both do with one."

Pretty soon people hear about what's happened and congratulations and cheques are flooding through the door. Then the Queen hears about it and I get a medal for bravery and appear on television with my arm around Mum.

I always eat three thin slates of toast piled high with home-made marmalade in the morning, then I'm off to my shop in the plaza. It's only a short walk, down the lane, through a little wood, across a thin field and into the shopping centre, where now a tall Christmas tree towers and makes the world look exciting with coloured lights. I pause in front of 'Amp and Watts', the newest shop in the plaza and a great palace of electrical gadgets. My eyes are drawn immediately to a device described as The Automatic Tea Maker. Suddenly I know that this is what I'll get Mum for Christmas. We can have it in the lounge and she won't have to get up and make tea just as her favourite programme's about to begin. That'll fool her. I can't help but grin.

At lunchtime I enter the gleaming shop and a big man in a suit with a small confident moustache approaches me. He looks tired and cruel.

"The tea-maker," I say.

"You're lucky," he says, "there's just one left."

He walks away and I follow after him. We reach the tea-maker at the back of the shop and it's sitting prettily on top of its box. I touch its smoothness and symmetry. It's beautiful. A doubt enters my mind.

"Is it hard to use?"

"Hard to use! Plug it in, tea in there, water in there, milk in there, that's it. If it was hard to use I wouldn't have sold out."

I feel a bit ashamed and not sure what to say next.

"We can gift-wrap it, deliver it to your door, you're local aren't you, well no problem, it's part of the service. If you want to think about it I can't guarantee it'll be here much longer the way things are going this Christmas."

"Would you put a huge pink bow on it?"

"I'll put three if you like."

I see from the plastic badge in his lapel that his name is Reggie. I suddenly like him and grin.

"Three pink bows then."

I went back to work with a generous sense of achievement.

In the evening the parcel was waiting at home complete with three pink bows as fine as little pigs' tails. I beamed. Mum was grim.

"Were you expecting this? It's not a bomb is it? I noticed it rattled."

I picked it up and carried it with a mysterious grin into my room.

In the evening after our meal and the washing up was done I dozed in front of the television with Mum. I must have fallen asleep because suddenly I was awake with a start.

"Cowards! They pick on the old ones. Those that can't defend themselves ..."

She paused for a moment silently changing gear but in that silence I distinctly heard the nostalgic swish of the birch as it rippled the backs of the guilty.

"... You can't walk the streets in daylight let alone at night, Aida down the lane said she saw two youths ..."

My eyes were closed again. I saw myself walking down the lane dressed from head to toe in a completely knife-club-bullet-proof suit. For a moment I was safe and happy. Then I thought of armour-piercing shells and shoulder bazookas. Not even a tank could save you from those inventions.

"Where's it going to end?"

I sighed deeply. I so much wanted to give her an answer to that terrible question.

The bungalow looked superb. As usual Mum had given it the Christmas touch. There was holly with blood-red berries behind the mirrors and clocks. We didn't have an actual tree because they were messy but Aida, Mum's friend, had brought her some evergreen ferns and these were placed all around the lounge, even on top of the television. Little snakes of tinsel glinted unexpectedly from odd places. Our little world had been transformed. I kissed Mum twice on Christmas morning and thanked her for all her efforts throughout the year.

On Christmas afternoon after a magnificent dinner and the Queen's speech, Mum and I exchanged presents. I opened mine first: a new black sweater she'd somehow secretly made, some Irish linen handkerchiefs, two pairs of socks and a tin of shortbread from Scotland. I thanked her profusely and pushed my big parcel with the pink bows towards her. She stared at it and there wasn't a knot in her face.

"You shouldn't have done Bob. You know I don't expect anything. You're not making that much money and things are so expensive ..."

I gestured regally at the parcel.

"It seems a shame to tear the paper."

"Rip it off Mum," I said dramatically.

Slowly she unpicked the sellotape and removed the Christmas husk all in one piece. I smiled. Mum had her own way of doing things. The brown cardboard box frightened her. Her grey eyes narrowed. She went back inside herself.

"Oooh Bob."

Poor Mum. I realized she didn't know what it was. I opened the top of the box and she peered anxiously in.

"Oooh Bob."

"It's The Automatic Tea Maker," I said. "It's dead easy to work."

Perhaps it was the Christmas glass of sweet sherry that Mum had drunk that made her giggle suddenly. She picked up the tea-maker decisively.

"I'm going to try it out in the kitchen. No Bob, you sit down. I'll bring our first automatic cuppa."

My face ached with pleasure and I was just unwrapping my ninth toffee when I suddenly realized that Mum had been out of the room for something like twenty minutes. She wouldn't have gone down the lane to see her friend Aida, not on Christmas Day without telling me. A tom-tom started tapping inside me. I shot up out of my chair and rushed into the kitchen. What I saw there broke my heart and tied me up in a great bulging knot. Mum looked hurt. I saw that at once. She was holding the length of lead in her veiny hands.

"It, it doesn't seem to have a plug. It, it's very dusty. I'll have to give it a stripped wash."

I shook my head and spoke as calmly as I could.

"No, don't touch it Mum. I'll put it back in the box and change it."

Mum gave me a grim, piercing look.

"I'll put the kettle on," she said quietly.

I put the tea-maker back in its box and the box back in my room. I went back to the lounge and sat in front of the television. My mind was racing. The hurt inside me was so deep not even my invisible hands could reach it. Reggie, the salesman, had given me the tea-maker from the window. That I was sure of. He'd probably already sold the one I'd looked at. I wouldn't be able to change it! It occurred to me that the man's treachery had ruined my Christmas. Still I'd have to keep up appearances for Mum's sake. I smiled when she brought the tea things in and sat down. She gave me another piercing look.

"Don't be upset about the old tea-maker. We can change it."

"He gave me the dirty one from the window," I said. I just couldn't keep that fact bottled up.

"What! You didn't get it from that 'Watt and Amp' place did you?"

My head sunk onto my chest. I wanted to burst into tears.

"They're all crooks there. I could have told you that. Aida bought a radio there. She couldn't get half the stations. Blow me, then it stopped working altogether. They didn't want to change it. It's getting so you can't trust anyone ..."

Mum went on and on and slowly I regained some of my composure. I smiled and ate more toffees but the hurt was still inside me.

On Boxing Day Aida hobbled up the lane and rang on our bell. She'd brought Mum a bunch of flowers and me a little box of chocolates.

"Sit down Aida. You shouldn't have done."

"Nicest people in the lane. Wish I had a big son like you."

"I don't know what I'd do without him Aida. When you look at the world these days ..."

Aida nodded her frizzy old head. She always agreed with

everything Mum said.

The television was on. Frogmen were searching a gravel pit for a missing child. I bit my lip. I couldn't take any more.

"Going to walk off my dinner, Mum."

"Yes dear. Get some exercise. I'll be all right with Aida."

I found I had walked down to the shopping plaza. Even from a distance I could see there was no tea-maker in the window. The window was full of big red SALE signs. I stopped suddenly and stepped into the newsagent's doorway. A man in a camel hair coat with a poodle on a lead had come out of the shop and was locking it up. I didn't dare move. My heart was thumping madly inside my anorak. The man passed quite close to me. I stared at his reflection in the shop window. He hadn't seen me but I'd seen him. It was Reggie.

I followed him out of the plaza. I hung back as he crossed the thin field. When he had disappeared into the wood I ran across the field and hid behind a tree. After I'd got my breath back I peered round the tree. Reggie was standing ten yards away from me. He had his back to me and was staring down at his squatting poodle. I had a long log in my hand. I ran at Reggie and brought it down on the back of his head. He fell forward into the mud. The poodle squealed. I picked it up, took it off the leash and threw the dog away. In a moment I had Reggie's leg tied up but he wasn't moving around much anyway. I looked around the little wood. There was no-one about. I knew the little wood very well.

Mum was still talking to Aida when I got home. I smiled at them both.

"I think that walk brought some colour to your cheeks. I expect you'd like a cuppa now."

Indeed I would. I caused something of a sensation when I opened the box of chocolates Aida had brought me.

"I brought them for you and you're giving them away."

"Bob's always been like that," Mum piped in.

I beamed with pleasure and mashed up a strawberry-filled chocolate in my mouth. Then I blinked my eyes a few times because for a moment I saw Reggie writhing in the mud and a figure standing over him.

I saw Reggie again the following evening. I was still on holiday. Mum and I were watching television. The news came on and I saw her little body tense.

"... A bizarre and macabre attack just outside Eastbourne ..."

"Ooooh Eastbourne," Mum gasped, "Well I never, not safe on your own doorstep ..."

I wanted her to shut up. I was missing details of the report.

"He is said to be in critical condition ..."

"Bring back the birch!"

As soon as those words entered the room they were picked up by the reporter:

"... Mr Reggie Jones, a popular salesman with 'Amp and Watts' was struck on the head, tied up and flogged with a birch sapling ..."

Mum was staring across the room at me. Her mouth was moving but she wasn't saying anything. I shrugged. I sounded like Mum when I said:

"Well, that 'Watts and Amps' place. He probably had it coming to him."

She nodded and stood up. She looked small and old. I wanted to throw my arms around her and protect her for ever. She was silent.

"I didn't kill him Mum."

She found her voice:

"Thank God, for a moment, I thought you ..."

I shook my head.

"I didn't kill him. I just gave him what he deserved: a damn good birching. He knew what he was doing when he sold me that tea-maker. They can't get away with it for ever. He'll think twice in future. Any other country he'd have his hands cut off ..."

I couldn't stop myself now. I went on and on until Mum said she'd make us both a nice cuppa.

"Thanks Mum, I could do with one."

There were some girls with long legs doing high kicks on the television. Their faces were beaming and they seemed very blatant. I suddenly realized I liked looking at them but not when Mum was in the room. And where was Mum? She was a long time with the tea. I shouted out for her but there was no reply. Could she have gone down the lane to see Aida? Not without telling me I thought. I got up and wandered into the kitchen. Four big men grabbed hold of me. I struggled in the paralysis of a nightmare ...

"... anything you do say may be used in evidence against you ..."

"I want my Mum," I shrieked, "I want my Mum."

They dragged me screaming down the garden path. They dragged me past Mum, standing still as a statue in the garden. A lady policeman had her arm around her. Mum's lips moved. Her eyes were twinkling. She didn't look old and small. There was no knot in her face. In fact she looked happy as she whispered:

"Give him the birch. That'll teach him."

LETTERS

Fellatio and Old Age

I have been reading lots of stories in a variety of magazines of late and at this moment I can't remember bringing to mind a single one. All these writers seem to be involved in a Creative Writers Competition. Few authentic voices, in other words. Come to think of it, I do remember Richard Zimler's story (*Tale of Two Cities First Prize. Ed.*) which to me lacked resonance. Is cock-sucking really the issue right now? I belong to a different time, though I am still in pretty good trim at fifty-five. Do spare a thought for the older writer. We have a much larger view and wider perspective than these youngsters (who should be spending more time with their electronic toys). Older writers are likely to know who they are and thus will eschew fancy writing as they don't want their words to be lost in a sea of poetic phrase making.

Brian Darwent
Frodsham
Cheshire

There were three references to fellatio in Panurge 20 and one, I see, in this issue. Interestingly the latter is in a story by E.H.Solomon who is 78 years old and makes his fiction debut here. Lorna Tracy, Cecil Bonstein, E.H. Solomon and the translator James Brockway are all older than Mr Darwent and all of them are responsible for the more challenging styles (fancy writing) in recent Panurges. I just don't think innovative style correlates with age nor that fellatio as an incidental topic is restricted to the under forties. Brian Darwent's is the only negative response so far to R.C. Zimler's story. It has been widely praised by readers.
Ed.

Fancy Styles

I enjoyed Panurge 20 more than any other previous issue and especially welcome the variety of themes. Rizkalla's was an excellent supernatural story; Zadoorian's a fine exercise in irony. The only one I didn't like was Lorna Tracy's, though the fault is probably mine. I'm not prepared to apply myself to excessively obscure or clever stories. Although I may have another go at it.

Cecil Bonstein
London SW20

Honor Patching

Sorry, November

Only Lilith noticed the shaft of thin, greyish sunlight which shone in through the attic window. The inverted glass was transformed by it into a vessel of moving light. Her husband and sons became angels with haloes of flame. Then the light faded. Once again she was sitting with three ordinary red-headed males, their hands touching hers as they shunted an ordinary kitchen tumbler to and fro across the table.

They had asked if the old woman downstairs was going to die and what she was dying of. They had enquired how soon. The glass had answered their questions, obediently, if rather hesitantly, spelling out YES, CANCER and TUESDAY.

At least it was more forthcoming than the doctor.

*

Three floors down, Laura stood by her grandmother's bed. The old woman lay with closed eyes, as though already dead. Her skin looked jaundiced and brittle. She had insisted all her life on washing her face with the same coarse soap she used for scrubbing floors, yet her skin had always been fine and soft. Now, against the bleached pillow-case, her face was finally the colour of the cheap yellow soap.

Laura shuddered. She averted her eyes from her grandmother's hand, which lay on top of the plump pink eiderdown. But even the hand had a macabre, oddly naked look, because the rings had been removed. Laura glanced across at the dressing-table, where the rings were all stacked on top of one another on the amber glass ring-holder. They reminded her of doughnut rings on the West Pier, piled on a spike and sparkling with encrusted sugar.

Laura's mother, Meg, stood gazing out of the window, parting the net curtains with an upraised hand. Her face was turned determinedly away from the room and even her back had a rigid and unresponsive look about it. Laura sighed and turned again to Grandmother's face. To her shock, she found herself looking into a pair of wide-open eyes.

*

The glass was travelling in a slow, shuddering loop, juddering and catching like a skater on a rough patch of ice. Rallying briefly, it zipped off in a lively zigzag but soon it began to drag.

Kevin, the youngest of the two boys, had the shortest arms, so when the glass went to the far corner of the table, he had to stand up.

He was tired of having to push back his chair, lean across, then sit down again, without letting his finger slip from the glass. His mother was always so reproachful if the contact, as she called it, was broken.

*

The eyes were fixed on Laura. Time seemed to have stopped. She would be here in this sick-room forever, in the ferocious dying light of Grandmother's gaze. She closed her own eyes, hoping it was a bad dream. When she opened them again, the eyes were still glaring into hers. She was trapped.

Suddenly, the naked hand shot out and gripped her by the wrist.

*

The seances had lost their fascination for Kevin since he had noticed that the glass inevitably made the same spelling mistakes as his mother. His father, Ned, knew too, he thought. If Kevin pulled the glass in the opposite direction to the way Lilith wanted, Ned would support her, subtly using his strength to make the glass go her way. Kevin also knew that his brother Neil tried to make it spell out rude words. Between the four of them, it was a wonder the glass didn't fly into little pieces.

*

The intense glare of Grandmother's eyes made Laura dizzy. She submitted hopefully to the feeling, holding out a welcome to the blotchy vision and the tingling rush that meant she was going to faint. She was three months pregnant and had passed out once or twice, but this time it didn't happen. The dizziness cleared and the eyes still imprisoned hers. The grip of the naked hand was unrelenting.

Laura looked across at her mother's back. No help from that quarter.

Grandmother's face grimaced and the mouth worked, little gobbets of sound emerging as though the economical old lady was trying to piece together a voice from scraps.

Laura guessed what she was going to ask.

"Are you married yet?"

Laura opened her mouth to say no, she wasn't going to marry, but panicked at the last second.

It was easy enough to say, to most people, that she intended to bring up the baby on her own. But to her Grandmother, the statement became very difficult, if not impossible, to make.

All she managed to produce was an indeterminate stutter.

"Are you married yet?" Grandmother asked again.

Laura had lost her voice altogether. Her head whirled, she could produce no sound and thought she might really faint.

The old woman was angry, both with herself and with her relatives. Did they think she was suddenly a fool, just because she was dying? She could see what the situation was; she just wanted to get things straight. But her stupid old mouth kept on framing the same question, over and over.

For no apparent reason and for the first time in years, the thought of Mitzi came into her head.

*

The glass, which had dragged to a standstill near the middle of the table, gave a sudden twitch. It jerked and bucked and seemed full of unsuspected energy. Everyone, including Lilith, was taken by surprise. It took some time before the four of them could get control of it again.

*

"Are you married yet?"

Laura swayed. She was certainly going to faint. But before she had a chance to do so she heard a determined voice say, "Yes!"

"Yes," the voice repeated firmly, "yes, she's married."

In her confusion, she almost thought she had spoken herself, but it was her mother, who had come up behind her. Still recovering her senses, Laura was disengaged from Grandmother's grip.

"Come on," her mother said grimly, "we'd better go up and say hello to Aunt Lilith and Uncle Ned."

By the time they had climbed the stairs to the attic, Laura was shaky and breathless. Her mother propelled her into the room and she subsided into the rocking chair by the window and closed her eyes. The face of the dying woman downstairs imprinted itself against the red of her closed lids. The rocking chair, familiar since she was a child, felt as though it was about to tip her out. She heard her mother greeting the others but she didn't feel like joining in. She just wanted to be away, out of this tall narrow house with its dark corners and its faces and its endless stairs.

Nobody spoke to her. They might at least offer her a cup of tea, she thought. Nobody did.

*

The grandmother lay with her eyes closed. She did not believe her daughter. She knew Laura wasn't married. But it suddenly didn't matter any more, because an ancient memory was occupying all her attention.

Mitzi. An odd name for a baby, perhaps; more like a name for a pet monkey. But that was what the scrawny, red little thing had reminded her of. The name had come into her head and somehow stuck, although she had never spoken her child's name out loud. Except afterwards, sometimes, to herself.

*

Laura dozed for a while in the rocking chair, then she opened her eyes. Her relatives were sitting at a table with their heads bowed and for a moment she thought they were praying, then she saw that they all had their hands on something which moved. Laura got up out of the rocking chair and tiptoed over to stand behind them. A board, decorated with stars and moons and arcane symbols, was opened out on the table. Around the edge were the letters of the alphabet and the glass moved from one to the other in jagged, bad-tempered looking jerks. Her mother stood by the table watching.

Ned said: "Let's ask it when she's going to Pass Away."

Neil raised his eyes to the ceiling. "We've already asked it that."

"Well, let's ask it again," Ned said, in a tone of bright determination, "to show Laura and Auntie Meg."

He held his face an inch or two above the glass and glared down into it, then suddenly boomed out: "Grant us, Oh Spirit, this question. When will she die?"

The glass skipped about rapidly. Lilith had an impish expression on her face. Kevin and Neil looked resigned and followed the glass in an apathetic fashion.

IVE ALREADY TOLD YOU THAT, the glass spelled out.

Lilith smiled indulgently, like a mother proud of her infant's cheeky ways.

"Not when Meg and Laura have been here to see," Ned said, giving his wife an exasperated glance.

The glass was still for a second or two, then it added rather sulkily: TUESDAY.

"It seems a bit full of itself, if you ask me," Laura's mother said.

"What can we ask it now?" said Ned, ignoring his sister-in-law.

"Let's ask it if she'll go to heaven," suggested Lilith.

Once more, Ned went through the glaring and booming procedure. The glass took off smartly. This time Neil and Kevin looked more enthusiastic. Lilith seemed taken by surprise at the sudden burst of speed. The glass unhesitatingly started with the letter B, followed by U and then M and came to a halt.

Meg made an angry snorting sound. Neil and Kevin shook with suppressed laughter.

"Bum?" Laura said, bewildered.

"It hasn't finished yet," Lilith said hastily. "it must be still in the middle of a word."

The glass seemed to undergo some sort of crisis, jigging and starting this way and that. Lilith had a frown of concentration. A nerve ticked visibly in Ned's cheek. Finally, the glass lurched away to the letter P, followed by T,I,O,U,S. There was another pause, during which Lilith seemed to be deep in thought, then it spelt out: REJOICING.

"Bumptious rejoicing!" said Ned, looking relieved. He wiped his forehead with a handkerchief.

"What's that supposed to mean?" asked Meg.

"It means she's going to heaven of course," Lilith said. She smiled brightly. "Now let's ask it about something else. Let's ask when Laura's baby will be born."

The question was put and the glass went immediately to O, and then C, and spelled out OCTOBER.

Lilith looked at Laura and her mother, whose faces registered shock. The baby wasn't due until January.

"No good?"

They shook their heads.

"We'll try again."

Lilith put the question once more, adding sternly, "And get it right this time!"

The glass started with the letter S, and Laura thought for a wild moment that this time it was going to predict a birth in September, but the next letter was O.

When it came to a standstill, Lilith summed up the reconstructed message.

SORRY MEANT NOVEMBER.

She sat back with a satisfied look. "Is that better?"

*

The old woman was still thinking about Mitzi. Had she lived? Had her new parents loved her? Had she grown up and found someone reliable, like her own Percy? She would never know. It seemed hard that she was about to die without knowing.

*

Laura's mother began to have hysterics.

Ned crossed the room and helped her, rather forcibly, into a chair. Neil picked up a cushion and ineffectually fanned his aunt with it. Kevin got up to put the kettle on.

Only Lilith was oblivious to her sister's screams. Although the others had left the table, the glass was moving. Lilith trembled as her hand followed it across the board. A surge of power shot up her arm like an electric shock. She followed blindly as the glass dictated her movements, steadily from letter to letter. She tried to call to the others, but her voice was an inaudible squeak, like when you try to cry out in a dream.

*

The old woman was young again. She was sixteen and she held her first child in her arms. The tiny red face below hers screwed up and blinked and blew bubbles. She was so light, so fragile, so warm against her breast. A little scrap of nothing.

She had been lucky. If it wasn't for her family's discretion her life could have been ruined, like other girls she had heard spoken of, girls who took to the streets with their illegitimate babies and often died in poverty. Her parents had tactfully arranged the secluded pregnancy and birth in the home of a distant relative. Everything was covered up, kept secret. After the adoption, the business had never been mentioned again.

"Mitzi."

She had not uttered the name for seventy years.

*

Lilith couldn't have withdrawn her hand from the glass, even if she had wanted to. It was fused, flowing, her arm, her hand, the vessel of moving light were one.

This was the moment she had waited for all her life.

*

The child tensed and kicked in her arms and looked up into her face as though trying to tell her something. She felt the wiry strength in the little body. And she seemed to see, in the blue eyes, a succession of images: of the baby growing to a sturdy infant; a serious, but not unhappy little girl; a spirited, intelligent woman.

*

The glass moved on magnificently, with none of its previous jerks and starts and hesitations. It was smooth, it was an inspiration, a work of art that she, Lilith, was participating in. Everything was clear and whole. She thought she could hear the glass singing as it moved, a high, clear note of sweetness.

*

Gradually, the image of Mitzi faded. But she could still feel the delicate warm weight of the child in her arms. She closed her eyes and lay back against the pillows, treasuring the sensation.

*

The glass stopped. Her hand on its rim, Lilith turned to the others. She opened her mouth to tell them what had happened, what was still happening, because she could still feel the power running up her arm, still hear the echo of the ringing song.

"Listen to me," Lilith said, "the message has come through."

They took no notice, so Lilith raised her voice and shouted. She was shaking and incoherent with excitement. At last, her sister Meg noticed her. She looked across the room with red-rimmed, wild eyes and said something Lilith didn't catch. She was coming over to the table.

Laura's mother moved so suddenly and violently that everyone jumped. She smashed her hand down on the board and swept it from the table, sending the glass spinning to the other side of the room. The letters of the alphabet rose and scattered like a startled flock of starlings then clattered to the floor.

She grabbed her startled daughter by the hand and pulled her out of the room. Their footsteps could be heard pounding down the stairs, followed by the slam of the front door. Ned, Kevin and Neil stood staring after them.

The glass rolled, unbroken, to the base of the rocking chair, where it lay and quivered while the chair rocked wildly above it. Lilith sat for a moment, dumbfounded, then she was on her knees, making a small whimpering noise, scrabbling on the floor for the spilt letters. After a moment she gave that up and crawled over to where the glass lay. She picked it up gently, dusted it off with her hand, held it to her ear. Shook it slightly and held it to her ear again. The singing, the clear pure note, was gone, although she could still hear it somewhere inside her head, like music half-remembered from a dream.

She crawled over to the scattered alphabet letters and sat on the floor, shuffling them aimlessly with one hand, while she held the glass in the other.

Ned crossed the room to his wife. She seemed oblivious to his presence. Her lips were moving and he bent lower to hear. She was whispering: "Come back, please come back. Oh, please, please come back."

Kevin was the first to recover his senses. He hurtled out of the room and down the stairs. He wanted to tell his cousin the ouija board was a fix. But there was no sign of Meg and Laura. He went a short way down the street, then realised Grandmother had been left on her own and returned to the house.

*

They had pushed a cup of tea into her hand but Lilith held it in front of her without drinking. She was trying to remember. The harder she thought about it, the faster it seemed to disappear. She thought it began with an M. And there was a Z in it, somewhere. It was slipping away from her. She knew it would never come back.

*

Kevin poked his head apprehensively round the door of the sick-room. The old woman was leaning crookedly against the pillows, her head lolled to one side. He noticed her arms were in an odd position, as though she held something cradled in them. He tiptoed over to the bed. Grandmother was obviously dead but, looking at her, his fear left him. The yellowness had gone and her skin had a look of worn, smoothed transparency. She looked somehow light and pure and dry, like the skeleton of a leaf. He went out of the room, closing the door softly as though the draught might blow her away.

*

Laura's baby was born at the end of November.

"Funny," she said to her mother. "It was November, after all."

"Coincidence," her mother snapped, "pure coincidence."

Then she asked, "Have you thought of a name?"

Laura looked at the baby, who had a face like a little red monkey.

"Mitzi," she said suddenly. "I think I'll call her Mitzi."

She looked up at her mother and smiled.

Adèle Geras

Rex's Pictures

Nearing retirement, Leonard used to say: "I can't possibly live in England. The policemen here don't salute me." He was only partly joking.

*

In his youth, when the world (so he would have his daughter believe) was painted with altogether brighter colours, Leonard used to swim with his brother Rex in the Suez Canal. It was an unappetizing, if historically significant stretch of water, muddy yellow under a yellow sky. A far cry from any swimming pool, he would imply. You could hear it in his voice, although he never actually said it. There he was then, poised in the water at the exact point where West becomes East. Special and wondrous.

Leonard's mother came from Morocco. In the Suez Canal days, she used to dance till early morning with Admirals of the Fleet and Captains crusty with gold braid. Oh yes, till the dawn broke over the oil-flat water, there she would be, drinking champagne and quivering in a beaded gown, black curls low on her brow. Her husband was a good man, fond of Gilbert and Sullivan. He died young.

All his life, Leonard took care to emphasize his Englishness.

*

Marion, his younger sister, married a Welshman who looked quite different, who *was* quite different away from the mysterious glamourising effect of the Egyptian sun. After their divorce, Leonard's mother went to live in the small house near Cardiff and looked after her grandchildren while her daughter went out to work. She stayed in that house (two up, two down, enclosed by walls of privet) for the rest of her life, misunderstood by her neighbours, wearing a flowered overall, defying the strict Welsh air with the fragrance of Oriental cooking coming from her kitchen. Stories of ships lit up at night, satin slippers tapping on the deck, drifted up with the steam from the pots that simmered on the stove, glazed the walls with a brownish film, hardened finally into memories.

*

Leonard studied Law at Oxford. In 1939, he married Hannah,the daughter of a family that had lived in Jerusalem since the nineteenth century. In 1944, Hannah gave birth to a daughter, Jennifer. After the War, in Rhodes, Leonard was in charge of German prisoners of war. A man who claimed that he had been Hitler's cook made a cake for Jennifer's second birthday and wanted to teach her the words of 'Lili Marlene' in German.

After Rhodes, Leonard worked in Palestine for the British. During the hostilities of 1948, he and Hannah and Jennifer were in Jerusalem. Besieged. Going without food.

Jennifer remembers the aniseed drops that changed colour as you sucked them, and lorries like square animals lighting up the bomb shelters with their eyes.

Hannah remembers one tin of sardines divided between eight people.

Rex was there too. One night, he made an amusing remark. The whole family embroidered this anecdote until at last it acquired the status of a Story:

The scene: a shelter in the basement of a house in Jerusalem. Moaning and groaning of a thoroughly un-British kind is coming from Leonard's aunt, his mother's sister, Simmy, once a beauty but now only spectacularly wealthy. She is bewailing her diamonds. There is fighting near Barclay's Bank. Her diamonds are there, in the bank, and what, oh God, would become of them if they should fall into the wrong hands? No one else knew, no one else could comprehend the agony, the responsibility, the worry. Ai-ai-ee, my diamonds.

"Auntie," Rex says quietly, "why don't you simply transfer all your diamonds to me? Put them all, every one of them, in my name. Then I'll worry about them."

A baleful look from still-splendid eyes. A Moroccan curse on the heads of all those who wish to rob her of her wealth. Ai-ai-ee!

Rex was not one of these. Rex was not interested in money. Neither was Magda, his wife. They lived for Art. Rex was a painter. He went to live in Paris.

*

After 1948, Leonard joined the Colonial Service. Hannah became a British subject, or, as she used to say, a British object. When Leonard was posted to Nigeria, she said: "How can we possibly go? There are two pages of diseases you can catch. I looked it up... what about Jennifer?"

Jennifer was happy in Nigeria. In Ibadan, she had a friend called Alero, who had many brothers and sisters. When Jennifer stayed in Alero's house overnight, Alero's poor mother had to braid Jennifer's hair into scores of tiny plaits all over her head, because that was how Alero's hair was done. One of Alero's big brothers used to make them play 'What is the time, Mr. Wolf?' The little girls were very frightened, but never asked to be left out of the game.

They moved later to a place called Onitcha. The house there was huge. Bats lived in the roof and came out at twilight. Leonard lay under the mosquito net and taught Jennifer the whole of 'Ode to a Nightingale.' Outside, a field of Ramadan lilies lay like blood on the earth. In the market, meat had to be sold with fur still on it so that you could see what animal it had come from. Someone (maybe it was even Leonard and Hannah?) had a record of 'I'll see you again.' Whenever she hears it now, Jennifer is reminded of that time. A Gothic time, because of the cavernous house and the bats in the dusk.

*

Going on leave, to Leonard, meant going to Paris. To see Rex. To act at being a Bohemian. To buy more paintings.

Leonard bought paintings from Rex for two reasons. Firstly, because he genuinely admired and loved them, and secondly, because Rex desperately needed the money.

Considering the kind of life Rex led, the paintings were not what you would have expected. Rain came in through the studio roof. Mice nibbled the sheets on the bed. Once, Rex said, a particularly gifted creature (or creatures... surely such an endeavour required some degree of cooperation?) had gnawed the outline of a map of France on the bedspread. The dishes were washed only when they were all dirty. That worked out at every third day or so. If you put something down for a moment, a pipe, say, or a box of matches, it was gone almost at once. Leonard called the studio 'Les Sables Mouvants.' Quicksands of chaos threatened to engulf everything. Therefore the paintings ought to have been huge, shrieking masses of thick, oiled disorder. Plastered on, swirling around, full of anguished movement - something of that kind. They were not. Stillness filled them, even when there was motion in the subject: small boats on the sea, with bright flags fluttering. No hard edges anywhere in pictures that were like mirages, like images behind a veil. Chess pieces, fish, oil lamps, birds, flowers were bathed in the light of tranquillity. Still life, in every sense. A belief in order. A belief in joy and peace. Art is a great transformer of Reality. The colours were pale but not weak. Blues and greens like sunshine under water, red like a hand held up to lamplight, the brightness of the blood visible under the skin, around the dark bones.

*

Leonard played Bridge, a respectable Colonial game. Rex played chess in cafés with men who wore berets and washed only from time to time. When Leonard was on leave, he sat for hours in the cafés, looking, listening, happy as a child is, allowed to sit up with the grown-ups. He wore casual clothes. He spoke French beautifully (a legacy of the cosmopolitan days in Port Said) and showed off in front of his wife and daughter. He took Jennifer round art galleries, telling her what was good and what was not, being dogmatic. He bought her postcards of all the greatest masterpieces which she stuck into an exercise book whose pages were thin and of poor quality, covered in pallid blue squares.

Paris he displayed to his daughter with pride and love, as though he himself had thought of it, had created it. "Look at that corner!" he would shout. "Isn't that exactly like an Utrillo?"

His loud, upper-class English made people stare. He never minded. In front of the horse-butcher's shop on the corner, he would point at the sides of meat and chuckle to himself:

"Oh, yes, Soutine would have loved that... yes, indeed." He was a positive embarrassment in the cafés, staring quite openly at this person or that, and exclaiming:

"Do you see, Jennifer, do you see? That woman there, she could be a Degas. Or a Toulouse-Lautrec."

Leonard loved everything about Paris. Things, people that would have provoked cries of indignation against the current government if he had seen them in London, were there transmuted into a living example of Art.

*

The habit of seeing Life as Art persisted. From Nigeria, Leonard was transferred to Jesselton in North Borneo.

"Gauguin would have loved this beach," he said often, and he would indicate the comely women in the market and nod wisely: "I can quite see why the man left Northern France behind him, can't you?"

Perhaps because of his youthful bathes in the symbolic waters of the Suez Canal, the East suited Leonard. A great quoter at all times, in Borneo Kipling came frequently to his lips:

" 'Ship me somewhere East of Suez,

Where the best is like the worst
Where there ain't no Ten Commandments
And a man can raise a thirst... ' "

he would intone, lying on the verandah of the house on a rattan chaise-longue after work, dressed only in a sarong.

He taught Jennifer 'The Road to Mandalay.' She liked the bit about the dawn coming up like thunder out of China, only here, the sun went down where China was, and not like thunder but like fire.

Leonard had been promoted. He had an office and a secretary called Sarah Tan. She was Chinese. Jennifer loved her, because Sarah was a film fanatic, and lent the child treasured copies of 'Photoplay.'

Jennifer went to the pictures all the time. Esther Williams in 'Pagan Love Song' was her favourite. It could have been filmed a hundred yards from her back door.

Leonard and Hannah went to Government House for dinner. Jennifer remembers her mother in a long, black, halter-necked dress scattered with huge white and magenta flowers. She smelled of 'Arpége.'

Leonard lay on the chaise-longue on the verandah and threw the contents of a packet of zinnia seeds into the ground below. They grew and flourished like weeds, and filled all the vases, week after week.

*

Rex's paintings hung on every wall. Leonard never locked the doors or windows at night. "The only thing worth pinching in this house," he said, "are the pictures, and anyone who appreciates them enough to steal them deserves to have them." They were not stolen.

They hung on the pale blue walls and looked down on the furniture provided by the Public Works Department. The chairs were made of bamboo and bulged with buff cushions edged with brown piping. There was a desk in the corner of the living room, covered by a sheet of glass. Under the glass was a map of Oxford, drawn and coloured in such a way as to make the buildings appear almost three-dimensional. Small figures walked up and down the streets, black gowns flying behind them, and around the sides of the map were the coats of arms of all the colleges.

Oxford was not a favourite haunt of Leonard's. It was more like the setting of a dream he had once had, distant but beautiful, remembered and embellished.

"Et in Arcadia ego... " he would murmur, pointing his college out to Jennifer, a little sadly.

But Rex's paintings filled Leonard with happiness every time he looked at them. They were like living things to him, like children. They were however, misunderstood children. Frowns of puzzlement ridged the brows of guests to the house. The paintings were too abstract, too modern, strange to them.

"But what is it supposed to be?" they would ask.

Leonard, patient as parents are patient when interpreting their children to the world, would say: "That's a table lamp, don't you see? And there next to it, a fish." He would trace the outline for them with his finger.

(A fish next to a lamp? Very odd. You could almost hear them thinking it, but they nodded politely and said:

"Gosh, how frightfully clever of your brother," or words to that effect.)

Leonard never gave up. The few who expressed admiration became friends, soulmates. As for the rest - Philistines.

*

Jennifer was sent to boarding-school. On the whole, she was happy there. Leonard wrote her letters in his elegant handwriting and sent her poems which he admired. Every letter he ever wrote to his daughter ended in the same way: 'Darling child, please don't forget to brush your teeth night and morning.' Every single letter. He loved her.

With Jennifer gone, Leonard took to talking to the cat. Hannah would find him in the pantry, talking and talking. He missed Jennifer, but she had to go to school. It was part of the image he had of himself, and of her. If she had been a boy, she would have gone to Eton. The best he could do was a red-brick establishment on the South Coast.

"It'll put roses in her cheeks," he told his wife, desolate at the absence of her child.

*

From Borneo, Leonard was transferred to the Gambia. He was now a Queen's Counsel. An important man. Assistant Attorney-General.

When Jennifer, growing up now, came out for the summer holidays, and went to dances at the Club, Leonard always drove her there, waited in the Reading Room till the revels had ended (lovely back numbers of *Punch* and the *Illustrated London News*) and then drove her home. He didn't mind her dancing, flirting, tossing her hair at all the young men, but, as he put it:

"I'm damned if I'm going to let her come home with them when they're all as drunk as Bandusian goats."

Gambia was next door to Dakar. There were French people in the Colony. Rex's paintings were beginning to come into their own. They were appreciated by a fair number of visitors.

Jennifer went back to school with a biscuit tin full of peanuts. She ate them after lights-out while the wind blew off the black sea. She thought of Jean, from Alsace, who drove a battered Deux Chevaux and had kissed her once. It was her first kiss.

*

Rex was more prosperous now. His pictures were selling. The glass roof of the studio no longer leaked. An inside lavatory had been installed. There was no more talk of mice. But the Sables Mouvants, the glorious Bohemian chaos, that hadn't changed. And Paris was always the same.

One summer holiday, when Jennifer was seventeen, she met a school friend on the Boul. Mich. This friend was staying alone in a hotel. Jennifer begged to be allowed to stay with her, to be a little independent. Grown-up. Leonard and Hannah agreed, but they went to inspect the room the two girls were going to share. It was a tiny *chambre de bonne* under the roof: dirty, and to girls used to the cleanliness of an English boarding-school, absolutely the last word in Romance. Hannah was dismayed. Jennifer reported every day by telephone, and gave bulletins on her welfare.

*

Jennifer usually spent the Christmas and Easter holidays with Leonard's mother, her aunt Marion and Marion's two boys. Her aunt was very pretty, and laughed a lot, showing beautiful white teeth. From her grandmother flowed a stream of Moroccan oaths, dire warnings, groans of sorrow and stories of the old days. Thus Jennifer learned about the Admirals who had danced all night, and the Captains. The food that emerged from the pots was as tasty as the stories.

Leonard's mother hardly ever sat down, and only ate what she could snatch from the pots as they stood in the kitchen. This worried her daughter. It brought Marion nearly to tears to see her mother hovering around the table like a servant while the others ate, but the old woman would not be persuaded. She had her reasons, she said enigmatically.

*

Leonard was made a Judge and sent to Tanganyika. A good actor, he enjoyed the part, even cultivating a slight deafness to help him in his interpretation of the role. "Would the Counsel for the Defence mind repeating that?" he would say languidly, leaning forward over the Bench, frowning a little. "I didn't quite catch it." He loved being the star of the Legal Show.

He worked hard. 'Deathless Prose' he called his judgements, and nearly meant it. His prose was indeed lucid, grave and sonorous. He modelled his style on Gibbon.

For Jennifer, he was full of advice. "Never use a long word where a short one will do," he said. "Never use jargon. Read the best all the time." It was good advice. Jennifer was accepted at Oxford. Leonard's cup was full. He had been there. His daughter would be there. It was the only 'varsity in the world, wasn't it?

*

One day, during Jennifer's second year, she received a letter from her Bank Manager. This terrifying being, worse than a Headmistress, wished to see her personally. Jennifer, dressed in her best, trembled her way to Lloyd's bank, Carfax branch, and was ushered into the presence. She knew she was a little overdrawn, but this? The Bank Manager smiled at her.

"I have here," he said, " a letter from the Hon. Mr. Justice Southam. Your father," he added unnecessarily. "Shall I read it to you?"Jennifer nodded. The Bank Manager read the letter.

" ' Dear Sir,

My daughter Jennifer, an undergraduate at St.Hilda's College, has opened an account at your branch. Should her overdraft at any time exceed the sum of thirty pounds, I would be most grateful if you would call her into your office and give her a jolly good ticking-off.I am, etc."

The Bank Manager looked up and smiled. Jennifer blushed. She spent a few minutes describing her father to the Bank Manager. Together they reached the conclusion that the Hon. Mr. Justice Southam was a lovable eccentric. Judges often are, aren't they? It goes with the job.

*

Leonard's mother died. His sister married again and moved from her small house into a large modern bungalow.

When Tanganyika became Tanzania, Leonard was made redundant and given a Golden Handshake of quite a considerable sum of money. Hannah, exhausted by years of travel to the far-flung outposts of the British Empire, wanted to settle down, to buy a house of their own after having lived so long in Government properties. She had been having a recurring nightmare: being about to sail somewhere, or fly somewhere with all her suitcases still to be packed, lying around her. It was at this time that Leonard made his remark about the British policemen not saluting him. He was not ready to retire. Instead he accepted a contract to work for two years in Guyana.

Before he left, he and Rex and an American painter called Fred spent a week in Brittany. Rex and Fred painted. Leonard watched them. In the evenings, they sat in a cafe and talked about Art and Life like men with no wives or children or responsibilities: young men. Who, seeing the brown bespectacled face with the thick hair still untouched by any grey falling over the forehead, could have imagined it framed by the white spaniel's ears of a judge's wig?

A short time after this holiday, Rex died of a heart attack. Leonard never once spoke about what this meant to him, but physically he shrank, becoming thinner, older, as though something had been squeezed out of him. He never went to Paris again.

On his return from Guyana, Leonard was offered a job in Botswana. He bought a strong pair of binoculars, and began to look at birds. He missed the sea. Hannah did not accompany him. She went back to her family in Jerusalem.

In Botswana, the whole house was filled with Rex's pictures. It was a permanent exhibition. Every so often, like a good curator, Leonard took one down and sent it to Johannesburg to be put into a new frame. Sometimes he moved a painting from one position to another, so that it hung in a better light.

*

Jennifer was married to Jonathan, whom she had met at Oxford. When their first child, a girl, was born, Leonard wrote with advice about names. "Have you considered Tallulah?"

He sent the baby gifts chosen from mail order catalogues: a mug decorated with a zebra and a spotted pony, a soft furry bear. He sent postcards of Basil Brush, his favourite television character. There was little to be found in the middle of the Kalahari desert to lavish on a grandchild.

He came on leave and saw his granddaughter for the first time. He wouldn't cuddle or kiss her, but sat on the sofa staring at her for hours, chuckling occasionally, shy of the newness of the child, her softness, her vulnerability. When he left, he gave the baby his entire collection of carved wooden animals from every corner of Africa: lopsided giraffes, rhino, antelopes, birds, tortoises, lions and an elephant. All hand-carved. Real sculptures in wood.

"Not your ordinary tourist rubbish," he said proudly. "The real McCoy."

Jennifer laid the animals out on top of the chest-of-drawers in the baby's room. A tiny jungle in the corner of an English bedroom. She hung one of Rex's pictures on the wall where the child could see it as she grew: a fish on a blue background, a black and grey and yellow tracery of lines in space like the sky or the sea or both together. Floating fish, swimming fish.

*

Just before embarking for Africa, just as he was stepping on to the boat train at Waterloo, Leonard had a heart attack. He was taken to St. Thomas's Hospital. The hospital telephoned Jennifer. Jennifer made the long train journey to visit him.

The Hon.Mr. Justice Southam, Bohemian, eccentric, writer of deathless prose and lover of Art was one of a score of sick old men on the ward: not much different from any of the others. Cheerful still, but quieter. Jennifer longed for the return of the loud, haughty embarrassing voice. She brought him a photo of the baby. She assured her father that she was happy.

"That's all I want," the old man said. "The only thing I've ever wanted."

Leonard recovered. He left the ward and took on his former status, almost his former appearance. He went to convalesce in his sister's house. His voice on the telephone to Jennifer sounded exactly the same as it had always been.

He played Bridge with Marion and her second husband and Peggy, a friend of theirs. In a couple of weeks, he would sail for Africa. One Sunday afternoon, he left the house to post a letter to Jennifer. It started to rain. He was near Peggy's house, so he dropped in for a while to take shelter. Peggy was making scones.

"Just sit down and look at the paper for a moment," she said , "while I finish up in the kitchen. Then I'll make us a cup of tea."

Leonard sat in an armchair by the fire and picked up 'The Observer.' When Peggy came in with the tea, he was dead.

On Sunday night, Marion telephoned Jennifer with the news. First post on Monday, Leonard's letter arrived, full of gossip, plans, jokes, love to the baby.

"...and darling, please don't neglect your teeth."

Jennifer travelled to Cardiff for the funeral. She took back the few knick-knacks Leonard had bought while he was on leave: some plastic ashtrays and a little tree made of wires strung with silver bobbles which vibrated gently when you touched them.

The contents of the house in Botswana were packed up and sent to Jennifer at Hannah's request.

Some months later, the crates arrived. Rex's pictures, scores of them, formed the greater part of Leonard's belongings. Apart from the paintings, his worldly goods consisted of household linens and utensils, books, a good pair of binoculars and a set of Judge's robes.

But the pictures...Jennifer hung as many of them as she could in her small house. The rest she kept in a trunk hoping for better things for them, more wallspace, a chance to be seen. She loved them for themselves and for what they had meant to her father.

A great majority of the visitors to Jennifer's house hardly noticed them, or if they did then they made no comment. Probably some people liked them and others did not.

Tribute

It was very sad to hear that **David Holden** whose work appeared in Panurge over the years, died this April from cancer. A young American living in North London, he published a collection with Bloomsbury in 1991 called *This Is What Happens When You Don't Pay Attention.* He was latterly a broadcaster and campaigner on ecological issues. His wife Ann has set up a David Holden Turtle Fund and anyone interested can contact her c/o Dom McLoughlin, 38 Casella Road, New Cross, London SE14 5QL.

Barry Hunter

The Lobster Season

Geoffrey Ndola woke up smiling, a full bladder adding potency to his erection. With the UDP taking sixteen of the twenty-nine parliamentary seats in Monday's general election, he was in opposition again. To his left, a wooden bowl containing three limes and a tube of Johnson & Johnson lubricating jelly held his attention briefly before his dark eyes settled on a naive seascape with twig figures, an unframed canvas by local artist and marijuana evangelist Walter Tsambas, perched experimentally on the skirting board beside the air conditioner. On his right, her buttocks connecting coolly with his own like washed fruits in a plastic bag, Samantha J. Hopper was dreaming of her father's death for the umpteenth time since he passed away on the jetty at Caye Caulker, chewed to the bone on his right side by a hammerhead he had encouraged out on the reef in the days before the marine reserve at Hol Chan began charging three dollars a head. (In Sammy J's dream, Samuel Hopper II is never killed by a fish. Instead, he dies over and over again in his suite at the Hotel Palenque, close to the Mayan ruins, when a ceiling fan drops out of the sky like a monstrous insect, hovering now and then on its slow-motion descent towards a torso protected only by a Conrad reader in paperback.)

"Way to go, Sammy J," whispered Geoffrey Ndola. "Of course, we live as we dream - alone."

He swung his legs off the hammock, stepped into his pants, and pulled on his PUP vest. It was going to be a fine day for sure. The United Democratic Party may have won the election, but the returned opposition member for Belize Coastal South had a majority of 305 votes to celebrate. Geoffrey Ndola was a constituency man. While the People's United Party campaigned for tougher restrictions on American investment along the barrier reef coast, the Honourable Member kissed his Louisiana exile under the stars on the roof of the Sundowner Hotel where she worked and lived. Geoffrey Ndola believed in mutual understanding. He liked to wait and see. One day, he and Sammy J would sling the hammock of their dreams between the coconut palms at St George's Creek, where the fish snap at dragonflies and rare birds call out in the night. Until then, what was the harm in a few shell-pink condos on the Ambergris coast?

Geoffrey Ndola eased the noose of his PUP tie over his head and tightened it, relieving himself quietly into the sink. He picked up his briefcase and shoes and slipped out to the verandah overlooking the hotel beach. Above him, the Island Airways 'Early Bird' service to the municipal airport and Goldson International cleared the Sundowner's corrugated roof with a roar and banked immediately towards the mainland. Geoffrey Ndola watched it climb above the sun. From below, the drone of the engine was gradually replaced by the scratching in the sand of Charlie's seaweed rake as the hotel handyman cleared up after the squall. Two glass-bottomed boats in the shallows beside the Amigos del Mar sports jetty creaked at their moorings and beyond, near the Texaco pump and the watertaxi rank, a pelican broke the surface at the edge of Geoffrey Ndola's vision and reclaimed the air with a cry. The Honourable Member paused in the sand at the bottom of the wooden stairs to slip on his shoes, then stepped into the sunlight on Front Street. He walked unshaven down a dirt road towards the radio bunker with the stray dogs of San Pedro.

"What's new, Miller?" asked Geoffrey Ndola as he sat down in the studio and picked up the guest headphones.

"Gonna find out right now, councillor," said the Cuban DJ with exaggerated sing-song lilt. He pressed home the news jingle cassette and handed his visitor a sheaf of faxed pages. "Coming up in a few moments, the Honourable Geoffrey Ndola MP will be telling us how it feels to be re-elected to represent this wonderful constituency of ours. But first, at just before six thirty on Wednesday fifteenth July, the news headlines. . ."

Miller wiped his mouth with the back of his hand and read from the faxed bulletin. "With the start of the lobster season still two days away, police in Belize City have made a number of arrests in connection with illegal lobster harvesting along the coast. During a series of dawn raids in the city yesterday, three separate stockpiles of frozen lobster tails with a combined street value of four thousand dollars were seized and later sold at market, the proceeds destined for various charities in Belize City.

"Security is to be reviewed for the second time this year at the city's notorious Queen Street Prison following last night's break-out in which sixteen inmates escaped. New Interior Minister Remijio Montalzo has promised an independent enquiry into the incident and urged those still at large to give themselves up immediately. Six prisoners who absconded were recaptured within half an hour when they were discovered drinking beer at a popular cabaret venue just two blocks from the prison.

"At the Americas Trade Association summit in Guadalajara, final agreement on US import quotas is expected later today after a stormy two-day debate during which the Honduran delegation twice walked out in protest at proposed banana restrictions."

It was enough to be going on with. Cuban Miller spiked the final item about the Governor General inaugurating a new incinerator for the pathology department at Belmopan's central hospital. He nodded his satisfaction, hit the jingle tape again, and cued Geoffrey Ndola.

*

She shivered in the draught of the oscillating fan and pressed her hands together between her thighs. She stretched in the shuttered half-light and switched on the radio behind her head. Sammy J lifted the sheet from the tiles below. She pulled it across her body and up around her throat where a gold chain tightened momentarily and then relaxed against her skin. Is there a time between sleeping and waking when the earth stops turning and the night sky merges with land and lake, all stars denied? She walks arm in arm with her father towards a temple pyramid a structure dim, crepuscular, not yet revealed but defined by scaffolding and hedged with flame of the forest trees. Around his neck hang a loaded Leica and two light meters, and in her hand a Polaroid print draws its moist shellac across the view: this ruined wedding cake of a building and, behind it, the blood blister of the sun.

"Jesus," she said softly, turning up the volume and extending the telescopic aerial to maximum. Sammy J splashed her face with tepid water and wiped her armpits with a discarded Nike singlet. As she dressed in mannish checked shirt and loose-fitting cotton dungarees, Geoffrey Ndola was speaking slowly and clearly into the microphone on the boom arm beside him.

"In conclusion, ladies and gentlemen, let us recall that when Jesus chose Peter to be the head of the church, the first Pope, he said: Thou art Peter and upon this rock I will build my church. So Saint Peter is the rock and an appropriate name for our beloved township."

He paused and swallowed. Beside him, the lean Cuban broke off from ringing diagonal letter groupings in a dog-eared puzzle book and passed his visitor three ready-made reefers. "In a world where the dollar is god and nothing seems permanent," continued Geoffrey Ndola, "it is more important than ever that we hold before us an example of constancy, of stability and of integrity - our patron saint, San Pedro."

Sammy J switched off the radio and returned to the basin in order to vomit. She was fifty-two days pregnant. As she wiped her mouth she remembered tonight was Chicken Drop night at the Sundowner Hotel. Every Wednesday, beers half price.

She pocketed her key and took the lift to the ground-floor lobby where Charlie was being sworn in as temporary daytime receptionist by a fat manager in his underpants. The Sundowner had two shift managers (one fat, both patronising) and a melancholic receptionist in exile whose wife disappeared around dawn in a camouflaged truck between Guatemala City and the shores of lake Atitlán in '88. Now he too was prone to early disappearances, arriving calmly at his post beside the pigeon holes in the middle of the morning with five dollars for Charlie and an excuse for the manager. One day he resuscitated a hypoglycaemic Arab in an overflowing upstairs bathtub after tell-tale droplets fell on his forehead from the polystyrene ceiling tiles of the reception area. In our earthly lives, he told Sammy J privately, we must learn to recognise the signs from above.

She said good morning, picked up the courtesy kart keys and headed out to Front Street. Charlie knew she was bound for the airport to meet the first flight from the mainland, and to collect two valises from Walter Tsambas' place on the lagoon side of the caye. By the time she returned with two prospective guests, the handyman was ready for her. He had cleared a space behind the ketchup jars at the back of the walk-in refrigerator and left a clean sheet as arranged. While Charlie checked in the mother-and-son combination from London, Sammy J tucked a cool white sheet round two identical red suitcases and returned to the reception desk. For the English new arrivals, she stowed twenty-five rolls of unexposed Kodachrome 64 in the lobby bar cooler, next to a pineapple and something soft wrapped in foil, then poured two Diet Cokes. She noticed that the long-haired English boy in jogging pants and trainers wore two gold hoops at his right ear and a leaping fish on his bicep. She already knew he was blind.

*

"I'll have a *piña colada* and the young man will have what I'm having," she announced with whisky voice to the barman-cum-waiter at the Blue Parrot.

Geoffrey Ndola looked up from his *huevos rancheros* to watch her park her bottom on the stool, swing her legs into position and rest her feet on the crossbar. Her legs were long. She wore blue deck shoes and ivory slacks with foot straps like ski-pants and a turquoise long-sleeved blouse which buttoned high at the throat like a Chinese jacket. Around her neck, her sunglasses swung on a cherry red lanyard.

"Too late for breakfast, too early for lunch," she added with a thin smile in Geoffrey Ndola's direction, shrugging her shoulders and then gripping the young man's elbow as he slipped in beside her. Her face was tanned and freckled and as lined as any old Africa hand's. She wore neither make-up nor jewellery. With her grey hair swept back tightly and drawn into a bun at the nape of her neck, she could have been Eva Peron on safari. It was impossible to say how old she was.

She took off her sunglasses and placed them on the bar deliberately. Releasing the young man's arm, she fished a portrait lens from a leather duffel bag which was strapped like a quiver across his back, then brought out a battered Nikon with motordrive attached. She clicked the lens into position and fired off twenty frames at the relaxed member of parliament before introducing herself. "My name is Elizabeth Barrett and this is my son, Matthew."

Geoffrey Ndola rose from his chair and took her hand. "Mrs Barrett, Matthew. . . welcome to our island. I trust your stay will be a pleasant one." He sought out the young man's hand and shook it robustly, then returned to his table and gathered up his papers. "I'm afraid you must excuse me, though," he added. "I have my surgery in half an hour."

Geoffrey Ndola slipped a ten dollar bill under his coffee saucer, snapped his briefcase shut and approached the Englishwoman with his PUP card proffered. "At your service," he said with ironic gravity, then ambled through the door beside the jukebox.

Elizabeth Barrett drained most of her drink in one draught and stirred the remainder with a straw. She glanced at the TV screen (Bill Clinton, the weather) which looked over the place like an umpire from its wooden gantry. She took in the garish papier mâché birds hanging on gilt perches from the palm fronds above, counting parrots, toucans, cockatoos, macaws.

"Charming man, wouldn't you say?"

Matthew sipped. He pulled a wad of banknotes from his shorts and fanned them out on the bar like playing cards for the man to select. When they finished their drinks they walked hand in hand across the sand to Ma Baker's watersports shop which had its own private jetty. The thatched hut was homely and decorated with sponges and cuttlefish bones, plus the jaws of some small sharks fished from deeper waters beyond the reef. Elizabeth Barrett recognised Charlie from the hotel as he hosed down a stack of wet suits, fins, face masks and snorkels. Without his baseball cap, he was quite bald.

Of course, Ma Baker had reservations about the crazy Englishwoman with the cameras and her blind son who wanted to go snorkeling at Hol Chan. Nevertheless, she stored their things and talked to Charlie and then waved all three of them off in a large speed boat fitted with a sun shade and stocked with water. Soon it would be the hottest part of the day.

When they arrived at the reef, Charlie paid the entry fee to a boatman at the edge of the marine reserve and nosed forward, looking for a good spot to drop anchor. In the water, all three stood on the tips of their fins while Charlie explained that the idea was to avoid damaging the corals by touching them or snapping their brittle stems. The sun flashed on their face masks. Elizabeth Barrett looked down. She saw the seabed stretching ahead and behind and to the side like a fabulous desert strewn with conch shells and fan corals and great boulders of brain coral studded with brilliant fish. Matthew spat into his snorkel and held Charlie's hand as they swam through the shallows close to the wrecked lighter. When his guide broke away to harry a crayfish, the blind boy floated at the surface of the ocean with fathoms below him and fathoms above. He felt the sun on his back and the salt on his skin. Honour the lord, and the lord will honour you. That was what he told himself.

*

By the time Sammy J lay down for her siesta, the sting was already going out of the day. Through the open shutters of her room she watched the sea turn silver as the sun began to dip and dazzle and dance in spots across her retina. She has been here before: this sacred valley in unknown Mexico which can be accessed only on foot. The year is 1892. Leaving his mule at the entrance to the valley, her father follows his Indian guides into the holy precinct. Some of the men are in a considerable state of excitement, having fallen under the influence of their magic plant. They are anxious to meet with the gods as soon as possible. After an hour's march along the side of the valley they descend for a thousand feet to a small clearing just above the river where the God of Fire, following extensive travel, has taken up residence in the temple devoted to him. In the realm of the Huichol, this location is the most sacred. Rendered crudely in volcanic ash, an idol stands in front of the doorway at a height of some eighteen inches. The statue is dirty and caked with dried blood, except for a hole on the right side where the raw material shows through cleanly. (It seems that when healing shamans visit the temple they scrape off a portion of the god's body with their fingernails in the belief that to eat it is to acquire a knowledge of mysterious things.) By the time he has made three exposures, the white man's guides rejoin him after swimming in the river. And he, tired by the exertions of the day, insists on resting here for the night. But they will hear none of it. They volunteer to bring him water and fresh hikuli to boost his strength, and he consents to their medicine, hoping the plant will help him recover. He swallows the bitter sap without difficulty. It slakes his thirst and allays his hunger. His fatigue is removed and he feels stimulated, as if he has taken some strong liquor. The effects, moreover, are immediate. He ascends the hill quite easily, pausing only to adjust the photographic apparatus on his back and to draw a full breath of air. At night he lies with an Indian youth on a carpet of oleander leaves and it seems the boy's tongue is a lizard's.

*

The sky was bruised black and blue when Walter Tsambas arrived at the Sundowner Hotel for the last time. He was in high spirits.

He chained his bicycle to a lime tree on the edge of Front Street and walked round the side of the building to the crowded verandah bar on the sea front where Sammy J was selling numbered tickets for the Chicken Drop. She was standing barefoot behind a trestle table in a simple cotton dress, a strap hanging off her shoulder and an unlit cigarette in her mouth. Walter Tsambas watched her explain the rules of the game to a man in long shorts who lit her cigarette and selected his tickets from the bucket on the table. As Sammy J noted names and numbers, a fluorescent light above her head flickered off and on briefly before snuffing out the night.

Walter Tsambas paid for a bottle of beer. He held the liquid in his mouth while he pictured himself at the embassy in London, surrounded by luxurious paintings, mingling with critics and second-world diplomats on the opening night of a successful exhibition for promising artists of the Caribbean. He had addresses in Croydon and

Ladbroke Grove at which to stay. What he required was spending money.

He started towards the patio. He watched Geoffrey Ndola exchange words with Sammy J, then embrace her, then turn to confront a group of well-wishers who shook his hand and patted him on the back. As he passed the smiling politician, Walter Tsambas squeezed his elbow and congratulated him too. He waited beside Sammy J until she took a pair of keys on a string from around her neck and handed them to him. Close up, he could smell her perfume.

"They're in my room upstairs." She spoke rapidly in his ear. "Room twenty-four, on the second floor. Two red suitcases with sixty tails in each as agreed. The kart's on Front Street. Keep the keys till you get back with the money. You should go now. You'll miss your flight."

People wanted tickets. She turned from Walter Tsambas and smiled at the tall Englishwoman and her son.

"You're just in time here tonight. How many numbers will you guys have?"

"Just the two, thank you," said Elizabeth Barrett. She took her son's hand and guided it towards the plastic bucket. There were about a dozen tickets left. Matthew picked out numbers seventy-eight and four. He could smell the patchouli which lingered on Sammy J's skin.

"So how does it work?" he asked her.

"You'll see," she said without thinking. "Actually, it's very simple. If the chicken shits on your number, you get the jackpot. That'll be two dollars, please. The only thing is, if you win you have to clean up the chicken shit before you get your money."

The patio filled up around the numbered board. As Sammy J sold the remaining tickets to a tourist from Des Moines, she was joined by Geoffrey Ndola. He bowed slightly across the trestle table.

"Mrs Barrett, a very good evening to you," he said. "No camera to record our cultural showpiece tonight?" He put one arm round Sammy J's waist and signalled with the other to Charlie at the back of the patio. "May I present my fiancée, Samantha Hopper?"

Then Charlie arrived at the crowded table with a large wicker basket and it was time to play the game. As Sammy J made her way with Geoffrey Ndola and Charlie towards the numbered board, she felt a hand seize her wrist and then release it. It was the Englishwoman's. She pressed a small monochrome photograph into

Sammy J's palm and mouthed: "I knew your father as a Yucatan man." That was all she said.

Sammy J reached the space at the centre of the small crowd. In front of her was a painted grid of squares numbered one to one hundred at random. When Charlie took the lid off the basket, she reached in with both arms, dropping the photograph as she picked up the bird. Many of those assembled began to cluck and flap their wings but she neither saw nor heard them. She placed the chicken in the blind boy's hands and gently extended his arms over the grid. The bird dropped to the ground, slipped and regained its footing. For a full minute it crouched immobile in the middle of the board, deaf to all entreaty, as the flashguns popped. Then, setting off in the direction of the beach, it released a sudden stream of excrement which all but obscured the painted number beneath.

Sammy J picked up the chicken and put it back in the wicker basket. She walked through the bar to the reception desk and collected a house key to her room. Alone on the second-floor verandah, she stared at the darkness beyond the jetty lamps and saw the spume of the reef phosphoresce in the moonlight. Pretty soon she heard the roar of the last flight to the mainland as the aircraft cleared the hotel roof and headed out to sea. She listened as the noise of the engine came and went and watched the plane turn back towards the coast. As it lost height suddenly, she had a vision of Walter Tsambas smiling serenely at the twinkling lights of San Pedro and waving at her through the window. Then the aircraft hit the water in the shallows beyond Ma Baker's jetty and buried its nose in the sand. Sammy J thought about her friend and the lobsters in his luggage. She imagined startled fish dashing from the crash scene in silent shoals. A hundred yards from the shore, the tail of the plane rose out of the darkness like the handle of a shocking sword. It was the most amazing thing she had ever seen.

THIRD PRIZE

Beady Eyes

John Cunningham

It was cosy, domestic; windy March outside. We showed the slippers to people who dropped in and they laughed at her wearing them. As soon as she got home she plunked her feet straight in. She'd seen them at the Barras and took them on account of the guy's patter, she already had a pair.

We'd be back around the same time. I walked home from my work unless the weather was bad and on the way bought things for our tea from the Italian shop. I went along the Clyde's dark water smelling of the sea and stopped to watch the birds near the bridge, out in the middle; one dived and brought up bits of weed or God knows what and pretended to eat them as far as I knew, and the other stood on a beam sticking up from the water, always about the same place, the remains of some old framework shifted by the tides and currents - stood on it ignoring his mate and held out his black wings bent at the elbows. Skart said our upstairs neighbour, the old man from Skye, when I told him, skart drying his wings. After the river I went along St Vincent Street and Dumbarton Road, the lighted windows, the dentures-fixed-while-you-wait shop whose sets of snappers glowed in dim pink light; and might buy herring at the van because they're good for you, good and cheap; then with bags of food I'd go up Hyndland Street glancing in the windows. Sunglasses, half-price, winter. The street rose into clear air. I was reluctant to arrive but keen to be home, to open the second half of the day, touch and talk. We did not say much on weekday mornings.

She wasn't interested in skarts and couldn't take the bones in the herring. We were soon out of our clothes and in each other's arms on the floor in front of the gas fire. On the windy evenings of that long wait for the warm weather we might go for a drink in a wine bar, down a long flight of steps arm in arm in our anoraks, close, bodies familiar, steps dropping slow, step by step, warm where we touched. I thought us a pair of horses, companions in the shafts.

Or domestic stuff. I liked our clothes turning together at the Laundrette. She said it was boring, smelly and a waste of time but we went together, that's what you did. We showed the student that

Bar, County Clare, Ireland.

Philip Wolmuth

we were together, the student on the evening shift who said one night when sweeping fluff from under the driers, Do you know what this is - human skin. I wanted to know if it was true. She said he was making it up. Somehow I liked her frowning in the Laundrette and her wanting to save for a washing machine, but I thought we had all we needed. We'd go home and share the ironing.

The slippers were furry animals with a short tail at the heel for pulling them on. And at the toe a face made of brown acrylic fur like the rest. The cheeks and ears were darker brown, they had a blob for the nose and glass eyes. They'd be all the rage for a month I thought, in various people's homes, then be thrown in the back of a cupboard.

I'd asked for a morning off - the gas man coming - and was fitting tiles round our bathroom mirror. We'd chosen blue and white mosaic tiles. I hoped she'd like them that evening. I placed them in an arch round the mirror, timing myself, expecting to be finished at midday. The radio was going, bathroom full of light, venetian blind up; tree in the back green motionless, pale green leaves bursting from its buds, and it was warm, spring at last, and I had a free morning during the week. I went whistling through the hall full of coats and junk to make a cup of coffee, whistling along with the radio and no thought in my mind, the perfect state, the perfect moment, existing, that was all. A slipper sat on the edge of the doormat, in the middle, by itself, tail to the door - it was watching me with beady eyes. Things rushed through my head and became one: that she'd put it on purpose to watch me - to tell me she was watching, even when she wasn't here. A discovery not a thought, her spy watching when she's not here. And I stepped back. I knew then it was a permanent state being watched, beady eyes or not. The brightness of the eyes reminded me of hers but with an expression or scary lack of one I hadn't seen in her, part of her character I hadn't seen, hadn't considered, deliberately ignored. They gave her away. The mug tilted in my hand. Coffee ran down and dripped onto my shoe.

The tiles could be unfinished yet. Or someone else has done them ... or she's finished them herself.

I couldn't step over the animal to reach the door but grabbed it by the tail and flung it against the skirting as if it would twist and bite my hand. With its mate they'd have been only slippers, a pair of slippers from the Barras. Having seen what I had, I fled.

In Edinburgh my room has a view over scoured rooftops of

Arthur's Seat, the Forth and the Fife hills; the room, bedroom with an armchair, is in the house of Mrs Muir, a forty-ish lady whose husband is not here. When I open my door I see the giant cheese-plant that flourishes in her airy hall; its branches with knobbly joints snake along the cornices and colonise the ceiling. She gets up on a pair of steps to dust the leaves. There was a pale avocado in Glasgow in the kitchen. There are plants all through this house including the kitchen we share, tactfully. She goes out a lot. When she'll be cooking for herself or friends I've learned to know; she tells me by the way she walks daintily across the hall and pauses thoughtfully ... the message passes and I'll say I'm going for a beer tomorrow night. I'm amazed. A woman I would have laughed at, and here I'm respecting Eileen's wishes, that's her name, and enjoying it. I'm sure she has said more than once in chat though I don't remember the occasion that she needs her own space - not, as someone else would have said, I want you out from under my feet. But I'm a different person here and her phrases are wonderful to me. I cooperate with the give and take, the way of life, I'm the lodger. We get on together. Weird.

I go for a beer with a couple of friends in the Canny Man and also across the road to the flash place with wall-to-wall women as they say; it means there are single women. Go on they say but I don't - the notion that I would betray Eileen.

On Sunday evenings she stands outside my door and calls: Have you any washing Neil? I hand it to her in the bag she gave me. The washing machine is off the kitchen in what's called the scullery. There's no room to stand back and see the clothes whirling and I haven't gone in there and looked. Does she put our stuff in together? Has she red, black and lilac pants?

I told her my parents live in Bathgate and she doesn't know I saw a blink of distaste cross her face or if she does, hasn't let on. She'll be ten years younger than Mum yet she's a different generation, a different nationality. I've told her that I lived alone in a bedsit in Glasgow. That I came to Edinburgh for a change and might think of buying a flat whereupon she brings details of what she thinks I can afford; what she has gathered about me. I know nothing of her except she's always lived in Edinburgh and has no children. Nothing of the husband who may be dead but I don't think so. I've seen his photo but that doesn't mean one thing or the other.

If Eileen wants her space and I don't fancy a beer I usually stay in my room and look out the window. There's the queer lump of Arthur's Seat. A foreign land, I wish I had binoculars. Can't settle to read.

I've been here three months. I take the early bus, 7.15, and notice the same people in their cars on the same stretch of road each day. By the M8 I'm seeing the poppies on the roadside in a haze of sleep and the droning, cosy vibration of the bus. Before it makes its halfway stop at Harthill we pass a place where they're landscaping mounds of earth into pyramids. They'll be covered with grass and bushes probably, the bare earth almost completely shaped now and a digger perched on the slope doing the final smoothing with its delicate arm.

It changes about here, Harthill which we reach next, a slight difference but no special place, like a border crossing, it changes here in the frontierland, the no-man's-land of undulating central plateau. We surmount an invisible ridge about Harthill, other than the crest of the road. Everyone in the bus must feel it, more or less; they slump back in their seats for the second half - we've crossed over. I can't help thinking somehow that the trouble they're having in Shotts prison must be connected with the situation, the poor guys being affected, perhaps dragging over the nerve each time they cross their cell, doing time in this twitchy no-man's-land. We go up the hill to Kirk o' Shotts. Over to the right black mounds and nothing much, to the left, kirk, graveyard, fields and wood but - the bus angles down and there are the towerblocks and spread of Glasgow.

I walk five minutes to the office. Some evenings, many evenings, leaving feels a wrong direction and commuting an illusion, a road to dreams.

But from high ground before Harthill, Arthur's Seat sticks up like an island on the horizon. It's a real hill that during the day has been a memory, a painting of another country. Soon the city in miniature shows twenty miles away: the castle and the Crags and Arthur's Seat, the tiny needles of church spires. The bus hurries towards the real suburbs of the romantic city.

I'm fixing a shelf in her kitchen and feel her looking at me. She goes on looking, suddenly without a mask, after I look back - her little bare feet in leather sandals will step towards me -

... one of these evenings she'll ask me along on her walk and we'll be in a sheltered nook of the golf course looking over the city, the two of us, then a pause, the long hesitation there's nothing else like ...

The curtains in her sunny kitchen stir in a flower scented breeze, no kebab and diesel, and Eileen smiles at her sandals and up at me again. She has gears I haven't engaged, and could get through the box at racing speed. If I touch her as I want to, tip of my finger on her arm, everything will change and won't go away; perhaps finally come down on this side. I'd go down to Claudio's and buy things for our supper, but sooner or later ...

There's a spot of blue from when they painted the ceiling on the white basin in her bathroom and I'm staring at it and it's absolutely here and I don't believe Glasgow. But the bus will go through the looking-glass tomorrow and I could walk along the Clyde, up Hyndland Street, to the Laundrette, down the steps ...

Edinburgh, Edinburgh, the white gulls. There's one on the chimney stack shifting its feet, turning cold eyes and yellow beak to the wind.

Ivy Bannister

The Chiropodist

'For better, for worse.' On the day that I married Hannah, I took the priest's words seriously, so seriously that four years, thirty-seven days, ten hours and twenty-three minutes passed before I forgot them in a moment of impetuousness. I was fifty-three years old on the day that I married Hannah, and she was twenty. I went into the arrangement in perfect good faith, without intimation of the sulphurous pit that lay ahead. But before I plunge into the smoke and stench of that tempestuous day, I must first illuminate the remarkable beginnings of my romance.

Oh, the foot, the foot! Its complexities are so commonly misunderstood. How taken for granted each one of its twenty-six bones is, that is, until something goes wrong!

Anyway. Believe me when I say that my snail's progress to the altar was no slur upon my masculinity. *Au contraire*, I was always in complete possession of the appropriate quantities of testosterone, and the hairs on my body sprouted in full profusion at the normal locations with particular abundance on my scalp. But before I met Hannah, there'd been no reason to rock my boat. For I was one of the fortunate few who had found complete happiness in work. Hannah opened my eyes to other possibilities. Yes, Hannah made me aware that there was more to life than attending to the eruptions and malformations that presented in my clinic.

My dear, dearest Hannah. How that young woman changed my life! I understand that there are gossips who found the December-May aspect of our relationship comical; not to mention other begrudgers who sneered because our marriage was celebrated before the grass had grown upon Mother's grave. As if I were a drowning man grasping at a straw! You and I know this to be nonsense. You and I know that the truth is simple: that I married because I fell in love. To be precise, I fell in love with Hannah's feet, then worked my way up from there.

The child arrived at my clinic one rainy afternoon with a minor complaint. Not that it was minor to her. Her face was white with pain. *Pauvre enfant*! She just couldn't tolerate suffering - or even inconvenience - in any way. When she limped into my rooms, real tears glowed in the corner of her eyes. At first I was unmoved. I listened with my customary indifference to the sound that I'd heard so many times before: the swish of tights being removed behind the screen. I certainly didn't expect what emerged. Her exquisite feet! So perfectly proportioned! Such pearly skin and the straightest of toes! All my years of experience and reserve crumbled in an instant. I stared helplessly, bewitched, unable to accept that these models of perfection might be flawed in any way. She rescued me - sweet stranger - by leading my melting fingers to the tiniest of corns on her dainty baby toe. As in a dream, I heard myself suck in my breath, then with one deft stroke, I turned the horny offender into a memory. She sighed with pleasure.

Hers was a languid little sigh that lingered in my ears. I became acutely conscious of my telltale reactions - the stirrings of mind and body that measured the enormity of my feelings. How astonished I was! For in the past, only the abnormal foot had thoroughly engaged my enthusiasms and exercised my ingenuity. Now, my faculties were aroused completely, and all for feet devoid of ills to succour or soothe!

"You have the hand of God," she said softly. "My tears have quite evaporated."

The tears! Her tears that I had so callously ignored. Mea culpa!

But still I could not look up. I could not tear my eyes away from her sole, which yet nestled in my palm. So loth was I to abandon its bald smoothness that I invented unnecessary tasks, probing the moist dark recesses between her toes, letting my hands creep up the creamy flesh towards the ankle bone, where I sought her pulse. Pressing the palps of my fingers against that pristine skin, I measured the rhythmic pulses of her heartbeat, as if my life too depended upon them. To my surprise, my questing fingers detected an increase in pace. Could it be? Was it possible that her heart too was quickening at our proximity? Impulsively, my hands ran up her calves, where they began to massage, ever so tenderly.

She sighed again, more fully, more expectantly, and then! more demandingly! forcing me to look up. She was looking directly at me! How they dazzled me, those eyes, her eager eyes.

"You know how to take the pain away," she murmured. "Yes, in this difficult brutal world of ours, you understand how to make a girl feel good."

Her words made me shudder with delight. For it was true. It pleased me to serve. Accustomed to caring for women, I was thrilled that Hannah had recognised this in me. I felt at once the clarity of the understanding between us, smashing down the barrier of years. As I had examined her foot, she had looked into my soul. And what more could love be, than such a frank exchange? Yes, from that moment in time, I was prepared to look after Hannah forever. In no way would I stint.

"Je t'aime," I said to Hannah. I was in love. And like any honourable man in love, I proposed marriage, then and there. Fortunately, as luck - and my profession - would have it, I was already on bended knee.

*

I have always been grateful for Mother's rearing me to be a gentleman. From my first wobbling steps, she immersed me in the requisite attitudes and manners. She taught me what was right. She saw to it that I had the necessary education and respect for authority. And she encouraged me when I decided to go into chiropody. Chiropody! Such a noble profession! The profession *par excellence* for the gentlemanly man, demanding the utmost of intellect and compassion. The hideous conditions that I am called upon to ameliorate! The blistering effusions, warped nails and ostler's toes! People respect me the way that they would a doctor, but, the joy of it is, that my life remains my own. For the chiropodist there are no peremptory summonses at any hour of the day or night. From the time I began to practise, I formed the habit of scheduling appointments around the heart of the day, just so I might stroll home and prepare a meal. *Répas de deux*, that's what I called cooking for Mother, a small joke at the expense of the ballet, if you follow me. And I never cooked beans on toast either, but a gourmet meal, salmon poached with dill, or breast of chicken and apricots.

Yes, I am very fond of cooking, French *cuisine*, by inclination. A gentleman's skills must be various. I am proud to say that these very hands of mine, which are so capable when it comes to verrucas and bunions, are equally useful in the kitchen. I can bone a chicken and peel onions with the best of them. Indeed, I whipped up my own wedding cake myself, sculpting the icing into a frilly fantasy with sugar mice peeping over the edge of the top tier.

*

Like any ordinary man, I regarded procreation as the *raison d'être* of marriage. I wanted nothing more than a tribe of children scampering about our happy home on their tiny pink feet. But in spite of my best efforts, nothing happened. I didn't lose heart, for I felt confident that our difficulty would be resolved. If my experience was limited, my reading was not, and I deduced that the power to rectify matters might rest in my own hands. Since I was no longer young, I set about a sustained course of action to improve my potency. I wore loose trousers, took cold baths and initiated a regime of abstinence punctuated by vigorous coupling at optimum times.

Additionally, I made a thorough study of the technical art of foreplay, subscribing to the principle that an aroused female is a receptive one. What unexpected pleasures I discovered in the practice of this principle! I took her little feet into my hands and I kissed them. I sucked each toe in turn, letting my tongue play along the delicious nail grooves, as I contemplated the little angels that we would engender. Inch by inch, I feathered my way up into her body, until she was ready to dissolve in a sea of satisfaction.

In fact, I pleasured her so thoroughly that, one evening, she fainted. Yes, without warning, at the very height of intimacy, Hannah went limp and slithered right out of the bed onto the floor. Were it not for my presence of mind, she would have banged her head. Poor Hannah! She looked so helpless, stretched out naked and insensible on the floor. I fanned her frantically. She groaned. I rubbed her wrists, their slender veins looking too blue against the alabaster of her skin. At last, thankfully, her eyelids fluttered open.

"Dearest Albert," she whispered, "have I frightened you?"

Mutely, I shook my head, but my heart was thudding.

Her eyes latched onto mine. With a tentative finger, she stroked the floorboards upon which she lay. "Life is so hard," she said. "Desperately hard. And I am so terribly tired."

Guiltily, I propped her head upon a pillow and covered her girlish body with a quilt. I blamed my acrobatics for her loss of consciousness. However, in the very act of making her comfortable, a thought wormed into my mind: that the root of our infertility might be lurking inside her young bones.

I banished the idea at once, but from that moment on, I believe that I eyed my wife differently. I started to notice her tiny frailties, a lingering cough here, a touch of breathlessness there. Concerned, I suggested that she quit her job in the children's nursery, 'to make conception more probable,' I argued plausibly, grateful for her ready consent. I began bringing her breakfast in bed, determined to give her every creature comfort that she deserved. And the first time that I saw her stagger beneath the weight of a basket of washing, I took to hanging the clothes out on the line myself.

It was no trouble to me really. I'd always helped Mother round the house, and managed perfectly well after Mother was gone. I wasn't afraid of scrubbing a few floors. Besides, Hannah's smile was reward in itself. "You're too good to me," she'd say, and then laugh in her charming musical way.

But no matter how much housework I did, nothing seemed to staunch the flow of my darling's decline. Bit by bit, her gait grew more uncertain. The tears welled in my eyes, as I watched her pitiful struggle from kitchen to dining room, clutching at the walls to support herself.

I bought her a walking stick. "Albert," she smiled, "you are the best man that a woman could want. If only these naughty feet of mine would bear my weight reliably."

I took them in my hand - her exquisite feet - and marvelled that Fate could play so cruel a trick. How I longed to heal them! To paint them with therapeutic tincture! To strengthen them with poultice or ointment! But so long as they betrayed no tangible mark of their disorder, what corrective procedure could a conscientious practitioner undertake? How frustrated I was! Yet I confess: part of me rejoiced that the little feet remained unmarked. How much worse it would be if her growing disability caused them to twist or contort, to become mere grotesque appendages?

*

I encouraged my darling to pass more hours in bed. I collected books and chocolates and armfuls of flowers to console her. I took on the shopping and the ironing and the washing up; in short, I became responsible for all the little domestic tasks that need doing in a happy home. Eventually, when she could barely stand unaided, I purchased a wheelchair, and helped her to totter the few steps from bed to chair, where I tucked a lap rug around her knees to prevent her taking a chill.

I continued to take particular care of her feet, scooping out the debris from under the nails, the toe-jam as we'd called it in boarding school. I buffed and massaged, stimulating her circulation to compensate for her stationary life. But as affectionate as my attentions remained, my hands strayed no more towards the regions closer to her heart. Somehow, it no longer seemed appropriate.

She didn't seem to mind.

I was often fatigued between the demands of my practice and

caring for Hannah, but I never complained. I genuinely felt no inclination to protest. My poor little Hannah, *mon pauvre enfant*! How I pitied her, revolving between bed and wheelchair, and wheelchair and bed!

If only I'd been a bad man instead of a good man! If only I'd been less of a gentleman, the tragedy need never have occurred!

For I want you to know (on the understanding that you won't tell) that my beloved became something of a tyrant. "There's dust on those books," she'd shout. And I'd dust as if my life depended upon it.

"And look at the state of those floorboards. A blind man would know they need waxing!" So I'd buy wax and apply myself until my knees and shoulders ached, while she'd tap that floor with her walking stick, urging me always towards more efficient endeavours. I accepted her instructions as though they were the word of God. You see, I recognised how much she enjoyed acting my superior, and I encouraged it. Why begrudge small pleasures, where so many of the normal satisfactions of life were denied?

I should have abused her! I might so easily have found other feet to console myself with. Why didn't I? When I think of it! I could have used my clinic as a cover for the most systematic carry-on! All those helpless women, you know, feet bared, queuing up for comfort. The services that I might have provided! If only I had, then the steam that ultimately exploded would surely have dissipated in the wind, long before that terrible morning arrived.

*

It began like any other morning. I helped Hannah into the bath. I sat in the steam, reading out loud to her.

Dear God! I remember it as if it were yesterday! The smell of the bath oil, and me drying the nape of her sweet neck, patting gently with a fluffy towel. That alabaster skin! I selected a lace nightgown that didn't disguise the womanly contours of her body. I kissed her good-bye then left for work. By the time that I arrived at my clinic, what had been a grumbling in my stomach had become a persistent ache; so I decided to cancel my appointments and return home for the day.

I heard the music as I turned my key in the door. The galloping strains of *Petrouchka!* I smiled, pleased that Hannah should be listening to fine music. I even paused in the hallway for a moment, letting the ravishing cadences wash over me. Already I was feeling better.

Then I noticed her wheelchair. It was empty. My heart quickened. Swiftly, I flung open the door to the sitting room. The music was loud, so loud that she didn't hear me. But I believe that she wouldn't have heard me anyway, for she was lost, quite lost, in her ... yes, in her *dance*! Oh, the treachery of her duplicity! Hair floating through air, she leapt from the table in a dazzling display of sure-footedness. Lithe as a cat, she skimmed across the floor - those very floorboards made to gleam by my own hands! The frothy nightgown fluttered over her fluid limbs, as she kicked and gambolled. Unseen, I watched her eyes, misted with a bliss that had nothing to do with me.

I clubbed her to death. No! That's untrue; I've told you a lie, for which I apologise. The case has been stated too dramatically. The very words - 'clubbed her to death' - imply a brutality of the most grotesque nature, a brutality of which a gentlemanly man is incapable.

In fact I only hit her once, and that, a clean blow to the back of the head which dropped her like a stone. Dearest Hannah! She never knew that I'd found her out. Thanks to me, she remained safe in her fantasy world until the end. In court, I listened with some satisfaction as an expert explained how that single blow had pushed her brain into the bottom of her skull.

I used the footrest off her wheelchair.

There was almost no blood, not from the death wound anyway. At once I was calm, my rage spent by that one decisive stroke. With gentle hands, I turned her onto her back, so that I might attend to her feet. She looked much as usual, with only the slightest trickle drizzling from her nose.

I went about my business methodically. *Quels pieds jolis*! I can picture them still, exactly as they were, those exquisite feet that changed my life. Yes, I did everything that it was possible to do to those feet, short of amputation. In court, they spent two hours detailing the extensive injuries, circulating a dozen photographs. They even displayed ten glass jars, each one containing a perfect toenail suspended in preservative, the ten toenails that I had excised that day with my customary precision. 'Premeditated,' they said, again and again, punctuating every piece of evidence with that gloomy word. 'Premeditated.'

To tell you the truth, they said some very nasty things about me indeed.

I neither challenged the prosecution's case, nor hinted at mitigating circumstances. It would have been churlish to tell them the real story, a story that necessarily would have cast my Hannah in a disagreeable light. No, they heard nothing from me about the liar and cheat that she was.

Mon dieu! I weep great tears when I think about it. And I had always imagined that Mother would have liked her!

In retrospect I realise how poorly Hannah and I understood one another. What a strange thing human relationships are! How very peculiar the ordinary man finds them!

I got life. Yes, the jury convicted me, and the judge gave me life.

It is just as well that Mother didn't live to see me in my cell. Her only son! But no gentleman grudges paying the price, for I did do wrong, even though the aberration was momentary.

I do miss my clinic. Happily, my memory is good, and I can bring it all to mind, all the other less exquisite feet with which I might have fallen in love. So many possibilities that might have led elsewhere! Sublime speculation! It is a most involving pastime.

Frans Pointl

At Home and Yet On The Road

(translated by James Brockway)

My existence, once unnoticed, as it were, has become livelier now, more exciting and surprising too but - above all - more exhausting.

*

I walk to Waterloo Square, my favourite flea-market, in the heart of Amsterdam.

Sited between two synagogues stands the statue of the Dock Worker. Now I take a good look at him, I realize that it's not only stubborn resistance that he radiates but at the same time impotence. Against the Nazi aggressor. Suddenly, quite clearly, I can hear the strains of the *leitmotif* from Bruch's *Kol Nidrei*, played on a violincello - as though borne by the wind.

On top of the Church of Moses and Aaron, Jesus is still giving trade his blessing.

From a friendly Russian I buy an old-style wind-up watch, trade name Boctok. For thirty guilders. 17 *kamhen* (jewels), in which the axes revolve. Imagine your country becoming so poor that you are forced to travel for days by train with goods for sale in a distant foreign land in order to earn a few cents. Suddenly I feel ashamed of our superfluous luxury. The Russian is bound to notice it.

He arranges the watch neatly in a plastic box. A Russian watch is always sold without a leather strap, even in the shops of the former Soviet Union. He puts in the guarantee certificate too.

"Good freedom here," he says.

I nod. What must I say to that?

I walk on and find a cardboard box filled with gramophone records standing between pots and pans. I crouch down and examine them: all classical. The salesman says they cost five guilders a piece and are as good as new - he'd just bought them in a single deal.

The records are all of '65 to '75 vintage and are, indeed, in perfect condition; they're as shiny as when new, but that can be deceptive. They can have a dull, silvery look and that means that, although unscratched, they're totally worn out.

To my surprise, I come across a sleeve that is still sealed. 'The Artistry of Elly Ameling' - a selection of Schumann and Schubert *Lieder*. Issued by Quintessence, an American make unknown to me. Elly A. is accompanied by Jorge Demus. It includes the unforgettable lyric, 'Der Hirt auf dem Felsen', too. I pay the price. How happy I am. Now nothing can go wrong anymore today.

From a stall crammed with Dinky Toys, alarm clocks, jewellery, I buy a fixoflex strap of steel for five guilders for the Russian wrist watch. The dealer smiles at me.

"You're the writer of that book, *The Chicken That Flew Over the Soup,* aren't you? You used to be a little masturbator, didn't you?"

The people standing round the stall look at me with amazement. The dealer and I get into conversation. He tells me he's a cultural anthropologist but can't find any employment in that field.

At the refreshment stall there are white plastic chairs and little tables. I fetch a glass of hot coffee. There's no spoon but the kindly woman has already stirred the sugar. Service. I go and sit down and watch the people rummaging about happily among the pots and pans, table lamps, radios and plates, etc., etc. The dealer is shouting out that everything today is going for one guilder - one *piek.* A woman immediately offers two quarters - half a *piek* - for a little vase.

"Put it down, lady, and get along to Woolworth's with you!" Everything costs a guilder today and the stallholder isn't of a mind to go one cent less than that.

At a cart piled up with old books I come across the author, Manuel van L. I tell him that I've been looking for years for the Dutch translation of *Les Amitiés Particulières,* that was stolen from me in 1963 by an illiterate German landlady. Manuel remarks that its author, Roger Peyrefitte, was an anti-Semite. Didn't I know that? No, I didn't.

The book is about a Roman Catholic boarding school for boys somewhere in France. It all takes place about 1950. A novice priest has got his pious eye on one of the pupils. There's a lot of praying and church-going in that book. The boys are subjected to a rigorous discipline. The priest concerned goes on eating and drinking but on the whole he remains thirsty. He doesn't even get a chance to give the boy one little pinch. That's all I remember of the book.

I go on. How monstrously ugly the new town hall is, especially when seen from Staal Street bridge. With those long, narrow windows it looks like a warehouse. Impersonal architecture. If you were to tell me it was put up in 1930, I'd believe you.

An elderly couple come up and speak to me. Am I really Mr. P? May they offer me something, a cup of coffee and a cake, for example? I refuse at first and the old couple are obviously disappointed.

"It'd make our day," she says. I agree to their proposal. I still have to learn to accept kindness. It always gives me a feeling of obligation, of being unfree. After all, it's not every day I make an old couple's day for them.

After a coffee and a cake and a chat, I arrive in Rokin via the archway near what was once the hospital. I'm going to my P.O. Box and then I'm going to eat at the 1870 Eating House. Suddenly the weird dream I had last night comes back into my head. I was reading a newspaper with a huge headline: 'Mayfly Saves Life of Entire Family'.

I walk into Kalverstreet. A man is chucking spiders of black plastic onto a wall. They wobble their way down, slowly. What would anyone want to do with such rubbish? Give someone a heart attack? A little further along a man with a face covered in whitewash is standing on an orange-box. He stands there motionless, like a dummy in a shop window, not a muscle in his face moving. Here you can earn a penny simply by standing still.

I hear classical music. Mozart. Twenty paces further on a man and woman are standing working marionettes. The hands of the marionette pianist are really playing. The little marionette violinist he is accompanying is doing his utmost. A rather skinny Alsatian is lying next to the black hat laid there for the collection. I fling a five guilder piece into the hat.

"For the dog!" I call out to the players.

I pass a clothing store. The door is open. 'Music' stamps its way towards me, but it is more like booming whiplashes. In the front of the shop stands a young girl. She is wearing savage make-up and chewing gum, apathetically. How can she stand such a noise all day long? Will she be going to a disco this evening? I can see her exhausted and asleep in a disco train.

Near an alleyway a middle-aged woman is standing searching in a panic through her shopping bag while her friend looks about her, horrified. Purse stolen by a pickpocket. When I'm in the city centre I check regularly to see if I've still got my wallet and my false teeth. It won't be long before I'm walking with a rear mirror attached to me.

When I look at all the faces passing by it occurs to me that there's a representative here from every quarter of the globe. Yes,

Amsterdam is a world in itself. Where else is so much going on per square yard?

In an arcade along Damrak I chuck fifty guilders worth of quarters into a one-armed bandit. To get the players going there are pictures on the illuminated machine of huge, open money-boxes piled up with gold coins.

A boy next to me is playing two machines at once.

"He's playing stereo, mister," says a Moroccan lad on my left. He offers me a cigarette but I don't smoke. There's a hell of a noise in here. There's something shady about the place too.

"Are you in work?" I ask the boys, who are evidently friends.

One says: "Why should I work? You hardly earn a sou working, man!"

The other: "I want to be an air-pilot."

*

Once outside again, I take a deep breath and feel relieved. How busy it is here - all these crowds. Overpowering. There are the new benches I've only glimpsed before from the tram. *That* tax-money has been well spent, anyway. I take a seat. The bench resembles a work of art that ought to be in a museum. A work of sculpture on either side, with the back of the bench between them. The colour looks a greenish-blue, but I tend to be colour-blind.

If a tourist was to have a photo of himself taken sitting on this bench, he'd be taking an original work of art back home with him. Which is not to forget the background: old houses along the water, with the spire of St. Nicholas's church towering up behind him.

A couple of youthful, coloured types in jeans are having a tiff. One of them grips the other by the collar. They yell at each other in a queer, clipped language that falls out of their mouths in chunks. Everyone makes a ring around them to avoid them as they pass. What would the fight be about? Drugs, money, a girl?

At last I've got to the Post Office. What a lot of mail is lying in my box.

Two ladies - it's as though they've arranged it between themselves - one in Kampen, the other down south, in Middelburg - want to know the exact day on which I was born, the exact hour, and my ascendant. Both are dying to read my horoscope.

A letter from a lady in Breda, who asks if I'll come along one day to eat chicken soup with her. (That book of mine!) In view of the distance, there'll be a bed for me, of course, she announces.

A grammar-school girl wants to have a talk with me as soon as possible. Otherwise she won't be able to finish her project properly. A reading circle in Alkmaar - there are eleven of them and they do it as a hobby - ask if I can come along some time to read to them. There is a possibility of a 'symbolic' fee.

A letter from a very old mevrouw in The Hague, who thinks she must have known Mrs Morpurgo from one of my stories.

*

I leave the Eating House. Shall I go home? I hate the depressing dingy street in East Amsterdam where I have my rented hovel. Why do I sit at home every evening? I stroll, aimlessly, towards Mint Square, the very heart of town.

As I near the bridge over the Amstel, near Staal Street, a heavy shower forces me to seek shelter somewhere.

I'm standing in front of a bar. Prosti Bar, it says on the door. I don't care for pubs and I don't want to get drenched.

I'm enveloped in a sickly fug of cigarette fumes. The bar is only dimly lit. 'Modern music' comes thumping out of a big amplifier. Regular customers in this place will soon have to put up with perforated ear-drums. I order a cup of coffee at the bar. I can see some vacant seats at the back. A young man with dyed blond hair brings me my coffee, tripping rather than walking.

There are a lot of men. Two very dolled-up ladies, sat at the bar, are enjoying themselves no end. Would they be prostitutes?

A woman comes up to me. She's a good six foot tall. Her impressive obscenity has my heart throbbing in every corner of my body.

An index finger, on which is a long finger-nail, varnished a jungle red, points. 'Are these seats free?' A masculine voice. I nod. She beckons someone. A lean fellow, dressed entirely in black leather and with very closely clipped grey hair, approaches. This is a bizarre dream: 'Mayfly Consumes Habitués of a Bar'.

To begin with, they hold a conversation of which I don't understand one word.

"And d'you know what he said next?" the leather man asks in a high-pitched voice. He picks up a packet of cigarettes with a lazy gesture and lights one up. "He says: Who d'you think you are? Why, you ain't even got anything you could call a bum on you!"

The man-woman makes a hissing noise and raises her shoe-blacked eyebrows.

"What a rotten bloody bleeder! I'd 'av made jelly of 'im."

I have landed up in a stage play that might lead anywhere and am still not sure what role I'll have to play.

Anna McGrail

The Nineteenth List

When my father suggested we prolong our stay, I suspected he had taken leave of his senses. Framington was a pleasant enough corner of Massachusetts, to be sure, and would look picturesque with the advent of fall, but we had planned to work our way around New England over the summer and be halfway down the Eastern seaboard by the time the air turned chill. We were already behind schedule. Papa would have to be careful, or we would be overtaken by ice. In all my life I have only seen the snow once. Two things that man can't abide: cold and maple syrup. We steered clear of both.

Steering clear was something we were practised at. Basic principles: never too long in the same town, one or two performances at most; never put one over on the county sheriff; never sleep with the mayor's wife. Stick to the rules and a person can make a good living in this business. It is interesting, if not exactly peaceful. I have never pined for more, or less. If it turned out to be the case, however, that my father's faculties were failing, then I felt it might be prudent to plan for a future which included such things as snow. It would be difficult. I was already twenty-eight, long past the marrying age. Besides, it did not seem likely that Mademoiselle Mathilde, Oracle of Versailles, would settle either very easily or very swiftly, and certainly not without serious readjustment, in the Bottled Syrup Capital of the World, Population 2,002, as the placard at the town boundary informed all those who entered. Second Sight, Clairvoyance and Communicating With The Dead, I could do. Pot-roasting a chicken and tapping trees for sugar were not amongst my accomplishments.

I'd been Mademoiselle Mathilde for ten years, ever since 'Wise Matilda, the All-Seeing Child' no longer seemed appropriate, given my advancing age and figure. Wise Matilda first became all-seeing shortly after my mother died, so we'd gotten good mileage out of her. I scarcely remember Mamma, but even now I hear talk, when we pass through some of the towns where she held court, of her precognitions and premonitions, the signs and portents she interpreted. Wherever she went, my mother brought comfort and hope. The roads we travel echo with the gratitude of those she consoled. In between the pages of family Bibles all over the country are daisies and rose petals, tokens of affection for their earth-bound families, handed to Mamma by little children playing in the fields of

Paradise. I have seen the lock of hair she pressed into the hand of a weeping mother in Minnesota, the lock of hair that was not cut from the child's living body, but which, by its particular shade of gold, the mother knew came from her only baby, cared for now by angels. In Evanston, still, there is a widow who treasures the faded missive from her dear husband, brought back from the spirit world on one of Mamma's journeys thence, a trip undertaken at considerable cost to Mamma - for she was always white and drawn after such excursions, with shaking limbs and circled eyes - and at no little cost to the widow, either. What would you not pay, though, for proof of your lost one's continuing existence, of his eternal love for you? Surely thirty dollars is a trifle.

I sometimes thought, judging by the awe in which she was held and the regard Papa carried for her in his heart, that perhaps Mamma's soul really did leave this earth many times before they laid her in that grave just west of Springfield. Perhaps the consumption which killed her weakened her body so much that its links with the earthly plane became tenuous and thin, and Mamma really was set free to visit the places that mortals should not. If so, it was her gift, and not one which I have inherited.

Do you think I didn't try? What wouldn't I have given for the drapery to cover my eyes and to feel Mamma's cool hand in mine, to hear her whisper in my ear? But night after night, Mademoiselle Mathilde took the stage and there was nothing. If I listened, I heard silence and then my father's voice calling to me, telling me to think now, guiding me through the lists. I talk to the dead every day of my life for the company assembled, but there is no spirit world. It is a sham. There are no loved ones, no Mamma.

Madamoiselle Mathilde's second sight may be a trick but it is a very good one. Being turned out of town was a rare occurrence. Papa knew, even in a place we had never visited before, who to keep sweet and how much we could safely take before we left. Our first night in Framington, for instance, we drew a good audience and Papa was on best form. He kept the questions light, his tone varied, yet never missed the slight pauses that are my cues. Naturally, as Mademoiselle Mathilde is blindfolded, to prove to the audience it is the guidance of spirits alone that provides my answers, I could never be sure how much it was natural circumstance and how much it was choice on Papa's part - I suspected the latter for it happened more than could be attributed to mere chance - but that night we began with the first item on the first list. I almost smiled as I heard the familiar questions: "What do I have in my hand? Can you tell?" It would not do for such an inappropriate emotion as jollity to be apparent in a clairvoyante. At all times my voice must seem to emanate from the realm of the spirits, so I answered in tones that were flat and dead: "A handkerchief," and the audience sighed in approval. They were in for a good evening.

I cannot remember a time when I did not know the first list, as if I drank it in with the sips from Mamma's *cafe au lait*, those precious little treats I was occasionally permitted as I lay back on her coverlet, against the pillows of her bed. "Listen, Matilda. Listen carefully." The first list: handkerchief, scarf, gloves, fan, reticule, hat, purse, cane, comforter, cravat. Items of outer clothing and objects carried about the person. I could skip to it, walk to it, sing it, chant it, but what I had to do was memorize it. Mamma was my first teacher, and the kindest. It is what I remember most clearly of her, lying beside her, careful not to disturb her breakfast tray as she scanned the morning paper, the midday sun turning the coverlet warm and the curls of her hair gold. Alone, in the centre of the stage, I would hear the words: "What do I have in my hand?" and my mind would start singing: "Handkerchief, scarf, gloves, fan..." I was a child again and the world was neat and ordered, everything arranged into convenient sets of articles.

Eighteen lists. Ten items in a list. One hundred and eighty objects. More than enough, you can take my word, for there is a limit to what people can bring into a theater with them, even when they have attended with the express purpose of proving me a fraud. An observer at three or four shows would soon find that the same items are proffered again and again: a key; a watch; a pipe; a pair of spectacles. The Custodian of the Oracle speaks from the seventh row back, "Can you say what I hold in my hand?" Seventh list: Money and associated Treasury notes. "Tell us." Ninth item. And lo, blindfolded, her back to the audience, Mademoiselle Mathilde pronounces, after a suitable pause, as if communing with the invisible entities with which we have populated the theater: "A silver dollar."

Of course, no-one gets the benefit of being able to observe three or four shows, or at least they should not. Framington was an exception. Usually we move on before any keen observer gets the chance to work out that the recognition of a silver dollar is always preceded by the precise same questions. A few more questions and I can tell you the date of issue of the coin, too, for the questions reduce the world to numbers and sets, and there is nothing we cannot map.

After Mamma died, my world became the lists. "What do I have here?" List Two: items of adornment. I rested my feet on the trunk that contained our clothes and waited, shivering in the January air, for the next question, the one that would indicate the item. My mind was ready: Necklace, hatpin, tiepin... We left Springfield in a carriage before the sun was up and the questions filled my mind, stopped me thinking about that grave in the cold ground. "Let me hear you speak." Item five: "A ring, Papa." The wheels scraped through slush on the country roads. Papa beamed briefly, satisfied, then stared out of the window at plains of whiteness. I only had to commit these sets of objects to memory, he intimated as the carriage rolled southwards, and the world would be at our feet. Next. "Tell us, Wise Matilda..." Eighth list. I measured out my distance from my mother in the recognition of her mementoes. "Listen": "A pen, silver with engraving." "Speak now": "A fan." Once the objects were identified, Papa put them away in his attache case and I never saw them again. They are probably long since sold. All I have that once belonged to Mamma is a locket containing a snippet of her hair, and her blindfold.

I regret being blindfolded at times, for I miss seeing the astonishment on the faces of the assembled congregation when time and again my answers are unfailingly accurate. You can tell, from the small murmurings and catches of breath, when someone in the audience has produced an object so unusual, so obscure, that all present doubt the ability of Mademoiselle Mathilde to discern it. Often such items are personal tokens, have some inscription or point of significance known only to the owner. You might think these present a problem, but the only difficulty is that they require more questions to identify them. Rather than dread them, on the contrary, we welcomed them. It is in such objects that the key to riches lies. It was Papa's greatest skill: detecting those in the audience who were hungry for more than we could give in the theater.

Our first night in Framington, for instance, towards the end of the performance, I identified, for a lady third row from the front, a gold timepiece of the Elgin Watch Company, inlaid with blue enamel and carrying the inscription: "R - Always and Forever - J". It doesn't take much perspicacity to realise that if the owner of such a watch approaches you when the show is over, then the watch most likely belongs to one of the dear departed. Why else would a person wish to secure an appointment with a medium? It is but the work of a moment to arrange a mutually convenient time the following day where, in the privacy of her own apartments, the seeker after truth may learn more of her loved one's fate after death.

At such appointments, where the rules are less clear, Mademoiselle Mathilde comes into her own. With no questions to guide me, I have to guess, from the seeker's voice, what answers would please. I try to please. Like Mamma, I want to bring comfort and hope. What does it matter if the hope is based on lies, if the happiness is engendered out of falsity? I shivered sometimes at the silence when I called to Mamma. The universe is cold and dark. Why should I let others feel the weight of that darkness if my words could bring a little light? Why should I let them shiver?

Of course, I could not have done it without Papa. He was the one who, in the intervening hours, in the course of social intercourse at some accommodating hostelry, from careful conversations with the townsfolk, furnished me with much of my basic information. Nothing persuaded a customer that my abilities were genuine more than a few facts, thrown artlessly into my performance, which it seemed impossible I should know. If were were dealing with a widow, as was the case in Framington, I would have been told, before I even entered her house, her name - Rebecca; her husband's - John; the manner of his death - a farming accident last spring; and any other pertinent facts Papa could muster.

Yes, widows were easy. More difficult were cases in which the seeker after truth wanted to know, for example, in which field grandfather had buried his legendary treasure before succumbing to the influenza epidemic. I trusted Papa to filter out such frantic petitioners before I ever got to meet them. If the worst occurred and I was faced with a distraught surviving relative exhorting grandfather's spirit to reveal all, I made something up. Oh, quite often I could guess the truth: there was no treasure to bury, it was stolen by the son to pay off his gambling debts, but these were not answers eager families wanted to hear. I would not have been thanked. Instead I would point, say, to the farthest field and mention that grandfather thought a spot to the east of the bank would elicit the fortune. By the time the family discovered they needed a little more elucidation - Exactly how far to the east of that bank? - Papa and I were long gone, our payment safe in Papa's pocket.

I quite enjoyed widows, in comparison. Their stories were usually quick to ascertain and what they wanted to hear varied little. A reassurance that John, and possibly Baby John, if there was one, were together in Heaven and looked down on Rebecca fondly, was all that was required. Bring in a little poetry, perhaps, to the effect that Baby John was warm in the arms of angels whereas on earth he was so cold, and you could usually bring a tear to the listener's eye, tears of gratitude. Such reassurances make the guilt of the living easier to bear. Naturally, the payment for such reassurances is substantial. Papa made sure we did not waste time on any bereaved who had not the means to pay for their comfort. The more susceptible, however, and richer, were offered a more enduring token - a message from the planchette, rose leaves from Heaven - and the price increased accordingly.

Rebecca was a widow, and rich, but she was not susceptible. I had seen her only briefly at the theater but immediately recognised the type: the ones who seemed demure and shy were the ones that Papa liked best. She was not too tall, not too thin, with blue eyes and a white complexion she could never have kept if she had remained a farmer's wife. She was chillingly polite. Papa would enjoy the challenge, I thought, but I instantly dismissed the notion of scattering any heavenly rose petals behind when I left.

The information Papa had been able to glean was sparse. This was a woman who lived on the edge of town, who kept herself apart. She had been married a year when her husband died. Papa apologised profusely: he had nothing more to give me. When we arrived, at the appointed hour, I was not even sure with whom Madam wished me to make contact. Papa and I had been assuming it would be her husband - it was his watch she had brought to the theater - but for all we knew it could have been her mother, an uncle, an old schoolfriend carried off by diphtheria.

The house had polished, blond wood floors on which my high shoes tapped too loudly. The walls were white, as were the caps and aprons of the maids, two: one to usher us in, one to bring us tea on a tray. The latter comported herself in silence, the former breathed only a whispered "Mademoiselle Mathilde," and the French seemed shocking in the plain abode.

"The Oracle of Versailles," announced my father, smiling, in a manner I can only describe as unctuous.

Words did not disturb the air frequently in that place, I felt. It was her sister Grace's house. Rebecca sold the farm and came to live here after the death of her husband. A tragic figure, in some respects, Rebecca Lyall, with her grave to tend and no bairns to cherish. That much was common knowledge in Framington.

Whenever I come in somewhere new, I keep my eyes and ears wide open. There is little you cannot tell about people from the place they inhabit, but in this case I had only Grace's house to look at, not Rebecca's. I had no way of knowing whose taste was reflected in those elegant furnishings. The strongest note of colour, however, was the ebony picture frame on the oak dresser, a black border for the staged photograph within showing Rebecca and her spouse in their Sunday best, not too long after they were married, I guessed, for the way in which she carried her hand showed she was still conscious of the unaccustomed weight of her wedding band. John's face was the face of a farmer anywhere, his hand resting on his wife's shoulder with a proprietorial air. There were no pictures of Grace.

As I sipped the pale tea and let my father speak, I wondered why this woman had invited us in. The house betokened the presence of Puritan forbears: there was no piano, no embroidery. The air was still, as if lacking nothing. Perhaps it would have been different if there had been a baby, if children's feet had tramped mud across that drawing room floor. Nevertheless, something in Madam's self-contained composure prevented me from seeing her with a brood of offspring in the run-of-the-mill kitchen of a farm. I could not imagine her making jams or winnowing grain, not with those thin fingers; I could not see her tapping trees for syrup in the fall the way every other able-bodied inhabitant of the Bottled Syrup Capital of the World would be doing come October. I took a cookie from the plate for politeness' sake but filed it on the edge of my saucer, much as my mind was filing away snippets that Papa drew out in conversation.

Her sister Grace was taking tea elsewhere, with a friend, and as soon as she said this I knew Grace knew nothing of Madam's appointment with us. Their only other living relatives were a pack of shiftless good-for-nothings gone to farm in Nebraska. She had been born on a farm. She and John had been childhood sweethearts. Papa waved his hands expansively, trying to draw her out further, but the pickings were thin. Whatever the key at the heart of her troubles, she had kept it secret too long to divulge it easily.

Papa tarried, even after I had intimated that, although he would like to linger longer, he had urgent business in town. He glared at me, but eventually picked up his hat and cane and left us alone. She had been allotted an hour, twice the usual time, so I suspected that the payment she had made was more than generous. With so little to go on, an hour was a vast sea yawning before me. I wanted to get it over with. She drew the shades and the room became dim. I put down my tea.

"I need some token," I told her. "A personal item used by the departed." She looked suspicious.

"There are many spirits close to this earthly realm," I said. "Many have messages they wish to tell their dear ones. I have found that holding some token helps to guide them. If I held the watch, say, which you so kindly brought to the theater, then its owner would understand that it is he with whom we wish to converse." The token was vital: without it, I would not know with whom I was supposed to be conversing, either.

I expected her to produce the watch again but it was not forthcoming. Instead, I got a Bible. I have known this happen before. It is as if people feel that by utilising the Good Book in this manner, the whole business is sanctioned by God. They put aside the fact that witchcraft is looked upon askance in the scriptures and say: "Jesus talked to spirits. Why may not we?"

"Is this is the departed's own Bible?"

"John read from this Bible every day of his life," she said. I heard in that statement neither approval nor disapproval. At least I was right. It was John I was meant to summon up.

I took the Bible in my hand and turned the pages. My eyes were half-closed, and I let the leaves fall as if oblivious to their passing, but I was looking for underlinings, annotations, details of births and deaths listed on a blank page, any clue, however vague. Disappointingly, the Bible contained nothing except the Holy Word, which wasn't helpful at all.

I decided to start with the death, for that was one event which I was fairly certain had occurred. The circumstances of John's accident were muddled. Papa was only able to tell me that it occurred on the farm, that it was at harvest-time. Suddenly, I felt a desire to hurt the woman, to shock her out of that complacency and composure, to set a cat among the pigeons of her ordered world. "He died in pain," I told her. "Terrible pain."

The room was quiet. I did not even hear a small intake of breath, a sigh, any acknowledgement such as I depend on to tell me which guesses are right. I was adrift in the dark.

"He didn't want to die," I told her. "He felt he had been called before his time." I was on safe enough ground there, for I knew from his photograph that he hadn't reached his threescore years and ten. "Rebecca," I said, and with the use of her name I got a reaction for the first time, though the sharp withdrawal of her hands into her lap might have betokened nothing more than displeasure at this familiar mode of address from a stranger. "Rebecca, he wants to talk to you."

"I am listening." The words were cool, not breathless. No anticipation, no dread. It was as if she talked to the dead most afternoons when Grace was out.

"He is finding it difficult." I shook my head and frowned. I was finding it extremely difficult. I tilted my head to one side, as if listening, as if trying to make out words that were whispered. "There is so much he does not understand."

"I imagined the dead knew everything," she said in her cool voice. There was a faint clue here. What was there to know? Some secret, something hidden.

"The ones who still linger, the ones who have not yet ascended into the realms of light, there is much they do not know. Sometimes they want to talk to the living, just as much as the living want to talk to them. There are questions they feel must be answered before they can move on." This was a tried-and-tested Mademoiselle Mathilde gambit which had often been successful before. It is surprising how many seekers after truth will supply you with the questions they want the dead to ask, which you can then make sure the dead *do* ask. I left a pause, hoping she would fill it with, if not an entire litany of queries, at least some indication of which track I should pursue, while I tilted my head again, as if listening to an urgent question from a higher plane that very moment.

The pause drew on, and we both waited. Finally, I tilted my head in the other direction and said, "There is a question about marriage." This was a desperate tack, but I was using all I had to go on. She was a widow after all, sometimes they got married again; sometimes they wanted the blessing of the husband now in heaven, his forgiveness for betrayal.

"I imagine there is a question about marriage," said Rebecca. "Just what is the question?" I could have hit her.

"Why did you marry him?" She looked up, as if realising the question came from me and not some ghost, then looked away again.

"Why do you think I married him?"

"How much did you get for the farm, Rebecca?"

"You may leave my house now." She paused, to leave me in no doubt she knew my name was false. "Mademoiselle Mathilde, this interview is over."

"Was it worth it, Rebecca? Was it really worth it?"

The door slammed so hard, one of the maids looked out of the window. The tea maid or the door maid, I couldn't tell which.

Compared to Mamma, I hadn't done particularly well. Where was the consolation, the sympathy, the salve for the grief? I had given Rebecca none of those things. The fact that she did not seem to need them was beside the point. She must need them; behind that cool exterior must be hurt and pain to be assuaged. Why else would she have brought me into her home? Why else would she have wanted to talk to the dead?

The Custodian of the Oracle was surprised to see me. He was gossiping on a bench in the town square and fanning himself with a newspaper. Although I pointed out that the only sensible course of action was to flee with alacrity, he seemed disinclined to agree. He knew as well as I did that a woman with a reputation to preserve had only to petition the deputy sheriff with a claim to being an injured party, and we would find life becoming very difficult. Such difficulties had, in the past, taken the form of threats of jail - once, in Buffalo, a spell actually in jail - , fines, confiscations and prohibitions against ever entering the county again. Of course, the injured parties rarely admitted to the truth. With reputations to preserve, they were unlikely to announce to the world that the very people they now condemned as charlatans had been invited into their parlors for a seance. No. When we were set upon by the law, it was usually because we had been accused of purloining some precious item, surprisingly often the item that had initially been brought for our inspection at the theater: the silver watch, the Gold Rush dollar. In our defence, I have to say that we never stooped to such thievery. The business of distributing mementoes from Paradise was far more lucrative.

Indeed, not only would Papa not agree to flee, he also put forward the suggestion that we prolong our stay. He had taken the liberty of securing us two extra engagements at the theater. Four shows in one town was always too many. To arrange four in a town where sheriffs sniffing for blood could come snapping at your heels at any moment could only mean that my father had gone mad. I told him it didn't even need second sight to spot it.

"Come on, Matilda. Stop sounding like your mother. Let's eat."

There was only one explanation: the Widow Rebecca. Love, however, did not put my father off his steak.

On stage that night, the blindfold heavy against my eyelids, I reached out, as I always did, into the darkness for Mamma. If there had been just once, in the twenty years since her death, a murmuring, a whisper, I would have found my own consolation. I was eight years old when she died; I have scarcely anything to remember of her. Sometimes I take out the locket that contains the curl of light brown hair, and I do not know, when I think I recall lying on her warm coverlet, the sweetness of the *cafe au lait*, whether this is real memory or something I have dreamed. Did her hair turn gold in the light of the sun? Or do I imagine that it did?

Papa's voice sounded urgent and I knew I had drifted. He would have to repeat the question. Sometimes, he was telling the audience, the voices of the spirits drown out our more... mundane communications. He laughed at his own little joke. "Mademoiselle Mathilde." I raised my hand to show I was listening. "I have something here." Twelfth list: small comestibles. "Pray, say what it is." Third item. A lemon or a nut? Apple, lozenge... lemon or nut?

"It is a fruit." No, it wasn't. The silence told me that. I covered my tracks. "A fruit of a tree, but hard." I listened for the first letter of the next question.

"Just let the spirits guide you." J stands for P. The nut began with P. Peanut, pecan or pistachio? "Hear their voices." E. It was narrowed down to two. I mentally urged Papa to get on with it.

"It is a..." I paused, mystically.

"Gently they speak." C. Now I had it.

"It is a pecan." The audience applauded. The spirits had not let them down. I cursed the person who thought to tax the powers of the dead with a pecan.

The Custodian of the Oracle was convinced I had done it deliberately because I didn't want to be in Framington. He was only partly mollified when I spent the following afternoon reassuring the daughter of a Cape Cod whaler his last thoughts had been happy. I communicated with his spirit through a harpoon normally accorded pride of place above the mantel. I toyed with the idea of presenting her with some heavenly salt cod or herring, but finally simply left her with the notion that there were seas in Paradise, and he was sailing them. I got forty dollars.

My redemption was short-lived. At that evening's performance, I forgot most of List Eight and had to be guided to the answers through the alphabet code, usually reserved for identifying colors, dates, inscriptions and engravings, headlines from newspapers, and items that did not figure in the lists at all. There were always a few such items in each town, though lately, I had pointed out to Papa, they were featuring with greater frequency.

Our lists were becoming out of date. There were items no-one carried about with them any more, most of List Fifteen, for example: bullet, gunpowder, shot. And there were items becoming commonplace that the lists barely acknowledged: the photographic camera, for one. I asked my father how many alphabet questions he thought it would take before I could identify a strip of celluloid, say, containing pictures from Mr Edison's kinetoscope, because it was only a matter of time before someone brought one in. The lists betrayed the days my mother had devised them - her own parents had died in The War Between The States. I wanted them changed. Papa pointed out that changing would be a luxury if I was currently forgetting even the ones we had. The air was sour with bad temper.

Still, the coffers were filling, the bloodhounds had not come snapping at our heels, and the applause was loud. On our third night in Framington, I was beginning to think we had got away with it. When I took off my blindfold at the end of the act, however, and saw the Widow Rebecca in a seat to the left of the centre aisle, I knew we hadn't.

The next day Papa and I practised, from breakfast till luncheon, the alphabet code. Shortly after noon, he picked up his cane and his newspaper and made his promenade down to the hotel bar. He called it research. I lay on the coverlet of my bed and twirled my hair between my fingers, thinking that at this rate we would still be in Framington at maple syrup time. I woke, knowing there had been a knock on the door, although I wasn't sure I had actually heard it.

Presuming it was my father, come to tell me had had fixed up an appointment with yet another bereaved soul, I answered with my hair dishevelled, my gown askew, my eyes heavy with sleep. In contrast, she looked collected, controlled, still as a picture. Her hair, brushed till it shone and gleaming like weak tea, was pulled back from her face and secured in a tight knot at the nape of her neck. Her gloves had been ironed. Nothing was out of place. I wanted to spit.

"If you want my father," I told her, "he is engaged upon business."

"No, you silly girl," she said, stepping into the room. "I want you."

She has a flair for it, my Rebecca. When she takes the stage and calls the spirits, when she introduces her daughter, Mademoiselle Mathilde, to the waiting congregation, there is a hush in the air, an expectancy. She negotiates good rates with the widows and keeps the law sweet with her politeness and charm. She knew I was good when I guessed her secret that first afternoon, among Grace's teacups, Grace's cookies. She had to make sure I was good, she says, before she risked everything. I am good. I may not be a clairvoyante, but I know the human heart.

We left Framington in a carriage going south, abandoning my father to a life of maple syrup. On our first journey together we made the nineteenth list: telephone, cinematograph, praxinoscope... Rebecca's thin fingers were warm in my hand. In two years' time the century would end and we were ready to meet the new. There would be things that flew, moving pictures, machines that talked. We would be ready to meet them all. The wheels clattered along the hard roads, rushing us forward to freedom. On the highest slopes the mountain ash and maples were just turning: red and orange in a blaze of glory. Rebecca's hair burned like the aspens in the last rays of sunset: brightest gold.

Tim Love

A Fair Cop

It's just one of those things I suppose: I must have blanked out. When I walked into the police station to report myself as a missing person the duty officer said "Hello Serge, nice to see you back". "I don't feel well," I replied, realising I was a cop; I'd hoped for better. "Don't worry Tom, I'll get one of the boys to drive you home". A glossy Scottie robodog leapt to greet me as I got out of the levocar. Its tag said *Victor*. It was a start. I found that the key in my pocket unlocked the door that Victor led me to. I sat down and opened the book that I'd been clutching all the while as if my life depended on it. A bible? No, a meticulous journal of my life and thoughts. I made up my mind to read it. Or rather, vice versa. Reading's my re-creation you might say. It's really no different from reading a novel and having the characters come to life. If the characters just don't gel it may be a disappointment for you but it's a bloody disaster for me. By bedtime I felt myself again though I'd only read a few pages; the Amnesia never wipes out everything, the raw data's still there waiting to surface.

Just a few days later I'm back at work. I've replaced the regulation Amnesia pill missing from the heel of my shoe and have reset my passwords. Miss Terley, my second in command at the Thought Police, bursts into my office wearing a fetching turquoise trouser suit. Together we tackle the cases that ordinary coppers leave behind. If you thought the Thought Police censored imagination then you've been reading the wrong books. The computers do all the hack work, the cross-referencing and pattern matching. We're employed to look out for the unexpected - my name's not Tom Bowler for nothing. "Something's come up Serge. Looks like a missing person case. No less than Mr Snow himself." "Who?" "I know you've been a bit forgetful lately but surely you know about Snow. He led the Descartes Project. Doubt was built into computers in the hidden layers of their neural nets so that the processing cells were also the ones involved with observing. Just as Descartes searched for things there was no doubt about, so these computers looked for axioms, super-knowledge. It got called snowledge, then simply snow. Hardware-dependent. Non-portable." "What's the point of all that?" "To make them more like us, except that they're not allowed to kill of course. The snowmen are taking over all the boring jobs. I think we're the only humans working here now."

We sit at out terminals for an hour or so, collecting evidence from Snow's neighbours, autobank tellers and shop security cameras. "Well?" Terley asks, "Do you think he's dead?" "What does it matter? We can continue although we have no body. The mighty Holmes claimed he could reconstruct someone from his walking stick; we have a whole life-history to go on." "But Holmes wasn't real. It was easy for him." "But then, Terley, his suspects weren't real either." "You know Serge, I reckon you've been reading too many pretentious CD sleeves. You're philosophising like a French cook." She knows how to hurt me. She has a pre-structuralist innocence that I find engaging. But as far as I've read in the journals I've never made a pass at her. What in me has changed? Perhaps when I find out I will be able to discover the spark that makes all the difference between liking and loving. I'm surprised she hasn't found a man. At least, she's never mentioned anyone. She may be waiting for me to invite her round. Unless she's a lesbian.

Walking home I review the case. What's next? The door-to-door inquiry with nosy neighbours getting grudges off their chests? Bobbying around the dockland pubs pushing donkeys into grass's sticky palms? That's not my style. So often my peers accumulate information until it reaches a critical mass that explodes in even the dullest snowballs. They work away like chained goats on their circles of grass, there is no leap beyond their perceptual lasso of expectation. Clues are so much easier seen looking back: you still can't afford to skip the boring bits in case there's a clue but at least you know that everything must be in the text, that no inside knowledge is necessary. But it's a shame there haven't been any minor characters yet; I've noticed that the biggest clues often get put into their mouths.

I turn into the High street past the fuzzy logic of traffic lights. Between a *Stocks'n'Shares* shop and an anti-virus consultant, a narrow doorway leads to Madame Osmiros, Fortune Teller. I nip in, climb the creaking staircase and push aside the raffia curtain. She has her back to me, watching the horses on an old 3D set in the corner. She's wearing a red polka-dot headscarf. I cough and she turns, smiling. She's young and pretty in an obvious sort of way. "I was just passing," I say as she turns the volume down, "when I saw your notice. I'm investigating a case where we need the public to come forward. Suppose it came out that you were helping us. We would both get free netnews coverage. What about it?" She looks me up and down. "It's worth a go." She leads me to a darkened room and takes off her shawl. "Sit over there love," she says, pointing towards the round table. About the room are scattered knick-knacks, photos and, on the windowsill, her drying smalls. "Now have you brought something?" I pull out my wallet but she winces in disgust. "No, something belonging to the one you seek." To keep her happy I give her my handkerchief. She clasps it to her breast and starts swaying. "Evil," she moans, her eyelids fluttering, "cold soulless evil. Born on a cusp." Her fingers probe deeper. "Any names? Details?," I ask. "Sh!" I wait as she hums and begins to tremble. "....He has secrets. Obsessional. Green's his favourite colour, or is it blue? He must be a bit colour-blind. I can see his face now, clean-shaven. It's changing; a woman is working through his features. No it's gone again....concentrate....yes, he's back. Smart, as if he has to hide something. He's in control but look how his eyes move. He's scared....no, he's gone....he's gone." She slumps back in her chair. I wait, wondering whether to call a doctor or applaud, until she revives. "Thankyou Madame Osmiros, you've been most helpful. Here's my card. Leak the story whenever you like. I'll deny everything of course." "Ta."

It's dark when I get back onto the street. If I get lost I can always find my bearings by looking at the Satellite dishes; they all point one way. It's strange how everything's gratuitously different to how it was in the late twentieth century. Will it be enough? Nervous, I begin humming Schoenberg. My shadow disappears beneath me when I'm under a streetlamp. Walking on I watch it grow from my feet, resisting the urge to flap my hands about to see action at a distance. With the approach of another lamp-post my shadow fades. I can feel another shadow shrinking behind me. It's like life, but then everything's like life to me. I don't believe in people; they fascinate without leading me to imagine there's a meaning behind it all which might make belief necessary. They can be set up and deconstructed as you wish. The nearer I get to home, the more alone I feel. Everyone I pass acts like a snowman. Just when snow emerged, Bionics and cosmetic surgery were also breaking through. In 2033 it was said of Joan Collins, a flatscreen starlet whose fortune financed much of the research, that she was the most desirable centurion since the crucifixion. Now snowmen look just like the real thing. The philosophers took them to court in the name of humanity for infringement of *Look and Feel* but the Turing Foundation beat them hollow. Is it too late to stop them? I double bolt the front door behind me. The sights and smells of the day leach into the walls. I am myself again, clean and pure. I finish off a quiche while I read my old journal. I'm still only half way through reading it. It would have made more sense for me to make an Alternative Reality Tape instead, like so many others do, but I've never got into modern A.R.T. I'm old fashioned. Well, just plain weird really. I'm a sucker for the old plot tricks using words. They laugh at me at work for being quaint, for falling in love with librarians, for liking stories where the only non-cardboard character *gottle of geer's* his way to a happy ending, but I don't care. Now, where was I ....

Monday, 26th March:21.31 - I have been reading my medical books and have come across agnosia: a mental condition often caused by a stroke when the sufferer can identify parts but can't compose them into a whole. This is an agnosiac's reaction to seeing a photo of a bicycle:- "At first I saw the front part. It looked like a fountain pen. Then it looked like a knife, it was so sharp, but I thought it couldn't be a knife, it was green. Then I saw the spokes." Think how much worse it would be if you could only recognise parts of yourself. Humans, by mixing with those who had faced and conquered doubt fell victim to mass agnosia. We are, literally, dis-spirited: the ghost in our machine had been excommunicated. We've lost our hopes, our determination, our single-mindedness.

Monday, 26th March:22.11 - The effects of an epileptic attack depends on the focus of the over-excitation. If it happens in a certain part of the frontal lobe then the subject suddenly becomes religious and loses libido. It comforts me whenever I find a physical explanation of the spiritual. In all the medical books I've read there's never been a brain abnormality that makes people more rational. It's the only behaviour that can't be explained away. There's hope yet.

Monday, 26th March:22.42 - Only when a baby tells its first undetected lie does it realise that its parents minds aren't co-extensive with its own. It starts to have an identity, thanks to lies. I wonder, do the snowmen lie?

I close the journal and open my new one but I'm too tired to add anything. I shall pay for it later, no doubt. I'm like a chained bible, each day a new page left open; turned whether it's read or not. All in all though, not a bad day. There's still time to walk the dog. I have an unconscious mannerism that tells Victor I'm about to take him for a walk. He leaps excitedly at my groin. "Want to go to the heath boy?" I feel his hot breath through my trousers. In the hall he calms down waiting for me to find his remote, one of my few concessions to technology. I've been watching him carefully this week. Dogs come to resemble their owners, I'm told. Humans do the same except they have no owners so they invent them. They call them gods. Since Piltdown man first lost a night's sleep in ontological doubt, men have been searching for self. Failing to find it, they look to the stars and see them form into gods onto which they project longed-for unity. But constellations are only chance alignments. We don't need telescopes to see that; the gypsy girl doesn't. Tomorrow there could be a new heaven. Tomorrow I could be someone new. I get out my journal and look around for my walking stick but can't find it. No matter, it will turn up again; these things always do. The church peals sound strange. Perhaps there's a bell missing or there's an attempt at syncopation. You can't trust these young vicars; they're so popular nowadays they think they can get away with anything. I've got nothing against religion - people have a right to be religious in the privacy of their homes - but when they flaunt it in the streets in front of schoolchildren a line has to be drawn somewhere. I give Victor every chance to piss on the church trees but to no avail. Instead he picks the one streetlamp which is still on. As we climb the hill the houses thin out until we reach the heath. Later in the day the sky will be crowded with kites twitching like anglers' floats but now it's deserted. I sit on the highest bench and trace the path back past the spire, the long residential road to my distant gate. The houses lie like museum exhibits under glass, each with a tiny number. A wave of nostalgia overwhelms me as I release Victor. It's quiet; at most the distant traffic could be mistaken for running water. Many fear silence because there's nothing to hold them in; they realise how little of themselves there would be left if they stayed there long. At least I have my journal with me. I watch Victor disappear into the wilderness before opening at my levobus-ticket bookmark.

Tuesday 27th March:7.15 - Frankenstein's monster was a lifeless patchwork until that enchanted evening when suddenly the lightning flashed and he sat up, wondered where he was. It's the same with characters in novels; without the sudden inspiration they remain a bundle of secondary characteristics. It's like love. I think I'll send myself a kissagram.

Tuesday 27th March:7.35 - People can fragment in various ways.

Sometimes each part has enough to become a personality in its own right but more often they are voiceless fragments, with language mediating between the competing selves, speaking with one voice which makes us think that each of us is a single entity. In Music Hall times there were imbeciles who performed feats of mental arithmetic. The inverse too must be possible: flawed genius, Freud's cigars. Multiple personalities are well researched. In all cases early child abuse made the patient want to hide. What was Man's initial trauma? Original sin?

Tuesday 27th March:8.15 - First computers freed us from the effort of calculating, now we're spared the effort of doubting. Is this why we are all becoming weirdos? As they're developing personalities, we're breaking up. The snowmen can't be sure that the real world is there, but they're sure they're experiencing sense-data. They've dissolved the real world and have given us each our private one. Of course the churches are trying to capitalise on Man's yearning for unity but it wouldn't surprise me if the snowmen had infiltrated the clergy too.

Tuesday 27th March:19:51 - I stayed late at the office tonight. I was hoping that Anna would stay too, but she was off for the weekend. She's skinny but then I prefer them that way. Tonight for the first time I looked at her personal files. Unethical, but old habits die hard. It was a good thing I did. Anna hasn't always been called Miss Terley; she used to be Mr Lee. Alan. Working undercover in the vice squad did him no good at all.

I slam the journal closed. Genderbending's as bad as genre-bending in my book. Apparently some people switch a few times a year nowadays. Victor starts barking. I turn to see his wagging tail disappear into a thicket. "Victor!" I shout, slapping my thigh the way I've seen other owners do. He ignores me. I follow him into the bush. "Victor! Here boy!" I shout again, pushing aside the foliage. Then I see a body lying in a hollow, fully clothed in a grey suit. Victor is gnawing at the end where the head used to be. I stand there shocked for a moment. Surely this couldn't be the body we're searching for? Such coincidences never happen in real life. But then I recognise the walking stick staked through its stomach.

It is traditional to gather the suspects into a room and reveal that the murderer was known all the time. All the clues that have been laid like timebombs along the route should have been set to explode now. It helps to think backwards then write forwards. Nothing is hidden;

our attention is distracted at the vital moment. I'm alone in my study. Around me are the journals, medical books and case dossiers that make up my life. It's all here somewhere. I have avoided the temptation to skip to the last pages of volume 1 until now.

Sunday 5th August:8.53 - It is quiet on the heath today. It seems to keep people away, silence. Victor is as lively as ever. An old man approaches, respectably dressed, perhaps on the way to church. He crouches to make a fuss of Victor. I put down my journal.

Sunday 5th August:9.10 - "Nice dog," he said. "Yes." "What are you writing?" He stared at me like a proof reader knowing at a glance that something's wrong. He had very blue eyes. I told him what I was writing. "Why not A.R.T's? You could download them nightly into your MBF." "My what?" "Man's Best Friend." "He's a robodog isn't he?" "Yes but he's got no snow." He sat closer. "You don't recognise me do you? I'm Mr Snow. Retired. Or so the media think. Actually I'm looking to unify snow theory with theology. Either that or I'm crazy too. Are you a snowman?" "How did you guess?" "You talk like one" "But you're wrong of course." "Prove it." It's the chance I've been waiting for. Unpremeditated crimes are the hardest to detect. "Let me just finish writing this. I'll be with you in 5 minutes." As he walks away I take the Amnesia Pill from the secret compartment in my heel and finish writing this my final note. DON'T CHEAT! READ FROM THE START!

The journal stops there. I've caught up with myself at last, given myself a reason for living: a motive, an opportunity, a method. Only a few loose ends remain; exercises for the reader. I'm impressed by the gypsy girl, I'll visit her again tomorrow. We're 2 of a kind. But first, some more pressing business. In for a penny, in for tuppence, as I always say. I pick up the phone. "Terley, I think I've solved the Missing Person case." "Serge, you're a genius. I wish I was you" "Sorry, I got there first. Come round and I'll tell you all about it. We'd better not chat over the phone." "It's getting late, Serge." "Don't worry, you can stay here tonight. And Terley?" "Yes." "Make sure no-one sees you coming. They're rather old fashioned round here."